IT HAPPENED
IN WISCONSIN

Ken Moraff

Text copyright © 2013 Ken Moraff

Published by Amazon Publishing
P.O. Box 400818
Las Vegas, NV 89140

ISBN-13: 9781477848180
ISBN-10: 1477848185

Library of Congress Control Number: 2013909117

FOR KARYN

For example, the quantization procedure applied to the action $S = \int x(t)\, x(t+a)\, dt$, for which there is no canonical momentum nor a Hamiltonian, gives rise to negative probabilities and imaginary energies.

—Richard Feynman

Five or six times, hitting against a guy with good stuff, I swung hard and—oomph—just fouled it back. Really hit it hard. And I smelled the wood of the bat burning.

—Ted Williams

CHAPTER ONE

It happened in Wisconsin.

It was April of 1939, but I still feel every bump in the road. The creak of the suspension, the sway of the springs. The throb of the engine as we rattled south on Route 12 in our Crown Coach Company bus.

Not like the buses today, with their plush seats, their headrests, their cushioned arms, with buttons that tilt you back to sleep. As if you were an emperor sprawled on pillows, some fat millionaire in a limousine. We were working men, and we knew that luxury softens your resolve, that comfort weakens your character.

To prevent such an erosion of the spirit, we sat on cast-iron benches, nine to a side, white enamel chipping off the cold metal arms. The seats were upholstered in ancient crimson leather, worn shiny over the years and beginning to tear in places, as the country itself was tearing. Roosevelt could talk all he wanted about a New Deal, but factories were still closed, men crowded the counter at soup kitchens, bankers and tycoons were hijacking the country while children went to bed hungry. And if you looked past the cracks in the leather, you could see the thin layer of cloth that held the seat together. Only a few heroic threads kept the fabric from splitting and releasing an explosion of stuffing.

The engine growled as we passed a tractor. The pistons fluttered, the exhaust pipe shuddered. The carburetor gasped for breath. But we couldn't slow down, because crowds in Kenosha and Wausau and Dubuque waited for us to take the field. Boys running alongside the bus, banging their gloves against the mud-streaked fenders as we pulled up to the ballpark. Fans lining the rusty bleachers around the diamond, eager to see us sprint from the dugout. Farmers and carpenters and mill workers who clapped and whistled in the stands, because times were hard, and life was a battle, and they knew which side we were on.

You know that feeling when you stand on the pitcher's mound, staring in at home plate? The batter doesn't even exist, just you and the catcher and the ball in your hand. You rock back on the mound, and your leg kicks up and your hip swings in and your arm comes around like the sword of justice. Your wrist snaps loose the fastball of your dreams—a bolt of lightning streaking toward the plate— and for one split second, the universe is balanced. The catcher's fat mitt is the center of *everything*.

That's the way we felt. We dazzled our opponents—they slunk back to the dugout rubbing their eyes. We flew around the base paths, kicking up plumes of dust, outrunning the cheers of the crowd. We hit doubles to left field and right, triples into the corner. We smashed home runs over stadium walls, bouncing balls into the back streets of Decatur, Rockford, and Terre Haute, breaking windows and frightening stray dogs.

It didn't matter that our uniforms were threadbare, that the bus had seen better days. You could still read RACINE ROBINS in faded red paint, and everyone from Cedar Rapids to Syracuse knew what that meant. They might not let us into Yankee Stadium, but what's wrong with a good, honest Class B league? If we'd had our chance, we would have beat those pampered boys in pinstripes—because we stood for something, and the crowds knew it. So they turned out for batting practice. They cheered us more than the home teams, they mobbed us for autographs. At the ballpark, on the street, outside the cheap hotels where we bunked four to a room.

"Hey, over here, will ya?"

"Come on, it's for my sister. She's in the hospital."

"Mister, could you sign this bat for me? Please, mister?"

One rainy Saturday, we drove to a rally in Green Bay. The building trades were on strike—wages had been cut three years in a row and forty cents an hour wouldn't pay your rent, even if you lived on potatoes and beans. The unions filled a park in the center of town, not just locals but plumbers from Oshkosh and Appleton, roofers from Waukesha, plasterers bused in from Fond du Lac. In the cold drizzle, they wore flannels and stamped their feet to stay warm. They passed around jars of coffee, blew on their hands in steamy gusts. That's what counts for spring in Wisconsin! But even in the rain they waved banners, they chanted, they cheered the speakers. We didn't mind the cold—the president of the pipefitters' local had invited us personally, and we went to as many rallies as we could. Because when we looked out at those faces, it lifted our hearts, all of that common purpose.

We stood at the back of the platform while the union officers gave speeches. A carpenter's wife sang "I Dreamed I Saw Joe Hill Last Night" while an electrician played the banjo. Then we sent Ozzie Gadlin to the podium.

Of course Ozzie was a big man—have you ever seen a little catcher? If you asked Ozzie how tall he was, he'd say, "Five foot eighteen inches," and that was no lie. He was as wide as a delivery truck, shoulders poured from cement, wrists so strong he could have made a living opening stuck jars.

The stage had been nailed together that morning, and it shuddered as Ozzie walked to the front.

"Friends," Ozzie said, and he stood like a mountain before the crowd. They started to clap, and the boys in the front row waved their baseball gloves and yelled Ozzie's name. The men in the back took up a cheer, and it spread through the park. Ozzie held up his hands for quiet—but the crowd kept on clapping. Because we *were* friends, and everyone knew it. Sure, we were leading the league, but we didn't let our heads swell. We worked hard, and the tickets we sold paid for diners and rooming houses, gasoline for the bus, a pool for our own salaries, divided in small but equal shares. And most important, as much as we could manage—a quarter of the gate, or a third, sometimes even a full half—for the cause.

A strike fund. A soup kitchen. A workers' council, in whichever town we were passing through. We gave what we could! In truth it wasn't all that much—you wouldn't want to stake your livelihood on us. But it made a difference when our bus rolled down Main Street, suspension swaying, jolting over potholes. People heard the roar of the engine, and they looked up and knew why we were there. And if our contribution was small, at least no one owned us. No one lined their pockets with the product of our labor.

When Ozzie stood on the platform with his arms raised, he stood there in all honesty.

"Friends," Ozzie said again, but the crowd kept on cheering. A group of men from the bricklayers' union whistled and clanked their trowels against the pavement. Around the edge of the park, a line of policemen in dark-blue jackets watched, their arms folded.

Ozzie waited it out as the noise began to settle. When a hush descended, he said, "They say this country belongs to the owners. They say it belongs to the businessmen."

There was a stir in the crowd, a shaking of heads. Ozzie shook his head, too.

"They say we owe our jobs to the bankers and tycoons. But have you ever seen a banker drive a run home? Have you seen a tycoon stand at the plate, take a swing, knock the ball out of the park?"

The boys in the front row shouted, "No!" The crowd booed at the very idea.

Ozzie looked from one end of the plaza to the other, and his voice boomed out. "You never have," he said, "and you never will. You know who drives in that run—the man with the bat in his hand!"

The crowd erupted again. They yelled and whistled, they stamped and cheered. Ozzie grinned and swung an invisible bat.

The policemen stood motionless, not even a twitch. They might as well have been lampposts. But their eyes followed that imaginary bat.

"Friends," Ozzie said, and again the crowd settled down. "Have you ever seen a stockholder strike out a batter? Can a board of directors save a lead in the bottom of the ninth? Or is it the man with the glove who makes that diving catch? Who throws that strikeout pitch?"

"The glove!" the crowd shouted. "The glove, the glove!"

"Listen to me!" Ozzie said, his voice rising. "You built the ballparks, you laid the bricks. You rolled out the carpet in the owner's box!" The crowd roared, all across the square, voices echoing against wet pavement. The boys in the front row tossed their gloves into the air.

"What banker laid an inch of track?" Ozzie shouted. "What stockholder shoveled an ounce of coal into the firebox? The chairman of the board could fly to Mars, and the trains would run just the same. It's *your* hands that make them run!"

The men bellowed and hooted, they waved their hats in the air. Ozzie stood tall at the front of the platform, shouting now to be heard.

"You paved the roads!" Ozzie said. "You strung the telegraph wires, raised up cities! You built this country, and it belongs to you!"

The crowd clapped and shouted Ozzie's name. They yelled so hard that one of the policemen made a tiny movement—he touched his index finger to the brim of his cap.

We ate a spaghetti dinner in the union hall. There were more speeches, and we sang around an out-of-tune piano and danced with the pipefitters' daughters. At one o'clock in the morning, we climbed on board the bus. We had a three-hour drive ahead of us, and an afternoon game the next day. But it was a great feeling.

We were conquering the world.

CHAPTER TWO

I wish my nurse could have seen us then. The spring in our legs as we raced around the bases, the set of our shoulders as we waited in that outfield grass, patient and strong as farm animals. Swaggering as we walked to the plate, swinging our bats as if demolishing a building.

She's the only good thing about this place, my blonde-haired nurse. Her hand is warm when she holds my arm. If I were forty years younger, I might have put my palm on her waist, just so. My fingers might have brushed the starched cotton of her uniform, traced the curve of her hip. Who knows what might have happened? In those days I still had sharp eyes, a strong back, a full head of hair. I had reason to feel confident. Even today people smile at me in the hallways, women turn their heads when I walk into the cafeteria. Unless it's my imagination.

My nurse's father worked in a coal yard, or maybe it was a lumber mill—the details aren't important. What matters is she knows that life is a struggle. I see it in her soft brown eyes, the way her fingers squeeze my arm as we walk around the lawn. She nods as I point out flaws in the system, injustices large and small—but none too small to notice. I tell her that labor is the source of all wealth. That history is a clash of opposing forces. That justice depends on collective action.

She listens patiently as I explain.

I wish my nurse could have seen us as we swept through Wisconsin on our Crown Coach Company bus. The win in Madison made us nine and two on the season—my sixth year on the team—and I'd never seen a start like that. Although it was only April, and of course the standings weren't the point. The point was it meant something when our bus pulled into town, the engine rumbling as we crawled past empty storefronts. Towns where everything was for sale and no one was buying. Where men stood in line at the Salvation Army, hands out for mugs of watery soup, when all they wanted was to work, to weld iron or lay cement or pound shingles into houses. But people far away had made decisions, people who waved their hands and closed factories, who sipped champagne in their corner offices while their bank foreclosed on your house. Who chortled over the *Wall Street Journal* in their limousines, and when they swerved off the road, dragged the rest of the country with them.

The point is we didn't ride in Pullman coaches, like certain other teams. We didn't stay in fine hotels. We didn't eat in restaurants with tablecloths, wineglasses, fancy silverware. We brought an idea to those dusty towns, from Iowa to Michigan to Pennsylvania, and fans whistled and waved banners and stamped their feet because they knew the idea was spreading. Working men were standing up—at the siege on Goodyear Rubber, the march on Republic Steel. Dimes and quarters rained into pails because a great movement was stirring the country, a movement on the side of children not going to bed hungry. We were out to save the world, because someone had to.

Effie Mendez sat behind the wheel as we drove the cracked asphalt of Route 12, cornfields drifting by, tires humming on the highway.

Effie's real name was Efraim, which was also his father's name, and his grandfather's, and the name of the family bean farm in Laredo, Texas. But Effie left Laredo before they could hang the farm around his neck. A lot of things must have run through his mind as he trudged behind the plow—the fact that the bank took half the crop because they had a piece of paper in a filing cabinet, and that the distributor stole the rest because he owned the truck and the warehouse. Well, who else were you going to sell to? Effie was only a teenager, but he could see who worked the plow and who reaped the profits. And he was the best shortstop in ten counties—so he packed his bag and went north.

He'd heard about the Robins, of course. Effie was only a boy at the time of the Racine Painters and Paperhangers Strike, but he knew the story—that all the union men wanted was fifty cents an hour and Saturday afternoons off, but they had to stop work to get it. While they cooled their heels, they tossed a ball around, and someone got the idea to put a team together and play an exhibition against the Racine Belles. They lost 12–1 but raised seventy-five dollars, and the run was a moral victory. The next week, they played the Madison Senators, and when they came within three runs, some of the union men decided they didn't want to be paperhangers anymore. By the time Effie joined, the Robins had picked up talent from the La Crosse ice workers' strike, and added more when the Oshkosh glove makers walked out and then the Marinette timber workers. Pretty soon they could hold their own against anyone in the Wisconsin-Illinois League—and beyond.

So Effie joined the team, and for the next sixteen years, he stood on the infield grass and figured out the details. If he wasn't on the field, he had his nose in a book, and he remembered every single thing he read. So while Effie had never gone to high school, he knew just about everything a person can know. History and philosophy and poetry. You have to be smart to read poetry, don't you?

When his bat slowed down, Effie slid right into the driver's seat. He bought newspapers in every town, and as he turned the pages, he'd raise his left eyebrow to tell you that everything in the world was open to question. Effie could show you how the threads are connected, the bankers and senators and chairmen of the board, the secret world of nods and understandings, the machinery that hums backstage while the actors smile in front. He could tell you what the newspapers don't print—that a hundred men labor in the mines to earn the boss's salary. That their lungs clog with dust while the members of the board loaf in the steam room at the country club, gossiping with the governor, the chief of police, the chairman of Lackawanna Steel. He knew there was something wrong when men with soft pink hands could run the world without touching a shovel or lifting a pick, when they could own a country built on other people's backs. And when the chairman of Lackawanna Steel walks out of the steam room, the governor hands *him* a towel.

Effie knew the score, is what I'm trying to tell you. He had history behind him, and logic, and it was foolish to argue with him, because he knew more than the encyclopedia.

Let's say, for example, you're talking about the day Ozzie Gadlin hit three home runs in Utica. It was a good fifteen years ago, in Ozzie's rookie season, and you and Effie have a difference of opinion about who was pitching when Ozzie hit the third one. You happen to know you're right, because you have the clipping in your hand, the story from the *Utica Observer-Dispatch* pasted in the team's scrapbook. You're reading directly from the paper while Effie works from memory—and he shakes his head and contradicts you. It drives you crazy, because it's right there in black and white. But then you take a second look, and you'd misread the box score.

It really *was* Scooter Dennett who pitched the ninth, a sidearm lefty the shape of a fire hydrant. Scooter left the game after that season, bought a radish farm in Schenectady, and married a woman with a wooden leg. All of that according to Effie, so it must be true.

The point is that Effie knew what he was talking about. He would give you the right answer even when you asked the wrong question. He could look four steps ahead without getting a headache. He was the smartest man I ever met, and I have been in almost every town in the Midwest.

The Robins didn't need a manager—we made our decisions together, all with an equal say. Why should it be any other way? But Effie drove the bus, and worked out the schedule, and stood at third base to wave the runners around. He had an eye for talent, too, a knack for finding men who'd rather swing a bat than work a trowel. If we'd *had* a manager, it would have been Effie.

* * *

The bus hummed along the cracked asphalt of Route 12 as Effie argued with Ned Kretzmann, our first baseman. Ned was almost as tall as Ozzie, and his legs sprawled across the front seat.

"I'm telling you, Ned, Texans always lie," Effie said as he stared at Ned in the rearview mirror.

Ned scratched his head. "But Effie, you're from Texas."

"Yep, that's right."

"So you're calling yourself a liar."

"I suppose I am."

You might think Ned was lazy if you went by appearances. At the plate, the bat would sit on his shoulder, heavy as lead, until the last possible moment. He'd swing late, without a hint of enthusiasm, and the ball would look lazy, too—a routine fly. But then the ball would carry deeper, and deeper still, the pitcher turning to follow it, the outfielders drifting reluctantly back, as if against their better judgment, until—surprise!—the ball dropped over the fence. "What do you know about that?" the pitcher would say, scratching his head.

In the field, Ned stood flat-footed behind first base, like a buffalo in the sweetgrass who saw no reason to move. Let's say the batter slapped out a ground ball. Ned would look surprised for a moment before he'd break into a trot, straining for each step as if running through water, compounding his late start with clumsiness, a stride so lumbering he couldn't possibly make the play—until, at the last second, Ned lunged, got his glove down, and came up with the ball.

"Listen, Effie," Ned said. "If Texans always lie, then you're lying to me right now."

"Yes, I am," Effie said.

"But if you say you're a liar, and *that* is a lie, then you can't really be a liar. Can you?"

"I have to admit you're right, Ned," Effie said.

"So you're not lying."

"Yep."

"You're telling the truth."

"Yep."

Ned thought for a good long minute. "But look here, Effie. If you're telling the truth, and you say that everyone from Texas is a liar, then you *must* be a liar!"

"I told you, Ned, all Texans are liars."

"But Effie . . ."

Buddy Brodsky and Sweetie Malone played catch with a bag of peanuts in the aisle. You'd remember Sweetie if you met him—he was that good-looking. High cheekbones, a nose he stole from a statue. A dimple in his chin that made waitresses and barmaids go weak in the knees. You know what I'm talking about. Wide green eyes, and I swear that they twinkled.

More than one heartsick blonde had watched Sweetie climb onto that Crown Coach Company bus. Redheads and brunettes wept as they waved farewell in Columbus, Topeka, and Battle Creek. Tearstained letters waited at every stop. Sweetie was embarrassed by all the attention, but when it came right down to it, if a pretty girl wanted to kiss him, who was he to say no?

Sweetie's uniform was ripped at the waistband, a reminder of a foul ball in Muncie, a flare headed for the stands. It wasn't Sweetie's ball to catch, but for some reason the crack of the bat caught his attention. So Sweetie sprinted all the way from second base, spikes tearing up clods of grass. In truth he wasn't moving all that fast— Sweetie was one of those people who run with idealism rather than speed. But he reached the fence as the ball was dropping into the second row, and he leaped as high as he could. On the way up, his waistband caught on a snag, and the leap turned into a somersault. Sweetie toppled into the seats, legs scissoring in the air. By some miracle, the ball found Sweetie's glove, and his head was cushioned by the welcoming lap of a plump brunette. She leaned down, wrapped him in her arms, and gave him a soft, wet kiss. So we called him Sweetie, although his name was James.

Ned Kretzmann had finished arguing with Effie, and was rubbing his bat with a beef bone. He'd brought that bone in his suitcase, from his mother's farm, when he joined the Robins—he said it hardened the wood, and who could argue after the day he'd had? Two home runs to dead center field, then a double to drive in the winning run. All in a day's work for Ned. Of course, we all shared the credit, and why not? Didn't we all work hard? Didn't we take the same batting practice, run the same drills? Why should one man get the applause when we all wiped the same sweat from our brows?

We knew how it worked on other teams. The star slugger had special privileges, the pitching ace had a private hotel room. They might even pay certain players a larger salary—as if a batting average had anything to do with a man's needs, or the needs of his family. Can you imagine? What reason could there be to divide men like that? To sort them into grades, one more privileged than the next. Effie used to say that you can't play the game until the groundskeeper cuts the grass, so it stands to reason the groundskeeper should earn an equal share. Why not, if he works hard?

Talent, some will answer—but where's the justice in that? Where's the logic in rewarding a man for gifts that nature drops in his lap? If a singles hitter gives everything his talent will allow, who's to say the home-run champion is a better man?

* * *

I'm getting excited, after all these years, ready to argue. My nurse tells me to stop, for a minute, to have a seat on the bench. She says I'll feel better after a drink of water.

My nurse would probably agree with what Nancy used to tell me, all those years ago. "The world is a big place," Nancy would say. "You can't fix it all at once." I saw Nancy whenever I could, in those days. I'd walk up her street after a game, as the streetlights were coming on, moving fast because the breeze was turning cool. I knew she was waiting, a pot of mint tea already on the stove.

I remember one time in particular. We'd driven across four states, and I hadn't seen Nancy in weeks—but there she was at her door, the smile I'd been waiting for since Kenosha. She took my hand. She led me to her darkened living room, the glow of the streetlight sliced by venetian blinds. She put her fingers on my arm. She wanted to talk, she said. Nancy sipped her tea as we settled into her overstuffed couch—threadbare chenille cushions as old as we were, but I didn't mind, as long as I felt Nancy's warmth against my side, her hip pressed against mine. A wisp of steam rose from Nancy's cup. I looked in her wide, serious eyes, which in the complicated light were somehow lake blue and ocean gray at the same time.

"You can't be at war all the time," Nancy said. "You can't lose yourself in the struggle. What about the people around you?"

She had a way of talking with her hands as if she were shaping the future, and it made you pay attention. Nancy didn't plan what she was going to say, the way some people do. She just laid it out, told you exactly what she thought, and when you looked in those blue eyes, you could see her think it. It made you realize how lucky you were, to sit next to Nancy on the couch, to breathe the cool night air in her apartment. All you wanted to do was make her happy—give her everything she needed, if only you could figure out what it was.

As she talked, I nodded, although she knew I didn't agree.

Nancy set down her mug, and I brushed my lips against her cheek. She sighed, as if she were thinking it over, then she sank back, settled her weight against me. I felt the fabric of Nancy's blouse, and I went all warm inside. What more could I possibly want than Nancy curled against my side, her heartbeat against my chest?

But you can't get too comfortable. How can you lean back on cushions when there are battles to fight? Don't you have obligations to the team, things you have to do? You can't sit on the couch forever.

"What about a little balance?" Nancy said. "You have your *own* life to live. What's the point of saving the whole world if you wind up alone?"

I nodded, again—I didn't need to argue. I didn't take it personally as Nancy's fingers drifted across my shoulder, the mint of her breath warming my cheek.

Why would I wind up alone?

My nurse hands me a cup of water. I sit on the bench and drink.

*　*　*

But we were talking about Wisconsin. Sixteen players plus Effie, rolling south on Route 12 in our Crown Coach Company bus. Late afternoon, the time on a bus trip when talk settles down, when your teammates lean back in their seats and you're alone with your thoughts.

You look out the window at meadow and forest, trees beginning to bud, a glimpse of a pond. Paint peeling from an old barn, although that's the least of its problems—the door of the barn is missing, the roof is tilting, the side boards are rotting. Shards of glass cling to the windowsills, like broken teeth. The structure sags, but the barn hasn't yet realized it's time to collapse.

The window is cold to the touch, but the air of the bus is warm. You listen to the engine's comfortable rumble, and you smile, because everything is familiar on the bus. Sweat and muddy spikes. Talcum powder and Rawleigh's Medicated Ointment. Oil rubbed into glove leather, grass stains on uniforms. A dry, woody tang from the boxes of bats. A smell you've known as long as you can remember, all the years you've been driving from one dusty ballpark to another.

The view out the window might change, but the purr of the engine is the sound of home. Everything you need is here: sandwiches in a hamper on the front seat, fresh uniforms for tomorrow's game, ironed and hanging on a cord across the back. Your teammates all around you—they know you so well after all these years, and you know them, the best friends you will ever have. You lean back in your quiet little world, a world that will last forever, a bubble of warmth and light on the darkening highway.

You don't have velvet cushions, but the bench is comfortable enough. Your muscles are tired but not sore. Who needs luxury when you have the hum of rubber on asphalt, the vibration of the engine through the seat, the bus speeding down the highway? All that weight carrying you along, all that momentum, and you know deep in your bones that you are on your way. That everything is exactly as it should be. That you have a destination, and you are traveling in a straight line as fast as you possibly can, and you know for sure that it's the right direction—as you go, everything falls into place around you.

Ozzie saw the snow first.

A line of darkness, off on the horizon. But the wind was up and it moved in quickly.

We thought it would be rain, and when we saw the first flakes, we mistook them for moths. But they came down faster and thicker, blowing in gusts until, incredibly, the snow began to stick. Wet, heavy flakes, covering the stubble in the fields, swirling and drifting across the road.

It was April. Not yet summer—a long way from the heat of August. But even so, you don't expect snow in baseball season. It was wrong, an injustice of nature. Although, when you think about it, it was no match for the injustices of man. Because there was no malice involved, no cruelty. No profit from the suffering of others. So maybe *injustice* is too strong a word.

It was only an oddity, a hiccup of chance. The kind of thing that can happen in Wisconsin.

Effie drove on. But after a few miles, the drifts were piling up, the wind was howling, and the snow was coming down faster than ever.

"Boys," Effie said, "it's time to look for a light."

We peered out the windows, but we might as well have been underwater, for all we could see of the outside world. The bus crawled through the black night until Sweetie said, "There! Over there!" And there were two lights, then three, then five.

Suddenly, we were in a town. A fire station. A general store. A little Lutheran church. All of them shuttered for the night.

Just when we thought we had seen the whole town—just as we were considering the idea of sleeping in the cold, in the dark, on those cast-iron benches—we saw sturdy white pillars. A row of lamplit windows. A welcoming sign: JOHN D. ROCKEFELLER BAR, GRILL, AND TRAVELER'S LODGE.

That was where we lost Mike.

CHAPTER THREE

When the sun comes out, my nurse and I stroll the grounds. Not a sprint, I'll admit, but I can still put one foot in front of the other. We breeze past men in electric wheelchairs, women hunched over their walkers, shuffling in their orthopedic shoes. Staring at the sidewalk as if they'd dropped some change.

My nurse does most of the talking. I don't mind if she wants to tell her life story—someone should listen to it! I've been here six months now, and she's told me all about growing up in Pittsburgh, her white frame house, the tire swing hanging in the backyard. You never forget a tire swing if you've had one, the frayed rope that makes your palms itch, the creak of the branch, your shoes scuffing at the bare dirt. So peaceful under the tree as you rock back and forth, the rubber holding the warmth of the sun. She used to sit on the swing for hours, my nurse says, and I understand.

"I would have built her one," I say. "A tire swing."

"What's that?" my nurse says, her face kind, perhaps a bit concerned.

It's humid in Racine, the clouds so low they could swallow a fly ball. A drop of sweat rolls down my neck, but my nurse's uniform stays crisp, her hand steady on my arm.

"Nancy," I say. "I would have tied a swing to the beech tree, in her backyard."

I didn't say *our* backyard.

My nurse and I walk past a neighbor from my hallway, younger than I am but more decrepit, which makes me secretly happy. He's propped on a bench under the willow, with some kind of cushion that keeps him from falling over. As always, he has a book of crossword puzzles but no pencil. I nod, and he scowls.

I would have built a tire swing for Nancy, if she'd wanted one. We could have stood at the kitchen window, chopping carrots or washing dishes, and as we chopped, we'd have looked outside to see a little girl on the swing. She'd have had Nancy's curls, her bright-blue eyes, a younger version of that thoughtful smile.

Nancy would have waved to the girl, through the window.

The lucky ones here have visitors on the weekends. Grandchildren who drive down from Milwaukee, who step out of the car holding a vase of flowers, a box of jams, a certain type of cake that has a special meaning. Young, strong arms propping up a grandfather or a great-aunt as they walk around the pond, gossiping about one thing or another. Nothing important—except to them. Their faces flush in the summer sun. I watch them hug good-bye.

Nancy and I could have had a tire swing. Why not? A seesaw, a sandbox. Piano lessons, birthday parties, Girl Scout meetings in the living room. I can almost smell Nancy's cinnamon rolls baking in the oven.

We would have watched our daughter grow. The seasons would change, the years would pass, but I'd have picked a sturdy tree for our swing—it would still be there. Why not, if that's what Nancy had wanted?

* * *

So there we stood in the lobby of the Rockefeller. All eighteen of us in our road flannels, as the snow piled up outside and Effie bargained with the desk clerk.

There was grumbling among the players. Four dollars a room was fair, no doubt about it. But the Rockefeller! As Effie negotiated, there were whispers about oil tycoons and robber barons. The old billionaire was barely in his grave—had we forgotten about the strike busters? The goon squads? The hired militiamen at the Ludlow mine, who had waded into the crowd, jabbing left and right with their bayonets? Cutting down men whose only crime was trying to feed their families and earn a living wage.

Ozzie Gadlin said we might as well put a For Sale sign on our souls right then, if our so-called principles didn't mean a thing.

But we had to sleep somewhere, didn't we? The storm raged on outside, as if good were in a final battle with evil. In the twilight, we could see the bus acting as a windbreak, snow piling up against the sides. So we weren't going anywhere. And wasn't it just a name? Not as if the old union buster actually owned the place.

So we grumbled, and waited for Effie to bring the room keys.

The lobby was comfortable enough. Walls paneled in Wisconsin pine, varnished until they glowed. Corduroy couches, upholstered footstools, brass lamps in every corner—layered with tarnish and crowned with shades of crimson velvet. Shelves piled with books and knickknacks. A wicker beaver trap, a collapsible telescope, a stack of fishing magazines. A fireplace made of round gray stones.

Mike stood in the middle of the room, and I followed his gaze to the wall above the mantel, to the monstrous head of a stuffed elk. The taxidermist was a true artist. He had frozen that awful moment when the elk's majestic body was brought down—by a two-legged weakling, a creature so cowardly that instead of using his own strength, his own teeth and hands, he left the job to a fire-spitting machine. Think of the injustice! One minute you're standing in the tall green grass, breathing sweet clover, the sun warming your back. An instant later your head is hanging in a paneled room, glaring for eternity at a gilt-framed painting of a Wisconsin lake surrounded by pine trees. And no matter how hard you try, you can't will yourself into the picture.

I knew why Mike was staring. We had seen that frozen glare before—in the two stone lions who guarded the steps of Edison High School.

Mike and I used to meet by those lions every morning. The school had imported them from Italy, hand-carved from marmalade-colored granite—and you couldn't miss the message in the lions' fixed, stony stare. The way they crouched on their pedestals, granite haunches tense, as if they were ready to spring right off their perch. Ready to leap at your throat if you stepped out of line, by even a quarter of an inch.

The pedestals had titles engraved on them: JUSTICE on one, MERCY on the other.

Mike was my best friend. Ever since that Saturday afternoon in third grade, the day we found ourselves in the dusty vacant lot behind Mike's house and discovered that Mike loved to hit a baseball as much as I loved to pitch it. That was it, the whole story. We knew at that moment what we would be doing every afternoon, for years to come. A pile of sand for a pitcher's mound. A rusty trash-can lid for home plate. A bat, a glove, a pail of baseballs. What could possibly be better?

Who needs bases when the runners are imaginary? Who needs foul lines when you have a well-placed pair of trees? We didn't need a backstop either, because Mike never missed. Fast pitches or slow, low balls or high. Inside the strike zone or out. As hard as I tried, I couldn't get a pitch by him. But I didn't mind. I liked pitching to Mike *because* he was so good.

You might think it would bother me, to see my best pitches knocked around the dusty lot. I understand why you'd see it that way—you probably think hitters and pitchers are opponents. And it's true that they square off on opposite sides, that they serve opposing teams. In that way, they are enemies—and don't you want to beat your enemy? Isn't that the whole point of *having* an enemy?

But you have to realize something about opposing forces, about things that push against each other. It's the pushing that makes things happen. Isn't it? Don't you rub sticks against each other to make fire? The struggle is the point—because what's the sense of a pitcher standing on the mound without a batter to face him? To dig in, set his shoulders, wiggle the end of his bat. Why would a batter step up to the plate, without a pitcher on the mound? Ball in hand, staring in, ready to let fly.

The batter and the pitcher are accomplices, no doubt about it. They may be on opposite ends of the equation—but it's the *same* equation. Everyone knows that an equation needs two sides, that an equation without two sides cannot exist. So why shouldn't a great hitter want a great pitch to swing at? Why wouldn't a pitcher want to stare in at the best, the most talented batter he can find? Mike and I were more than friends—we were partners and teammates and allies, and you couldn't separate us any more than hot dogs and mustard.

As the summers went by, I added to my bag of tricks. A little dip on the fastball, a sharper hook on the curve. But as quickly as I found new angles, as quickly as I changed speeds, Mike would figure it out. I could slip a fastball past anyone in the neighborhood, but Mike would crush that same pitch every time.

We played on every team we could find. They let us on the junior high school team when we were still in fourth grade, made Mike the starting center fielder while I climbed the mound. Then came high school, where Mike was always the strongest hitter. There was no one even close, as if some special gift had been provided only to him.

You'd think it would have gone to his head, like those hotshots who strut around the dugout. You can keep your .400 hitter if he's going to walk around the locker room like he owns the place. That's the last thing you need! Give me a player who works hard, who puts his arm around his teammate's shoulder.

That was Mike—he stood on the dugout steps and rooted for the man at the plate. As good as he was, he didn't brag about his last hit, he wanted to talk about *your* at bat. He could cheer you up if you missed a tag, if you booted a ground ball. He knew what to say when you were in a slump, and what not to say. He knew how to give advice, and when advice was the last thing you needed.

People asked Mike for pointers, they wanted to know his secrets. And Mike would do anything he could to help. But the truth is, Mike couldn't explain how he hit the ball any more than an ear of corn could explain why its kernels grew in nice straight rows. It just happened. He stood in the box, took his swings, and everything worked out.

The whole world was like that, for Mike.

People, for example. They warmed right up to Mike, without him making the slightest effort. You knew with one look that you could talk to him. He'd take in your problem, nodding so you knew he understood, thinking it through. And when you finished, he would say exactly the right thing, something you could use, a helpful starting point that might never have occurred to you.

You could put Mike in any situation, strange or uncomfortable or downright awkward, and he'd take it right in stride. As if he were stepping into a warm bath.

He had the same effect on objects as he had on people. Mike understood broken clocks, toasters, radios—he'd pick up some damaged gadget, turn it around in his hands, weigh it, feel it, stroke it—as if he were communicating, in some way. Sympathizing with it. And then he'd fix it.

Traffic lights turned green when Mike approached.

Not that I was jealous. I had my own talents, although I had to work a little harder to hone them. It took years to train my arm—if I wasn't in the vacant lot with Mike, I'd go behind my house, where I had nailed a board to the wall and outlined a strike zone in bright-blue chalk. I had ten or twelve baseballs in a metal pail, and I'd take them out one at a time. I'd stand on a little mound of dirt I'd made, sixty feet and six inches away from that blue square, the most beautiful distance on earth. I'd stare in at my imaginary catcher, then I'd wind up and throw at the chalk line—because that's what it's all about. Anyone can hit the middle of the strike zone. The trick is to find the edge.

A dozen pitches, then I'd run in and pick up the balls and carry the pail back to the mound. Back and forth, throwing and running, an hour or two at a time. The leather was nicked, scuffed, blackened—it didn't matter. I felt the weight of the ball in my hand and kept throwing, trying to hit that line. Happy only when the chalk turned my fingers blue.

My muscles ached, but they learned the strike zone.

When I could hit the corners every time, I split the strike zone into smaller squares, three by three so there were nine squares in all, and I'd throw at each one until I could smudge the chalk in the exact spot I wanted. It didn't matter if my fingers blistered, if my wrist was sore. I threw until I could aim my pitches like bullets, until my arm felt ready to fall off.

I worked even harder at learning people.

Don't get me wrong. I *like* people—but when you're on the pitching mound, the path of the ball is up to you. Most of it, anyway. Maybe a gust of wind comes up, and blows your curveball half an inch to the left. Your grip is slightly off, your knuckle grazes a seam, and the ball kicks a hair up or down. But 90 percent of the control is in your own hands. It's different with people—there's a *lot* of wind. You can have your own plans and intentions, but with people, things get blown off course, not just half an inch but into the next county.

You get in a rhythm when you're pitching, a flow as smooth and predictable as water rolling down a river. With people, there's no easy flow—something always goes wrong. It's not like bobbing along with the current, it's more like getting sprayed by a broken faucet, a geyser that soaks your clothes and floods the kitchen counter and overflows the sink. You grab for the handle but you can't shut it off, and there's nothing you can do but stand in the spreading puddle. Because as hard as you try to figure people out, half the time you're wrong.

I don't always make a good impression, is what I'm trying to say. I can be clumsy at the start, a bit awkward, before I find my footing. But I do my best. I try to understand, which after all these years is still not easy. People are *hard* to understand, and at my age, I'm as good at it as I'm ever going to be.

Mike and I practiced every day after school, with whatever team we happened to be on. Then we went to the vacant lot. I threw him pitch after pitch as the afternoon wore on, as our shadows stretched along the ground. Baseballs ripped through the weeds, fly balls clanged against the chain-link fence. Squirrels jumped to avoid line drives. When the pail of balls was empty, we poked through knee-high weeds, gathering up scarred leather until the light faded. Then we'd climb the back steps of Mike's house and spread out our books on his kitchen table. That's where I found out that Mike was the same way with school as he was with hitting.

I was a straight-A student. I don't mean to brag—I'm not applying for a job! At this point, it's enough to be alive. But I want you to understand. When I say that Mike was more than a good student, what I mean is, if he didn't know *every single thing,* he might die.

Some people nibble at their schoolwork. Mike was like a starving man tearing into a loaf of bread. He flipped through his books like a maniac, scribbling like crazy on a pad of paper—endless pages of notes, because all of it was important, not just what was in the book but all of the thoughts it triggered in his mind. One question leading to another, ideas flying like a shower of sparks.

His curiosity took him in all directions. Like a dog scampering around a field, sniffing first in one place, then charging off toward another.

I was happy enough to learn my lessons, to make my grades. But Mike had to go further. He had to look at things from every possible angle, and if you took one side of an argument, Mike would take the other. If you came around to his point of view, he'd switch over to yours. He wanted to poke at every side of the question, to see it in every conceivable light. He had to see what was behind it, and then what was behind *that.* There was always one more thing to understand.

It was a problem in school.

CHAPTER FOUR

What you noticed about Mike in school was that he always had a question. You should have seen him with Mr. Walters, our civics teacher in tenth grade, who was a nice enough man, for a pawn of the system. He wore white cotton shirts with the collar open, sat on the edge of his desk, and told us to call him Walt.

I remember a lecture on transportation. The miracles Walt had seen in his own lifetime—horses giving way to automobiles and electric streetcars. Train tracks stitching the country together. Not to mention ships steaming across the ocean, and airplanes. You could be in one place for breakfast, and five hundred miles away for lunch! How much progress we had made, in such a short time.

Mike raised his hand.

"There's something I don't understand," he said. "You're right that we have all these new inventions, all of this machinery. But every day in the newspaper, factories are closing. People don't know where to find a job—they can't afford steamships, a train across the country. They can't even pay for a streetcar! We have all these new things, but people can't use them. Or only a few people. Is that really progress?"

Walt taught us that vigorous discussion is healthy for society. That openness is the path to understanding. So he considered Mike's question carefully.

"Of course there are problems," Walt said. "There's a *long* way to go—you're right to point that out. It would be foolish to think that everything can be done at once. But we are moving in the right direction."

Walt moved over to the window. "Look out there," he said. "Buildings filled with offices. You don't have to break your back in hard labor anymore. You can *think* for a living—imagine that. You go home to modern conveniences. My father washed in cold water all his life. Now we have hot water." He looked around, to make sure it was sinking in. To see if his ideas had penetrated. Walt *wanted* us to learn.

"But what about the people who are out of work?" Mike said. "Every day, you see furniture out on the sidewalk. They shut off my neighbors' gas, they can't cook anymore. They have cold beans for dinner, they do homework by candlelight."

"There will always be stragglers," Mr. Walters said. "The world is not perfect, a few poor souls may not find their way. But you can't be distracted by the exceptions. The exceptions are not the point— on the *whole*, we are better off. And things are getting even better."

You might have heard a hint of impatience in Walt's voice—but he was happy to clear things up, glad that Mike had given him the chance to emphasize this crucial point. It is the *trend* that matters, not the details here and there. If some unfortunate person had watched the sheriff take his home, or lost his savings to a shaky bank, or watched his pension turn to dust, those were detours, and not the main point. Every road bends, Walt said. The important thing is where it takes you in the end.

But Mike was not done. "Mr. Walters," Mike said. "I understand that things are better for *some* people," he said. "No one can argue with hot water. But what if you don't have food? What if you lose your house? You see that all the time now, people living on the sidewalk. How can that be progress?"

By that point Walt's smile was too fixed, too unchanging, to be genuine. Why couldn't Mike see the obvious? That the factories were bound to reopen, that the machinery would grind to life and furnaces would belch smoke. Eager men would stream onto the shop floor, the assembly lines would hum and fill up the boxcars faster than ever, and all those canned beans and Studebakers and three-piece bedroom sets would stream across the country into the welcoming homes of those very same workers, in a complicated glorious system that was the envy of the world.

Progress was inevitable. With all of our goodwill, our boundless energy, our accumulating knowledge—things *must* be getting better! It was a point that did not need to be proven. It was so fundamental, so essential, you just had to accept it.

"It takes time," Walt said. "You need to look at the long run. And in the long run, there is no doubt that things are improving. History only goes in one direction."

Here's the difference between Mike and me: Mike would keep the discussion going. He'd stick around after class, he'd go in early the next day. He was curious, and he would want to talk it out, to see if he and Walt could agree on something.

I was content to let it pass. I knew Mike's question was important —and Walt was taking the easy way out. If you believed Walt, you didn't need to worry. The world was moving forward, and there was no reason to rock the boat. No reason to make changes, at least not serious ones. All people had to do was wait, according to Walt, and progress would lift them up.

Even then, I understood that this was a dangerous idea.

But I didn't need to argue about it. Why should I care what Walt thought? What difference did it make? Let Walt have his own beliefs. He was welcome to them. I had mine, and I didn't need to bicker over the details. I never understood why it bothered Mike so much, but at least he made it through civics class. The problem— where Mike really got into trouble—was with Mr. Polk.

* * *

Here is what started it. Mr. Polk stood at the chalkboard and sketched out a simple problem. About a baseball, of all things! Maybe that's why Mike paid so much attention. Too bad Polk didn't use an apple in his example, instead.

Anyway, the question went like this. Say that you are standing on a train, maybe a flatbed car. The train is rolling down the track at twenty miles an hour. You lean back, and you throw the ball— hard, but not too hard, let's say eighty miles per hour. But hang on to your hat. There's a man standing next to the rails, waiting for the train to pass. He watches the train roll by, he sees you throw the ball. He watches it fly—*at one hundred miles per hour.*

That's right. You throw the ball at eighty miles an hour, but add the speed of the train, and it's going one hundred. Simple arithmetic.

Mike watched carefully as Mr. Polk laid out the problem on the board. You could tell that something was bothering him, that an idea was bubbling up inside. That a question was gathering momentum.

I thought, *Please don't ask it.*

You could tell that Mike was fighting the same battle, because he kept half raising his hand and then lowering it. He knew as well as the rest of us that you didn't interrupt Mr. Polk.

Polk was the oldest teacher in school, and the grumpiest, and you could tell just by looking that he wasn't going to put up with any nonsense. The way he set his mouth in a permanent frown. The way he stared at you, his eyes like ice, his military hair cropped close to the scalp—turned white from years of aggravation.

Why shouldn't Polk's hair be white? Look what he had to put up with, he might tell you. The smart alecks and troublemakers. Year after year of delinquents, of wiseacres, and somehow they kept getting worse. Didn't someone have to keep order? Show them who was in charge?

Polk was in charge. You could tell from his tone of voice—a tone that said he had worked hard for his degree, had fought in the Great War, had lived through two depressions. He had been married forty-five years, and had taught physics in this very classroom for four decades, and by God, he was going to teach it *his* way. He certainly wasn't going to put up with ignorant questions.

Mike didn't interrupt. But the next day, he was ready.

If you absolutely *had* to ask Polk a question, the time to try was the very beginning of the class. Even then it was like tiptoeing up to a lion, and you had to hope that Polk would be in a good mood, which was so rare that none of us had ever seen it. But if you had to ask a question, that was your best chance.

"Mr. Polk?" Mike said.

"Yes?" Polk was already at the chalkboard. The board was a pure, deep black—Polk washed it every day, with a clean sponge and a pail of steaming water. He wouldn't use erasers, because he didn't like the streaks they left behind. Streaks that suggested a lack of discipline.

Polk had papered the walls with charts and diagrams. Tables of numbers and formulas, which you had to memorize, so you could repeat them on demand when Polk barked your name. There were posters of scientists, too, scowling men in white coats, every one of them glaring at you.

The shades were always lowered. Polk preferred incandescent bulbs to sunlight.

"Mr. Polk?" Mike said again.

Polk had already begun to write out a new problem, two trains moving in opposite directions. But he turned, chalk in hand, to address the interruption.

"I'm sorry," Mike said, "but there's something I don't understand. In the problem from yesterday, where you add the speed of the train to the speed of the ball."

"Yes?" said Polk. He already looked distressed.

"Remember last month, when you told us about light waves? Well, you said that the speed of light is as fast as things can go. Nothing can go faster than that."

"That is correct," said Polk. "It is a fundamental law."

"Well, then, what if the train is moving at the speed of light? What would happen if a man threw a ball? I mean, if you have to add the velocities. Wouldn't the ball go faster than light?"

"That is impossible," said Polk. His jowls had tensed up. "A train can't go anywhere near the speed of light."

"I know that," Mike said. "I mean a *real* train can't. But suppose you had a train that could? What would happen when you throw the ball?"

"It's not possible," Polk said. "At even a hundred miles an hour the engine would shake to pieces. It's not worth talking about." He turned back to the chalkboard, his back straight, shoulders firm. People who are wrong are always certain.

"But if it *could*," Mike said. "Let's say they figured out how to build a really fast train. Maybe some kind of track without friction. Or it could be a rocket, and not a train, a rocket that can go at the speed of light. It's the same problem. If you throw a ball and add it to the speed of the rocket, then the ball will go faster than light. Won't it?"

"Now look here," Polk said. He turned around again to stare at Mike, abandoning the problem on the blackboard. He slapped his piece of chalk down on his desk, harder than necessary, and walked over to Mike's side of the classroom, shoes clicking on the linoleum. Polk always wore a jacket and slacks, shades of gray and tan—not expensive, but clean and neatly pressed. You had to look carefully to find a loose thread, a worn patch at the elbow. Although if you paid attention, there weren't that many outfits, and they didn't change that often. A teacher's salary.

Polk stood in front of a portrait of Isaac Newton, framed in black. He drew himself to his full height. He glared down at Mike.

"I am going to explain something to you," Polk said. "And I will say it only once. Physics is not a game. It is not a toy. It is a *science*. And science deals with the world as it exists, not with figments of the imagination. It is impossible for a train to move at the speed of light, and there is no point pretending that it can."

"But—"

"It is *impossible*, and we will hear no more about it."

At lunchtime, Mike and I were walking in the schoolyard. Mike didn't want to let it drop. He had a *good* question, he said, and Polk hadn't answered it.

I didn't understand why Mike cared so much. What was so important about the speed of trains? About a man throwing a baseball on some imaginary flatbed car? Out of all the things you could worry about, all the wrongs and disorders, all the injustices of the world. But Mike couldn't let it go.

There was a fence at the edge of the schoolyard, and five or six boys leaned against it. We knew them by reputation, the kind of kids who snickered in the back of the class, who slouched through the halls. Who smoked cigarettes in the bathroom, then threw the butts on the floor, right next to the wastebasket.

One of them left the group and sauntered toward us, hands in the pockets of his olive-drab coat.

It was Andrew Flood. We knew his name because they called it for the detention list almost every day. Andrew Flood had green eyes, frizzy red hair, and clothes from a secondhand shop.

We couldn't imagine what he wanted with us.

"Hey," he said.

Mike could talk to anybody—teachers, bus drivers, the school janitor. The old women who ladled soup into our bowls in the cafeteria. I'd seen it a thousand times, Mike would meet someone and in five minutes he'd be lost in conversation. Some odd topic, some subject you might never have predicted.

Not just because he was polite. It was more than that—Mike was interested, no matter what the topic. He liked the surprise of it, the fact that you never knew what someone else was going to say. It might turn out to be really important. Just the piece of information you needed to help you understand something special, something you didn't even realize that you needed to know.

Mike stayed that way. Years later, when we drove around the countryside in our Crown Coach Company bus, Mike was happy to oblige anyone who wanted an autograph. He would stick around and talk to every last straggler in the crowd. If you gave him a ball to sign, Mike would ask who it was for, and what grade the kid was in, what position he played. Before he gave it back, he'd know all about your family. Maybe it turned out your uncle went to the same high school as his father, or your grandmother lived in the same city as his cousin. So he'd talk to you some more about that.

Mike would sign until his hand was sore, and then in the diner where we ate our meatloaf and peas, he would gossip with the counterman until closing time.

So it was no surprise that, although we had never exchanged so much as a word with Andrew Flood, Mike turned and said hello.

"I heard what happened with Polk," Flood said.

"He didn't answer my question," Mike said.

Flood nodded. He looked at us, as if he were making up his mind about something. Then he said, "Come over here." He motioned toward a corner of the schoolyard, where you could slip behind a toolshed and be hidden from the rest of the yard.

We walked over there. We went behind the shed.

Up close, you could see that Flood's skin was as pale as the moon. He had cinnamon-colored freckles around the jawline, which formed an illusion of a five-o'clock shadow, making him look unwashed. Flood's hair was longer than it should have been, and it might never have been combed or brushed. Sometimes, people who look like that don't care about anything. But you could see in Flood's eyes that there was something he cared about.

"Listen," Flood said, and looked back and forth between us. You could tell that he was nervous. He wasn't exactly fidgeting—it was less obvious than that, more of a shifting of weight from side to side, his head bobbing a little, like a pigeon's.

Flood pulled a cigarette out of his coat pocket. He lit it with a wooden match.

"Listen," he said again, breathing in smoke. He leaned against the shed as he spoke. "The speed of light is always the same. Right? Polk must have told you that much."

It surprised me that Flood paid any attention to physics, or any other class, for that matter. But Mike nodded his head.

Flood took in a lungful of smoke, then looked all around, making sure that no one had followed us.

"Forget about a train going at the speed of light," Flood said. "That's a distraction. Polk will tie you up in knots over whether a real train could go that fast."

"That's exactly what he did," Mike said. "But it isn't the point, because—"

"I know," Flood said. "Forget about it." He took in more smoke and let it trickle out of his mouth. His green eyes narrowed.

"Think about an *ordinary* train," Flood said. "A train traveling at an ordinary speed. Now think about this. *What happens when it gets dark?*"

Flood paused to let that sink in. I couldn't imagine what he was getting at.

"The train is moving," he said. "The sun starts to set. What happens when the headlights go on?"

Mike's eyebrows shot up. "That's it!" he said. "You're right, that's it!"

Andrew Flood watched as Mike began to pace around behind the shed.

"You add the velocities together," Mike said. "So it's the same problem. The train is going twenty miles an hour, then you turn the lights on, so you add twenty miles to the speed of the light—but that won't work, nothing can go faster than light. It's impossible!"

Flood took a long drag on his cigarette. "Yeah," he said. "It's impossible."

"So what happens?" Mike said.

Flood edged over to the corner of the toolshed and peeked around it. No one was near. Lunchtime was over, but Mike wasn't going to leave until he heard the rest.

"Listen," Flood said. "You're standing by the track when the train goes by. You measure the speed of the light from the train, how fast it's moving away from you. With the right kind of equipment, you could do that. Do you know what you're going to get?"

Flood paused, to sharpen the drama. He took a puff from his cigarette, then exhaled.

"Nine hundred and eighty million feet per second. Because the speed of light is always the same, never changes."

"But what about—"

"That's right," Flood said. "That's exactly what the problem is. The man on the train measures, too, and you know exactly what he is going to find. Nine hundred and eighty million. The light is moving away from him at exactly the same speed. But what sense does that make? How can the same light travel away from both men at the *same* speed? When one of them is moving, and the other is standing still?"

Flood threw his cigarette on the ground and crushed it with his foot. He took out another one, and offered it to Mike. Mike waved it away. He was lost in thought.

"How can it be the same?" Mike said. "How can it possibly be?"

* * *

You know what's coming, don't you?

The next day, Mike had his hand in the air as soon as Mr. Polk walked into the room. But Polk didn't call on him. He picked up some papers from his desk, turned his back, and began writing on the chalkboard.

"Mr. Polk?" Mike said.

There was no answer, just chalk scratching on slate. Polk's shoulders were rigid.

"Mr. Polk?" Mike said again. "I have a question."

More scratching, then a few sharp taps on the board as Polk punctuated his sentence. The entire class stared at Mike. Mike watched as Polk moved slowly down the chalkboard, still writing.

Mike looked down at the paper on his desk, a page of diagrams he had drawn. He cleared his throat.

Mike said, "What happens when the train turns its lights on?"

The class was silent for a moment, a stillness so perfect that you could hear the gurgle of plumbing from deep within the building. A small blue bird fluttered to the windowsill outside the classroom. You could hear the tips of its wings brushing against the glass.

And then, very slowly, Mr. Polk turned around.

"I am absolutely certain that I did not ask for questions," he said.

"But I'm talking about an ordinary train. I'm only trying to figure out—"

"Silence!"

Mr. Polk fixed his stare on Mike, to prevent him by sheer force of will from saying another word. But there were already whispers in the back of the room. A couple of people started to scribble on paper. Everyone else was looking back and forth between Mike and Mr. Polk.

Polk looked unsure for a moment. He continued to stare at Mike while taking in the fact that pencils were moving, that two or three hands were starting to rise. Slowly, to be sure, but rising nonetheless. Polk's neck went from pink to red.

Mike decided to continue.

"Mr. Polk, if you could just explain—"

"Silence!" Polk slammed both fists on his desk, upending a coffee can filled with sharpened pencils. The can clattered, and pencils rained across the desktop. A picture frame slipped off the edge of the desk and tumbled to the floor, landing with a crash. Mrs. Polk smiled through shards of broken glass.

A few seconds of quiet.

And then chaos—a dozen voices at once, everyone trying to be heard. Polk shouting that physics was not a game. Mike insisting he had a valid question. A boy in the back of the room suggesting that Polk draw a diagram on the board, and then Mike offering to draw it himself. Polk wagging his finger at Mike and demanding that he keep quiet. Mike saying that he only wanted to understand the problem.

Polk threw open the door to the hallway, shouted that class was dismissed, and ordered us out of the room.

Of course the school supported Polk. What do you expect? The system defends itself, right or wrong.

Mike's real crime was not that he challenged Mr. Polk in the class. The school didn't care about etiquette in the classroom—that was an excuse. Isn't there always an excuse?

The *idea* is what they were afraid of. Because what is more powerful than an idea? The school could have all the rules they wanted, but Mike had people whispering in the back of the room.

Mike's real crime was that he tried to unlock a door. A door the system wanted closed, because if you walked through it, who knows what might happen? Fundamental things could be called into question.

It came down to this. A full written apology, or Mike would be suspended. That was unthinkable—if Mike were suspended, he would be off the baseball team for an entire year. Can you imagine? Even in tenth grade, Mike was the best hitter the school had ever seen. How could they *think* of suspending him? But that was the threat.

In two weeks we'd start practice. Spring was in the air. Do you remember that feeling? That startling green when you jog out to the field, the first time you've seen it in months. Your shoes sink into spongy earth—as if you were the first person ever to walk on it.

The equipment is waiting, lined up in patient rows. You pull on your glove, pick up a ball. You feel the roughness of the seam, the weight of the ball in your hand. Its balance. It makes you feel that *everything* is in balance.

You trot out to the mound, that old strength in your legs. It feels good to shake the winter out of your muscles, to jog across the bright new grass. You climb that little hill. You toe the pitching rubber, a fresh white strip set in the dark earth, the last time that year you'll see it unscuffed. The catcher settles in behind home plate. You nod in, then go into your windup, the most natural thing in the world—your leg kicks up, your arm comes around, and the ball sails in, the way it always does. Right into the catcher's mitt, that satisfying *smack*.

What could Mike do? They told him what to write, and Polk posted the apology on the classroom door.

Dear Mr. Polk,

I admit of my own free will that I was wrong. A train can never travel at the speed of light, and there is no reason to imagine that it can. I promise not to engage in idle speculation, and in the future I will never question the established laws of physics.

Mike

Mike never raised his hand in Polk's class again. But we met Andrew Flood from time to time behind the toolshed, because Flood had a brother in college, who knew a lot more than Polk did. We'd huddle behind the shed, and Flood would carefully open a manila envelope. He'd pull out his brother's lecture notes, a couple of smudged diagrams, a mimeographed sheet of equations.

Time is the problem, it turns out. How's that for a kick in the pants? Time is like rubber, not steel, and it means one thing to the man on the train and another to the man on the ground. They measure the same speed but in different times—which all works out, if you don't mind twisting your brain into a pretzel. A clock is a kind of imagination, is the bottom line. You were standing on solid ground, but now that ground is dissolving beneath your feet and you're not even sure what ground *is*.

We had some lively discussions behind the shed, keeping an eye out for teachers. Even so, there were a couple of close calls. We'd be scribbling a formula when we'd hear footsteps, a shadow would fall across the grass, and we'd have to hide the paper and quickly change the subject. One of us would make a comment about girls or President Hoover, and the others would pretend to laugh.

When Mike wrote out his apology, I told him it was a lousy deal.

"It's OK," Mike said. "Everyone will know they made me write it. But I'll tell you what bothers me."

Mike looked at me, with that serious expression he got sometimes. "If they're wrong about this, what else are they wrong about?"

CHAPTER FIVE

Sometimes I think about that rally in Green Bay, the cold, rainy Saturday when we stood on that makeshift stage in the middle of the crowded square. We listened to the speeches and the chanting and the carpenter's wife singing about Joe Hill. We watched people in worn jackets wave handmade signs in the gray drizzle. Electricians and plumbers who were ready for battle, who knew what was right and were ready to stand up for it.

Most of all, I think about a little black-haired girl.

She sat on the ground in front of her father's muddy boots, her legs crossed on the damp pavement. Seven years old, maybe, eating peanuts from a paper sack. I told you that my recollection can be hazy—but even now, I see that girl as plainly as I see you. The wrinkles around her nose as she bit down on those nuts. Bits of shell on her gray woolen sweater.

She reached into that paper sack, took out a peanut, and cracked the shell with her teeth. She emptied the nuts into her hand.

It bothers me that I can't remember a word the union president said. That a thousand people filled the square, their hearts filled with purpose—and I don't remember a single face, except for this girl and her satisfied smile. Her hand reaching into her bag, her teeth biting down. The peanut shells making a pile on the wet asphalt. An image that has no significance at all but has stayed in my mind forever. Explain *that*, if you can.

Why this girl? If Nancy had been there, she might have had an idea. It was the kind of thing Nancy seemed to understand. I wish I could ask her now.

Seven years old. That girl would be eighty or so now—younger than me, but still old.

She has lived an entire life, a life that has had nothing to do with mine. Although who knows? I've passed through Wisconsin any number of times. I might have seen her in one place or another. I wouldn't have recognized her, once she was grown. She might have served me breakfast in some roadside diner, stood in line behind me at the grocery. Sat by my side one night in a movie theater, the two of us watching some Hollywood romance, our hopes rising and falling with the fortunes of the lovers on the screen. Ignorant of the secret history we shared.

She might even be here now. Why not? She's old enough to be one of those women playing rummy on the deck, her eyes a nest of wrinkles, her young girl's body lost to time. The chrome of her wheelchair growing warm in the sun.

* * *

But we were talking about the Rockefeller.

Effie paid the desk clerk and walked over with our keys. A stranger followed him, a heavyset man almost as tall as Ozzie Gadlin. A black wool overcoat, buttons fastened all the way to the top. Snow still melting on his shoulders.

The stranger had one of those smooth faces that made it hard to tell how old he was, with sharp blue eyes. Nose slightly larger than necessary. Forehead wide as a billboard. His thin brown hair was steadily receding—you know the type, in a couple of years he'd comb the last few strands over his scalp, and they'd float there like a wispy fog. You can't fool anyone that way, but what choice do you have? People expect you to try.

The stranger followed Effie, leaving wet footprints on the varnished pine. He looked around the room until he caught Ozzie's eye.

"Hello there!" He gave Ozzie a big smile, maybe in solidarity over their matching height and breadth. The man was not fat—no potbelly filled out his coat, no fleshy jowls padded his neck—but there was a heft to him. You could tell he was well fed.

Ozzie looked at him as though he were a block of wood.

"It's a genuine privilege," the stranger said. He drew out the word "gen-u-wine," taking pleasure in it, stretching that single word out to the length of a sentence. Nodding his head emphatically, as if agreeing with himself.

He stuck out his hand.

"Do I know you?" Ozzie said.

"Spencer," the stranger said, holding on to his smile. "My name is Spencer, and it's a pleasure to make your acquaintance."

Ozzie shrugged and put out his hand. "Gadlin," he said.

"I know," said Spencer.

It turned out that Spencer knew all about us. He'd been a fan for years, he said. A *true* fan. Reading our box score was the only reason to buy a newspaper, according to him, and the Robins were the only team worth watching. We played the game like it meant something. In fact he had stolen away from his business trip that very afternoon, sneaking over to Madison to cheer us on from the first-base bleachers. Imagine how surprised he had been to see our bus in the parking lot! He was pleased—no, thrilled—no, *deeply honored* to wind up in the same hotel.

"You ought to be proud," Spencer said. "You're a talented bunch. Dare I say it? Almost good enough to play in the major leagues."

You could have heard a pin drop.

"Almost?" Ozzie said.

Tall as Spencer was, at that moment Ozzie towered over him. But more than his height, it was Ozzie's glare that did the work— that special look catchers have, the one that can knock you over if you're not careful. A glare they earn in the heat of the battle. Who else but a catcher crouches in the line of fire, in the very shadow of the enemy? No green grass for him, no sweet outfield prairie. A catcher hunkers in the dirt, sweating into his chest pad, his shin guard, his scuffed helmet. He crouches until his legs cramp, until his calves ache. His thighs burn like molten lead. He'll crouch there forever if he has to—because he knows what every catcher knows, that victory goes to those who stand their ground.

So he waits, bracing for whatever comes his way. That blazing pitch, that swinging lumber. A runner hurtling toward the plate, spikes flashing in the sunlight. There are collisions, bruises, broken bones—but catchers don't mind. It toughens them into tree trunks, weathers them into boulders. The best of them become immovable objects.

You can't have a revolution without a catcher.

Ozzie fixed Spencer in his catcher's glare.

"Let me tell you something," Ozzie said. "You take any one of those so-called major league teams. Put them on the field with us, and we will teach them a thing or two about this game. We'll play them for nine innings, and they'll leave with their tails between their legs. We'll see who's good enough!"

"Oh, I don't mean to offend," Spencer said. "Don't take it the wrong way. You're a fine team, no question about it. An *excellent* team. But I'm sure you'd admit that you're not quite at that level, not for lack of talent, of course. You have plenty of—"

"Not at that *level*?" Ozzie fixed Spencer with that catcher's glare again. "If you don't mind telling me, exactly what level are we at?"

"As I say, you have plenty of talent, but you're not exactly set up to take advantage of it. Of course, I admire your ideals. You all want to be *equal*, you want to be the *same*. Those are beautiful ideals, they really are.

"But you can't deny," Spencer went on, "that some people are more talented than others. It isn't anyone's fault—that's just the way it works. Why would you fight against nature? If you're going to compete, why hold back players whose talent should lift them to the top?"

Ozzie stared at Spencer in disgust. The rest of us looked on, some sharing Ozzie's feelings, others merely hungry and ready to head for the dining room. After so many years in the league, we had heard this all before—the natural order, the way things work. As if there were anything natural about making one man a boss, and another a servant. As if it were natural for one man to own another's house, or his land, or his livelihood. One man wallowing in luxury while another sleeps in an alley. Why should I gorge myself on bread if my neighbor is starving? How is *that* natural?

Your principles are fine and good, people would say, but you have to be practical, you have to understand how it *is* out there. An old argument—why should it surprise us to hear it again? Especially from this fleshy businessman, with his shiny black shoes and smooth pink hands. Why should *he* understand?

Effie stepped in.

"Mendez," he said, looking Spencer in the eye.

"Effie Mendez!" Spencer's smile grew even wider. "I saw you play in Binghamton, years ago. You stole home twice in one game. Once is something to remember, but *twice*—incredible!"

"Buffalo," Effie said.

49

"I remember it well. Amazing baserunning. And now you're the manager?"

"You said you knew all about us," Effie said.

Spencer made a show of slapping himself on his wide forehead. "Of course, I forgot! No managers, no coaches. You're all equal. Well, as I said, I admire your principles. But don't you think you hold yourself back, with some of these ideas?"

"We're in first place," Effie said.

"Yes, I know. In a league with Scranton and Battle Creek. Akron, for heaven's sake." Spencer shook his head. "I don't mean to offend," he said. "I told you, I'm your biggest fan. But what kind of competition is that? And how old are those uniforms? When was the last time you bought shoes? That bus you ride around in? In the big leagues they ride in sleeper cars, they stay at the best hotels. Restaurants! Broadway shows! That's the life of a ballplayer.

"I'm not criticizing," Spencer went on. "I'd be the last one to do that. But you have so much talent—why not take advantage of it? I'm not talking about luxury. I know you have your ideals, and I admire them. I do! I *share* them. But why not enjoy the fruits of your labor?"

Spencer looked around at the rest of the team, for a moment, at Mike and Ned Kretzmann and Sweetie Malone. "You're twenty-one years old," Spencer said. "Twenty-five, twenty-eight. You have your cause, I understand that, and it's all right for now. But one day you'll want to settle down. A little house, a nice green yard. How about some money in the bank?

"Think about it," Spencer said. "What's going to happen when you fall in love?"

There it was.

The rest of it didn't matter—not a single one of us cared about fine hotels or Broadway shows. We didn't need sleeper cars when we had our Crown Coach Company bus. Who needs a restaurant when you have a hamper full of sandwiches? That's not what we played for.

But what about love? How *did* you fall in love, in the kind of life we were leading? Hand to mouth, always on the road, everything for the team. A woman smiles at you in Bloomington or Dayton or Fort Wayne—so you have a cup of coffee, a nice dinner. Maybe a little more. But the next day, the bus rolls out of town, and *that's* the question. How does love blossom when you live for a cause? How does it put down roots? How do you get it to grow?

My mind went immediately to Nancy.

But wait. If I'm going to be perfectly honest—and why should I be anything else? What's the point of all this, unless it's to get at the pure, unvarnished heart of the matter?

If I'm going to be honest, my thoughts did not go directly to Nancy. They stopped, just for a moment, with Ella.

CHAPTER SIX

I t's only natural. Ella was first, after all. Why shouldn't I think of
Ella if we're going to talk about love?

I met her in an elevator.

I was eighteen years old. I had just interviewed for my first job,
as a mail clerk at the university, which would keep me in spending
money while I played in the City Summer League.

The interview was in the administration building, the tallest
building on campus. Nine floors up and two basement levels down.
Halfway between the personnel office on the fourth floor and the
lobby, the cable jerked and the elevator lights went out.

It was pitch-black.

"Hello?" A woman's voice. In the darkness, the sound had a
physical weight. I'd noticed her when I'd stepped in—so pretty I
was afraid to talk to her, but now it was dark.

"Hi," I said. And then, "I guess we're stuck."

"You're smart. You must be a graduate student."

I smiled in the darkness. There was a breeze on my cheek. The
ventilation was still working.

"I just applied for a job," I said. "In the mail room, but I'm really a ballplayer."

"I'm a sophomore. Political science," she said. "Are you cold?"

"Are you? I could give you my sweater."

"No, thanks. Do you have any food?"

"Sorry."

"Let me have your sweater."

I pulled it over my head. A shower of pumpkin-colored sparks.

She felt around in the darkness, and our fingertips grazed. The static triggered one last spark.

"Talk about a blind date," she said.

I could hear her pulling on my sweater. I liked the sound of her voice—I mean, I *really* liked it. I liked the fact that she said "blind date." I liked the idea that she was putting on my sweater, if that makes any sense. I wanted to keep talking, but the best I could do was, "It's dark."

"I noticed that." She laughed. "My name is Ella."

I couldn't help myself. I wished that the elevator would stay put, exactly where it was, at least for an hour or two. Wouldn't it take a while to check the machinery? To inspect the cable, the gears and pulleys, while Ella and I got to know each other? There must be other elevators to attend to. There was no emergency here. Couldn't the repair crew find something else to do, at least for a little while?

Even as I made that wish, there was another jolt, and the lights flickered on. The elevator began to move.

Now I could see that Ella had chocolate-colored eyes, and hair that fell in a smooth curtain to her shoulders. The color was darker than her eyes—closer to black than brown. She said, "Would you like to get a cup of coffee?"

When she said "coffee," Ella touched me on the arm. Her fingertips brushed my elbow while she looked at me with those chocolate eyes.

Of course we had coffee.

We sat in a cramped luncheonette, sipping from steaming cups. Our knees touched under the chipped Formica table, and Ella nibbled at a brown-sugar muffin while I asked every question I could think of. She was a double major, it turned out—economics on top of political science—and when Ella talked about her classes, she made them sound exotic, like distant foreign lands. She was twenty years old! Two years older than me. Two years to accumulate experiences I could only imagine.

She had her own apartment, at least for the summer, while her roommate was in Philadelphia organizing restaurant workers.

I could have watched Ella all day. That straight dark hair. Strong cheekbones that gave her a look of determination. Some people might have said those cheekbones were too prominent, and it's true that they made her look angular, maybe even hard, in a certain way. But I loved them, and I loved her wide brown eyes. I loved the way Ella set her jaw when she had a strong feeling about something, which seemed to be just about all of the time.

She was an only child. Ella's father was a newspaper reporter, and he insisted that life is a battle, an endless striving between righteousness and injustice. They talked politics at dinner every night until she went away to college. The world is shaped by struggle, Ella's father had said, as he sliced his roast beef. At every moment, the path branches and you have to make your choice. Which side are you on?

Ella knew which side she was on. The side of the workers, not the bosses. The people, not the owners who enslaved them. She was on the side of justice!

As she spoke, Ella's fingers stroked her necklace. A double chain of blackened gold, studded with some kind of antique beads. From Egypt, she said. In the center, a dark stone drew the chain below the fabric of her shirt and I couldn't help looking there, trying to make out the darkness of the gold against Ella's pearly skin.

Although it was probably not gold. Ella was against that kind of extravagance. It was a sign of moral weakness, she said, and I agreed with her. Aren't luxuries a distraction? A detour from life's higher purpose?

But if we're going to be honest, Ella's conscience was not pure. There was a luxury Ella had to have—she couldn't go a day without chocolate, *expensive* chocolate. A slab to nibble after dinner, a chunk packed with her sandwich at lunch. Shavings stirred into a cup of hot milk. Somehow, Ella had found a supply of the real thing: hard, grainy bars from Italy. I never knew where she got them, but they were wrapped in gold foil, and they were dark and bitter, sharp on the tongue. Chocolate in its very essence.

Not those milky, insipid bars from Hershey.

But chocolate is a small luxury, not like diamonds or mink. Don't we all have some petty indulgence? Some minor flaw in the purity of our ideals?

I sat with Ella in the luncheonette, as she dropped cube after cube of sugar into her coffee. The hum of conversation around us, the clatter of dishes. The air steamy from the dishwasher, and growing warmer every time I looked in Ella's brown eyes.

I had never sat with a woman in a coffee shop. I had never had this kind of conversation, this back-and-forth of likes and dislikes, of personal histories. Circling around each other. Maybe even *toward* each other.

I felt that I had set off on a great adventure.

If anyone had looked at Ella and me—steam rising from our cups, muffin crumbs scattered across the table—if anyone had looked at us, they would have thought we belonged together.

I had spent a lot of time picturing a moment like this. Why not? How could you *not* think about it? Women were everywhere, drifting through the hallways at school, in giggling clouds. Floating through the cafeteria, a glimpse of crimson sweater, a flash of a smile. Of course I thought about them!

Brenda McAdams, for example.

I sat behind Brenda every day in math class, close enough to admire the smooth skin on the back of her arms, to smell the sweetness of soap. Inches from the crisp cotton of her shirt. I could have reached out and felt it crackle on my fingertips, I might have traced the lines of her shoulders, the muscles of her neck. There was geometry on the chalkboard, but I only wanted to look at Brenda. Wasn't that geometry, too? Her honey-colored braid. The arcs of her shoulder blades. The way they pressed against the fabric of her blouse when she raised her hand.

It is possible to fall in love with someone's back, in case you are interested.

Day after day, I sat behind Brenda, looking at the ridge of her spine. I imagined the things we would say to each other, if only she would turn around. The way her eyes would shine as we dawdled in the hallway after class. As we walked home from school. As we sat on her living room couch, Brenda sipping from a glass of lemonade. For some reason, I always pictured us in Brenda's living room, although I didn't even know where she lived.

We'd go over there to study. The house empty, her parents at work. We'd get halfway through our homework, and at a certain moment, after we had solved some particularly difficult problem, I would push the book aside, and Brenda would set down her glass of lemonade, her eyes already closing as we reached for each other across the coffee table.

I sat behind Brenda McAdams for a year, and I never spoke to her. Maybe it was hard because I was already so close to her. Maybe sitting *behind* Brenda for so long made me afraid to approach her from the front. But I spent a lot of time thinking about her, and a big part of what I pictured was the two of us sitting together in a restaurant. In a bakery. In a coffee shop. Just sitting and talking. And people would look at us and know that we were together.

Anyone looking at Ella and me in the luncheonette would instantly see that she was pretty. They might wonder, for a minute, whether she was *too* pretty for me. But only for a minute. I had my own appeal, if you took a good look. I wasn't handsome in an obvious way, but I was presentable. I might not have turned women's heads like Sweetie—but I had steady blue eyes, a square chin, an honest face. So when people looked at us, they would see that the match was within the realm of possibility, that it made sense for us to be together.

That we were a couple.

I thought a lot about how that would feel. I mean, a *lot*.

After all these years, that's the part I miss the most about that time—the way it felt to imagine what love *might* be like, before anything had happened. When it was all just an idea.

In real life, it happened slowly. All that summer, Ella and I sat in cafes and lunchrooms across the city, drinking coffee and sharing biscuits and chicken sandwiches. We ordered doughnuts dipped in powdered sugar, and Ella picked at the sugary coating while I favored the tender dough inside. It took time, I found out, to get to know each other, although one thing I learned right away—Ella was sure of herself. So sure, as a matter of fact, that you couldn't possibly argue with her. If you disagreed, whether the matter was large or small, Ella would pause for the briefest moment. She would raise her eyebrow a fraction of an inch. She would look at you with a blank expression—as if your comment did not deserve the slightest response, even the effort needed to shake her head.

Then Ella would go on, as if you had never spoken.

It drove Mike crazy, because he liked to kick things around, to look at them from every side. To chew on them until he was sure.

But you couldn't chew on things with Ella. She knew from the start that she was right, so what was the point of endless discussion?

The three of us had lunch one day. I thought it would make things easier, I don't know why. We squeezed into a booth in a diner, we ordered the blue plate special, and just as the food arrived, Mike made a comment—some small issue, something he knew better than she did—and Ella ignored it. Just passed right over. Mike looked at me and shook his head, and Ella caught the look and gave me a perfectly calculated glance, not quite rolling her eyes—more subtle than that. A glance that made it clear that Mike's comment and his head shake were unworthy not only of Ella's attention, but also of mine. Mike saw Ella's message, as of course he was meant to, and waited a minute to see what I would do. As if I had any choice. Ella was sitting right there! Then Mike stood up, put on his hat, and stomped out the door, leaving his turkey and mashed potatoes to cool on the plate.

I heard about it from Mike later, you can be sure of that. I didn't understand why he took it so hard. Mike got along with everyone else—why not with Ella? The truth is, I wished I could be more like her. I like the way it feels when you're sure, when you don't need to mull things over. Because the answer is right in front of you. You just *know.* I didn't want to feel the way Mike did, that the world is endlessly complicated, that you always have to puzzle things out, weigh one side against the other, look from every angle. What does it get you? You'll never feel satisfied once you go down that path. There are always subtleties, questions of interpretation, consequences that are hard to predict. What if you overlooked some critical fact? What if you didn't see a crucial connection?

You might miss the most important thing.

Ella didn't get tangled in the subtleties, in questions of interpretation. She knew what was important—all you had to do, she said, was open your eyes.

She smiled at the waiter who cleared a neighboring table, at the cashier behind the counter. The busboys, the kitchen staff. Why did the hardest jobs pay the lowest wages? We passed breadlines as we walked around the city, we walked by soup kitchens, and Ella told me they had not formed by chance. The system had created soup kitchens. The system *needed* breadlines. What better way to hold wages down than to keep people hungry? They'll take whatever work you give them if there's not enough to go around. They'll settle for what they can get if their neighbors are starving, and they won't make too much noise about it.

But things had finally gone too far, Ella said. Poverty is one thing, a depression is another. People were desperate, they had nothing to lose. They might even join together.

Ella was sure that this was about to happen. I believed with all my heart that she was right.

*   *   *

It rained for two weeks toward the end of July, and one Sunday morning, Ella and I sat in the window of a cafe. We drank chocolate, strong and thick, the way she liked it. Steam rising from ceramic mugs.

Ella was quiet, for a change, her expression serious. She looked at me through layers of thought.

I was used to Ella doing the talking—I had never seen this mood before. We sipped from our mugs, looking out the window at the traffic. I did my best to make conversation, but Ella had no opinions to offer, no lectures to give. Finally, she put her hand on my hand, her fingers warm from the mug of chocolate. She said, "Come with me."

We walked down the street, around the corner. Up the stairs to her apartment. And there I sat, on the edge of Ella's sofa, while she paced back and forth between her living room and her kitchen. Ella brought me a glass of water, then went back to get ice, but forgot and came back without it. She sat down next to me and then stood up. She went back to the kitchen and poured herself a glass of wine, which was odd, since it was morning, but then she left it on the counter.

I had never seen her nervous.

I was nervous, too. Because I had a feeling something was about to happen, something I had spent a long time waiting for, since that first afternoon in the coffee shop. Or before that—since the moment Ella touched my arm, as we stepped out of the elevator and she looked at me with those deep brown eyes. Or even before! The truth is, I had been waiting since I first heard Ella's voice, that bright "hello" in the blackened elevator. A voice that filled the darkness.

I wasn't quite sure what to do.

We had kissed before. Of course we had! In the park, where a gazebo was set off from the footpath. On an old stone bench, next to the river. On the sidewalk in front of Ella's apartment, as she leaned against the trunk of an old sycamore, which curved in a comfortable mold of her back. We would stand in the glow of the streetlight and talk for a little while—then I'd move closer, and Ella's arms would go around me. There's nothing like that moment! The warm night air, the darkness broken by an occasional firefly, the look on Ella's face as we would draw together. As her eyes would begin to close.

But now we were in Ella's living room, and that was an entirely different matter. When it comes to this kind of thing, there is a big difference between inside and outside, as I am sure you are aware. What was I supposed to do? *When* was I supposed to do it? How was it all supposed to work?

Suddenly, the fact that Ella was two years older than me seemed very, very important.

Ella took a deep breath and sat down again. Not next to me, on the couch, but in an armchair directly across. So she could look right into my eyes.

She folded her arms.

"What do you think about love?"

It was still raining outside—there were little streams running down the windowpane. It was humid in the apartment, and it felt difficult to breathe, for some reason. Ella's dark eyes were hard to read. Her lips were parted, just a little. She wore a peach-colored blouse.

There was a thin glaze of sweat on her forehead.

What did I think about love?

"It's fantastic!" I said.

Ella sat there in her armchair, looking at me. Then she sighed.

"I need you to understand this," she said. "It's very important."

So she explained it to me.

"It starts with capital," Ella said. "Don't look surprised, that's where everything starts."

I nodded. I wasn't sure why economics were important at that moment, but if Ella wanted to talk about capital, I was going to go along. I was ready to agree with anything she said.

"Men want to own things," Ella said. "They want to control them. Do you understand? There's nothing to be done about it, that's just the way things work."

I looked at her. What else was I going to do?

"Men store up capital," Ella said. "Because that is their fundamental urge—to multiply their power, to reproduce their wealth."

I confess that as Ella spoke, I felt a fundamental urge.

"But," Ella said. Her dark eyes locked on mine. I could not have moved an inch from that couch. I would not have wanted to.

"Capital is not enough," Ella said. "Capital by itself cannot make a product. It can build a factory, but a factory is only a place. Capital can buy machinery, but machinery does not run on its own. There must be a partner."

I nodded again.

"Someone has to *work* the machinery," Ella said. "Someone must operate the means of production. Do you see? This is important, I want you to understand the social context."

Ella leaned forward in her chair, and I could see the outline of her shoulders through the fabric of her blouse. The slope of her muscles, the ridge of her collarbone. Her peach-colored blouse against the skin of her throat.

I was eighteen years old. It was easy to lose myself in Ella's dark eyes, her hair falling like satin in a glossy sheet. If I could touch that hair, I thought, I would be the happiest man in the world.

Ella knew so much more than I did. She understood mysteries, the deepest secrets of life. And I had all of her attention! My heart was pounding, Ella's cheeks were flushed. She put her hand on my leg.

She said, "Capital is not enough. There must be *labor*."

I could not open my mouth to reply. All I could think about was the pressure of Ella's fingers on my leg. I could hardly breathe, let alone speak. As if the earth itself had stopped spinning.

Time had slammed on the brakes.

History had ground to a halt.

The order of events had vanished—there was no past, no future. All you could see, the only moment that truly existed, was this exact instant on the couch.

While time had stopped, space was having its own problems. I was no longer sure there was a world beyond Ella's living room. The universe had narrowed to a single point, and only Ella and I were left, sitting together, staring into each other's eyes.

"There must be labor," Ella said. "To run the machinery, to produce the product. Labor to make everything work."

Ella picked up my glass of water from the table next to the couch. She took a sip, and set it back down.

"There is one question," Ella said.

I nodded. I knew we were reaching the crucial point.

"Capital needs labor. Capital is *helpless* without labor. So the bosses need to make an arrangement." Ella looked at me, and I nodded.

"But why should labor cooperate?" Ella said. "The bosses pile up wealth while workers fight for pennies. Capital steals the profits while labor feeds on scraps. Why should labor want any part of the deal?"

Ella's face was so close to mine, and her hand was on my leg. Suddenly, the relationship between capital and labor was the only thing in the world worth caring about.

I thought carefully.

Before I could say anything, Ella was on the couch. I don't know how it happened—I didn't even see her leave the chair—but suddenly she was curled right next to me, her side warm against my side, the length of our bodies pressed together. She reached for my hand.

Then she answered her own question.

"Labor *has* to work," Ella said. "Work is part of life. I'm not only talking about money. What does life *mean* if you don't add anything to the world? What kind of dignity do you have if your hands are idle?"

Ella looked in my eyes. "Do you see?" she said. "Do you see why they need each other?"

I told Ella that I understood. The fact that labor and capital needed each other was as clear to me as anything in the entire world.

Ella's fingertips grazed my hair, the side of my neck. The kind of touch that creates a need for more touching. Her face so close to mine that I could feel, on my own cheeks, the heat from her skin. I had to kiss her—but as I turned my head, Ella put her hand on my chin to hold me back.

She said, "Why should capital be in control?"

I waited. What else could I do?

"Why should capital reap the profits?" Ella said. "Why can't there be a different kind of arrangement, a system that's fair? If capital depends on labor, why can't they *share* control?"

Ella was as close to me as one person can get to another. I was wedged between her body and the armrest of the sofa, and as we sank together into the upholstery, I held on to the arm of the couch. I liked the feeling of the wood, the pressure of polished maple against my fingers. I felt solidarity with that couch, its maple frame heavy as a battleship, and now it carried Ella's and my weight, too. I imagined all that weight sinking to the foundation of the building, to steel pilings that drove through layers of soil, through compressed clay, until they finally hit bedrock—the living, breathing heart of the earth.

Ella was right.

I looked in her eyes, and I knew there *could* be a different system. A system where profits would be shared. Wealth would be divided. Labor would be free, no longer dependent on the whims of others. No longer serving the desires of capital, while her own needs go unaddressed.

"What do you think?" Ella said.

I nodded my head, and that must have been enough.

Because Ella smiled. And at last—she pulled me in and kissed me.

What can I tell you? We indulged ourselves. We wallowed in it. At first the kiss was warm and sweet and deep, soft as velvet. But then the tides began to shift—you know what I'm talking about. Things which had been asleep began to awaken. There was something pressing, even urgent, that needed to be done.

Impatience crept into the kiss—it grew forceful. Revolution was in the air. Rules were being rewritten, the old government was tottering. Crowds were massing in the street.

We undid buttons and snaps. There were cheers as doors were broken down, as people raced into liberated buildings, as deposed leaders were forced to slink out the back door.

Nothing tastes as good as freedom! We made all kinds of discoveries, found all sorts of surprises as labor and capital explored new markets, removed barriers to trade. Crisp fabric slid over that gorgeous landscape, those beautiful hills and valleys.

I touched Ella's smooth skin in places I had never seen before. The wheels of commerce turned—my palm slid down her warm stomach, and our profits increased. As they did, the wheels turned faster.

Revenue soared to heights that neither of us had imagined.

There was wealth to share, an economy of lips and fingers, a world of marvels to treasure and caress. We discovered that there are times when giving is better than taking. Do you know what I'm talking about? *Much* better. There were times when giving was the only thing we wanted to do. There were times when it mixed together so completely that we didn't even know whether we were giving or taking.

Capital and labor were in perfect harmony.

We found all kinds of hidden connections, all kinds of un-mapped wiring. What happens on the surface can cause other things to happen below the surface. We were surprised, we were dazzled. We were so caught up in our progress that I found it hard to keep track of the social context.

I confess that at one critical moment, I forgot who was capital and who was labor.

* * *

So I knew what Spencer meant when he brought up the question of love. Although even today, I feel a little guilty for thinking about Ella. As if the thought were disloyal to Nancy in some way—even though Ella *did* come first. Isn't it perfectly natural that I would think of her?

And it didn't last long, with Ella. She was heading back to school, at the end of the summer, which meant the end—Ella made that clear halfway through August. Like a conductor on the Baltimore and Ohio announcing the last stop. I might have found a way to go with her, but she shook her head. We had fun, she said, but that's not what happens next. I wish I knew what ever happened to her.

I looked around the lobby of the Rockefeller. Spencer's question about love had kept us quiet, for a while, as each man followed his own memories, traveled his own path.

That was when Spencer offered to buy us dinner.

There were two ways to look at that kind of invitation. We huddled in the corner to talk it over. The hard-liners said it was tainted money, and we should refuse. Ozzie Gadlin, of course, and

Buddy Brodsky. On the other side were those who were just plain hungry and didn't care who paid for dinner.

In the end, Effie said it was all for the best. If the money was tainted, why not help Spencer spread it around? If the profits belonged to the people, why not share some of them right now?

So we walked out of the paneled lobby and headed for the dining room.

Outside, it continued to snow.

CHAPTER SEVEN

My nurse has a steady, reliable grip. Not that I *need* her to hold my arm. You may have heard that I fractured my ankle last year, but that was the fault of a patch of ice, and could have happened to anyone.

I let my nurse hold my arm because I like it. I like the pressure of her fingers. I feel warm when she is next to me, if you want to know the truth.

I may as well admit that there is something about her, my blonde-haired nurse, that reminds me of Nancy. Not in any obvious way. Nancy's hair was dark, not blonde. Not straight, like my nurse's, but thick and wavy. I remember the feel of Nancy's curls, the way they sprang back when I traced them with my finger. My nurse's hair is different—wispy and soft, like corn silk. Nice, but not the same.

Nancy was shorter than me, but to look in my nurse's eyes I gaze *up* half an inch.

The truth is, they're not alike at all. Except for a slight resemblance—it's not even a resemblance, it's more of a *reminder*—around the eyes. Something about the slope of my nurse's cheekbones, the curve of her eyebrows as they fade into the bridge of her nose. I wouldn't fault you for thinking that I've imagined it. Sometimes, people see what they want to see. But I am sure it's there, and for some reason, this similarity has a great effect on me.

* * *

"Sit!" said Spencer. "Sit down!"

Spencer waved us into the dining room, where a waiter was pushing tables into a long row. An elderly man, who from the look of his shoulders had once been strong but was starting to give in to gravity. His back slumping, his posture curling. You can't resist the earth forever.

The waiter's forehead was furrowed as a cornfield, but he had a tremendous head of hair, a snowy sheaf as massive as a polar ice cap. He left it uncombed, maybe through laziness—or maybe it was deliberate, a statement against vanity. Whatever the reason, he let his hair grow wild, tangles and curls forming ivory-colored peaks, like the top of a meringue.

The waiter grunted as he pushed the tables, slabs of solid oak. But he waved us away when we tried to help.

Spencer nodded at the empty seats. "Sit!" he said again.

Not a suggestion but a command. Which might have rubbed some people the wrong way, but Spencer's tone was so enthusiastic, his manner so spirited, that you couldn't take offense. Some people have a talent for that sort of thing.

My nurse, for example—"Take your cane!" she'll say as we set out on our afternoon stroll. I don't like to take orders. Who does? But my nurse smiles, and I give up any desire to resist. There is something in my nurse's voice that suggests a conspiracy, a kind of game between us. She knows I don't need that cane, her tone says— but why don't I bring it anyway? As a favor for her. To satisfy some quirk of hers, an exaggerated sense of caution. A charming excess of concern.

My nurse goes to all of that trouble to save my pride. The truth is, I *don't* really need that cane, I *do* carry it as a favor for her. But the least you can do, when someone tries to save your pride, is let them think it's working.

We walked toward the tables.

A true Wisconsin room—paneled walls as dark as buckwheat honey. The floors varnished oak, like the tables, but aged to a deeper brown. Wood that had a friendly feel, a fine, honest grain the trees had worked hard to produce.

There were gas lamps on the walls, burning pale yellow. They gave the room an antique glow, a light that flickered with the movements of the air. In a gesture to the modern world, there were also four electric lamps, one in each corner of the room, their frosted globes perched on brass pedestals. The two sets of lights produced a competition of shadows—the electric lamps cast crisp, charcoal-colored silhouettes with sharp edges. Shadows that meant business! The gas lamps were less precise, creating shadows with vague, blurry outlines. Like old photographs, or memory that has begun to fade.

It was the kind of room where a hunting party might go to celebrate, to boast about their kills. The kind of room where the local mayor, a couple of bankers, and the county judge might gather to make an important decision—about whether to allow a subdivision, perhaps, and how to divide the spoils.

Spencer said a few words to the waiter, who listened intently and then disappeared into the kitchen. We all sat down. Spencer in the middle of one side, Effie directly across. The rest of us up and down the length of the table, settling in our chairs, unfolding our napkins. Each man looking at Spencer with a different expression on his face.

Mike full of curiosity, of course.

Ozzie Gadlin a bit pensive, wondering exactly what kind of trouble Spencer would turn out to be.

Ned Kretzmann noticing Spencer's comfortable bulk, the way he filled out his clothes. Thinking that was a good sign for the dinner we were about to have.

Sweetie Malone was distracted. He had met a woman in Madison earlier that afternoon, a cashier in the bakery across from the ballpark, who'd helped us when we stopped to buy food for the road. She was pretty, of course—they always were. Nice green eyes, red hair tied in a ponytail, not strawberry red but bronze red, glinting with the kind of light you see at sunset. A few freckles, in just the right places.

Sweetie had looked over the counter, and she'd looked back at him, and that was it. Sweetie could get a lot done with a glance. We all knew what would happen the next time we went back to Madison.

Effie pulled his chair up to the table. He looked quickly at Spencer and then looked away, in a way that said none of this mattered. We were on *our* path, and Spencer was on *his*. What difference could it make, what significance could it possibly have, if for a moment those paths happened to cross?

Spencer looked at all of us, and smiled.

"I must say that it's a privilege to dine with such an accomplished group of men," Spencer said.

"It's a privilege to dine at all," said Buddy Brodsky. The rest of us laughed, because we knew exactly what he meant. Don't get me wrong, we earned enough to keep ourselves in sandwiches. There was always something to eat on the bus—a sack of apples, a loaf or two of bread. A tin of hard-boiled eggs.

We didn't starve.

But Buddy wasn't talking about the food. He was talking about the polished oak table, the clean china, the silverware laid out neatly, *two* forks next to every plate.

The napkins folded on the side.

The kitchen was in another room entirely—not a grill behind a counter. We wouldn't hold our plates in our laps here. We wouldn't pass bottles around. There were *wineglasses,* for heaven's sake.

And the aroma from the kitchen—like a taste of heaven. Smoke and spice, browning onions. The food itself might have been simple, like buttery potatoes and slow-roasted meat. But the fragrance got complicated when things were mixed together. You could spend the whole night scratching your head and not be able to describe it. You simply couldn't come up with the words.

I know what you are thinking. We were enjoying ourselves. I admit it! We worked hard, and it felt good to sit there, to relax, to be pampered for a change. But I can assure you of one thing. This is very important, something you need to understand. *We would not be seduced.*

We might have enjoyed a nice meal. We might have appreciated, once in a while, a little bit of indulgence. What's the harm? But we knew which side we were on. Not a single one of us would have changed places with Spencer, no matter how comfortable he was. No matter how fat his wallet.

We had made our choices, and we were satisfied. They were the *right* choices.

But there we were, trapped for the night in Wisconsin. So why not enjoy ourselves? It was only a diversion, a temporary detour—before we knew it, we'd be back on the road. Right back on our path.

CHAPTER EIGHT

The waiter returned from the kitchen, carrying a crockery pitcher. Fat at the bottom and glazed blood-red. He walked slowly around the table, filling our glasses with wine.

"Tell me," Effie said to Spencer. "What line of work are you in?"

"Buying and selling," said Spencer. "Nothing as interesting as what *you* do. People don't pay to watch me!"

"They must pay you for something," Effie said.

"I'll bet it's quite a feeling," Spencer said. "To stand there at the plate, all those eyes on you. Hundreds of people, maybe thousands! Waiting for you to take your swing. The chance to be a hero."

Spencer looked around the table. "But we can't all be ballplayers, can we? We each have to do our part. Business has its place, too. We couldn't live without industry, without commerce. Could we?"

"It depends," Effie said, "on how business is conducted."

Spencer nodded, as if the two of them were in complete agreement. "You are absolutely right!" he said. "There are principles involved, there's more to life than profit. We are meant for higher things. Although there's nothing wrong with making a living, is there? Someone has to run the machinery. Thank heaven there are still people willing to get their hands dirty!"

Spencer unfolded his napkin. "But we must conduct our business properly, I couldn't agree with you more. We must remember the most important thing, our duty to our fellow man. Our teammates."

Spencer looked around the table and raised his glass for a toast. "To the greater good!" he said.

We lifted our glasses to Spencer, some with more enthusiasm than others. The wine was sweet and dark. As we drank, the waiter brought baskets of steaming bread and set them down next to plates of butter. The plates were snow-white china with golden rims, and next to each plate was a small knife with a carved ivory handle. Whoever worked on those handles must have had incredible patience—if you looked closely, you could make out miniature cows and barns and butter churns, and a tiny milkmaid sitting on a stool.

What a way to live!

A gust of wind rattled the windows. "Hard to believe this snow is still coming," said Ned Kretzmann, nodding at the weather.

Heads shook around the table, mouths full of bread and butter. But Buddy Brodsky frowned.

"I've seen worse," Buddy said. And of course he had. It was not just that Buddy had reached the ripe old age of thirty-six and had seen more winters than anyone except Effie. The fact is that whatever you were talking about, Buddy had *always* seen worse.

If our bus got a flat tire, then Buddy had been on a bus with three flats and a fire in the engine. If the police tailed us out of an unfriendly town, Buddy told us about working as a leafletter for the C&A Railroad Strike when a National Guardsman fired what Buddy thought was a warning shot—until he got home, and found a bullet hole in the cuff of his pants.

"My *good* pants," Buddy said, and we all laughed.

"I've seen worse, too," said Spencer. "In January, or February. Maybe even March. But this much snow in April—it's an outrage!"

There were nods around the table. We knew it was an outrage. We should have been driving through Illinois, enjoying a nice spring night, looking forward to tomorrow's game.

"But look at the bright side," Spencer went on. "The storm has brought us all here. To this fine hotel, to this very table! You have to admit, without nature's misbehavior, we might never have come together, and I for one would be the poorer for it."

"You're going to be poorer after this dinner, that's for sure," said Sweetie Malone. There were chuckles around the table.

"Don't give that a second thought!" said Spencer. He waved his hand generously. "There's no better way to spend money than on a pleasant meal, with the best of friends. And I for one never question the work of destiny. You can't argue with fate!"

Effie looked up from buttering a heel of bread. "What do you mean?" he said.

Spencer looked at Effie, his eyebrows raised. As if he didn't understand the question.

"The work of destiny," Effie said. "What do you mean by that?"

"Only the obvious," Spencer said. "That there is a purpose to all of this, a higher meaning. There has to be! Why else would we find ourselves on the same highway at the very same time? How did we end up at the same hotel? Don't tell me it happened by chance."

Spencer must have seen the disapproval on Effie's face, so he went on quickly, leaving no time for an interruption.

"There are too many things that could have been different," Spencer said. "I might have stopped for lunch, for example. I might have taken the western route out of Madison. Your game could have gone into extra innings. So many things might have happened! How do you explain a blizzard in April if it isn't fate?"

Effie snorted. "We were on the same highway because that's how you get from Madison to Chicago," he said. "Our game stayed out of extra innings because Sweetie Malone made a diving catch. I am willing to bet that you didn't stop for lunch because you were in a hurry to get where you're going. Right? I don't see fate, I don't see any mysterious forces."

"You misunderstand," said Spencer. "I am not suggesting anything *mysterious*. We live in the real world, after all. We are enlightened men!"

Spencer took a drink of his wine and gazed judiciously around the table. The very picture of an enlightened man.

"But there are connections," Spencer said. "Events that are linked. You know what I mean. There are patterns, and you can't explain the cause. If you look carefully, you see that there is a direction to things, a *momentum*."

Spencer set down his wineglass. "The pattern might not be visible," he said. "At least, not at first. You might think there *is* no pattern as events unfold. But then an outline begins to emerge, if you pay attention. Things move on a certain path. In the end, when you look back, the blueprint is clear. Everything happened for a reason!"

The waiter circled the table, refilling our glasses. He rolled his watery blue eyes as he passed behind Spencer, although that could have been a trick of the light.

We understood what Spencer was saying. Of course we did! Things start out hidden, sometimes, and show themselves later. Buddy Brodsky used to pull a trick when he was guarding a runner on third base. Let's say a hotshot rookie is edging off the bag, an overconfident kid too fast for his own good. Ready to turn on the gas, to sprint home at the drop of a hat. In his mind, the kid is already standing on the plate, dusting off his pants. Waving his cap to the crowd.

Buddy would catch the umpire's eye, and call time. He'd stroll to the pitcher's mound for a chat, stroking his chin thoughtfully, where his beard would have been if Buddy had had a beard. Who knows what he wanted to talk about—something Buddy had noticed in the batter's stance, maybe. Or how they should play a bunt.

Then Buddy would saunter back. Nodding as the rookie took his lead, three or four steps toward home plate—a friendly nod, to say they were in it together. Sure, they might be on opposing teams, but didn't they share the dazzling sunlight, the soft green grass? Weren't they neighbors, at third base? Shouldn't neighbors be friends?

Buddy gave the runner a friendly nod, then reached out his glove to brush a piece of lint off the runner's shoulder. Ever so casually, a neighborly gesture. And then he opened the glove, to show the ball nestled inside.

"You're out!" the umpire would cry.

You've never seen a neighborly gesture cause such a stir. It took a second to sink in, for the runner to figure out what Buddy had done. Then there were strong words. Some yelling. The runner would be hopping mad—but it was good for him, in the long run, part of his education. A lesson that important things can be hidden, that you can miss the reason behind things, and later on it will appear.

But a hidden reason is not the same thing as fate. Maybe you just weren't paying attention.

Effie looked at Spencer. "So you believe in destiny?" Effie said. "That's how you think things happen?"

Spencer nodded. "No question about it," he said. "Everything happens for a reason."

Effie looked down the table, and said, "Let's see what Ozzie thinks about that."

Of course, he already knew. You could see Ozzie's blood rising as he scowled at Spencer, and it was natural for Effie to turn in his direction. Ozzie was the man you wanted at the plate if you were in a jam. The one we sent to the podium, to rile up a crowd. The one who could take the great and fundamental truths and make them easy to understand, even for a man like Spencer. We watched Ozzie compose his thoughts for a minute, choosing the right words. Then he cleared his throat, and said, "Things happen for a reason, sure. But fate is not the reason. *We* are the reason."

Buddy Brodsky, sitting next to Ozzie, nodded emphatically.

"*We* are the reason," Ozzie said. "The people here, at this table. Things happen because of *us*. There is no mysterious design!" More heads nodded in agreement.

"We are not puppets," Ozzie went on. "No one moves your arms for you. No one sets the path of your feet. Do you know what's wrong with that kind of thinking?"

Ozzie stared at Spencer, who scratched his head and shrugged. *We* all knew what was wrong with that kind of thinking.

"It's what the bosses want you to think," Ozzie said. "They want you to believe in a pattern, that everything is set, laid out by fate. That your path is fixed. Of course they want you to think that way! So that you will accept the way things are. So that you'll give in."

Ozzie fixed his catcher's glare on Spencer. As if Spencer were an opposing base runner, and Ozzie was daring him to step off the bag. *Just one inch.* So that Ozzie could nail him with a blazing fastball.

Spencer didn't take the bait. "I understand," he said. "You are men of action. You want to choose your own path. You want to drive the car, not sit in the passenger seat."

"That's exactly right," Ozzie said. "We drive the car."

"You are young men," Spencer said. "You have that strength, that wonderful enthusiasm. Why *shouldn't* you want to choose your own path?"

Spencer looked around the table and saw nodding heads. He went on.

"But wishing doesn't make it so," Spencer said. "You want to set your own direction, right? But the world has its own ideas. Did you plan to stop at this hotel tonight? Did you choose to be caught in this storm? You think you set your own path—but you didn't even choose to be in this *state!*"

You have to admit that Spencer had a point. Or at least half of one. Sometimes you head in a certain direction but wind up somewhere else. Does that mean fate sets our course? It sounded like blasphemy, to our ears, and it's not the way we lived. It's not what we chose to believe! But when I really stop to think—when I pause, for a moment, on the lawn with my blonde-haired nurse, leaning on my aluminum cane, watching visitors step out of their cars with flowers and jams and cookies—I understand the way Spencer felt.

How did I get *here*? When, exactly, did I choose this path?

I understand Spencer's point, but you can't take it too far. It's one thing to let the river carry you along once in a while, to give in to the current when you're happy with the trip. It's another thing for *everything* to be like that. To trust your entire life to the flow of the water.

Ozzie answered Spencer. "Bad luck brought us here," he said. "Blind bad luck. And bad luck is not the same as fate."

Spencer looked at Ozzie. "Call it what you will," Spencer said. "I know you want to think that way, I can understand your point of view."

Spencer picked up his wineglass, and looked at it with great concentration. He studied the pinpricks of light reflected there, the curve of the wineglass focusing the light, concentrating it into bright points. White from the electric bulbs, reddish gold from the gas lamps. Spencer rotated the glass slowly, then set it down without drinking.

"There is one thing I don't understand," Spencer said. "Let's say you're right. Let's say that you are free to choose your own direction."

"We *are* free," Ozzie said. "We *do* choose our own direction."

Spencer ignored him. "Let's say, for the sake of argument, that nothing is determined by fate. Let's say your destiny is so loose, so unconstrained, that you can choose whatever path you'd like.

"What I don't understand," Spencer said, "is this. If you can choose any direction you want—anything in the world—why would you choose *this* one? A life so difficult, so full of hardship. Why would you swim so hard against the current just to barely stay in place?"

For some reason, although Spencer's argument was with Ozzie, he looked directly at Mike.

Ozzie didn't notice. "I'll tell you why we chose this life," he snapped. "I will explain it so that it's clear even to—"

"*Great* bread," said Sweetie Malone.

Ozzie turned to his left and stared at Sweetie. Few people had the nerve to interrupt Ozzie. Especially when he was gathering momentum, when he was building up a head of steam. When he was about to put Spencer in his place.

But Sweetie shrugged off Ozzie's glare. "I'm just saying, it's really good bread."

He was right—it was fine bread, the crust thin but with a delicious crackle. The inside tender, with just the right amount of chew. There must have been whole wheat in the dough—it had a rich flavor, a hint of earthiness. Bread with character.

"All right, it's good bread," said Ozzie. "But the point is—"

That's when Mike decided to jump in.

"I don't know, Ozz," Mike said. "Maybe the bread *is* the point."

Ozzie turned to stare at Mike. He couldn't believe there was a *second* interruption. But Mike was one of the few people who wasn't rattled by Ozzie's glare.

"Maybe the bread *is* the point," Mike said. "Think about it. A lot of places serve lousy bread. You know? Soft and mushy, bread with no personality. Every slice is the same."

"That's right," Sweetie Malone said, spreading butter on another piece. "They ought to be ashamed."

"So?" Ozzie demanded.

Mike went on. "I'm talking about loaves of bread that have the right shape, that have the right color, but they're missing something. They don't have the *essence* of bread. They pretend to be bread, but the soul is out of them."

We could all picture the kind of bread Mike was talking about.

"They make that bread on an assembly line," Mike said. "A thousand loaves at a time, every loaf the same. Think about the people who work there. Some long brick building without any windows—if you looked at it from the outside, you wouldn't even know they baked bread in there. But there are hundreds of people, and it's hot from the ovens, and they're sweating all day long. They have to punch off the clock to even get a drink of water.

"It's dark, because why replace a burnt-out bulb? A new one costs money. If a fan breaks, why fix it? You'll save power if it's not running. Every ten minutes someone starts to cough up flour dust, and when they step outside to clear their lungs, they have to go off the clock. They *hate* bread by the end of the day."

"Not *this* bread," said Sweetie Malone.

"Not this bread," Mike agreed. "This is real bread. Bread with dignity."

"Come the revolution," said Buddy Brodsky, "*everyone* will eat bread like this."

"Now wait a minute," Spencer said. "Just hold on. You can't tell me that you're against assembly lines, that you're against factories. Against progress!" His wide face was incredulous.

"Of course we're not against progress," Mike said. "But it has to be the right *kind* of progress."

"I admit," Spencer said, "that there may be places like that, like the one you describe. I'll go further than that. I may have seen one or two of them myself! But there are good places, too, where the owners are decent men. Where they pay a decent wage."

"If they choose to," Effie said, joining the argument. "If *they* choose to. The owners decide how things will be, and the workers are stuck with it. Where's the fairness in that?"

Spencer buttered his own piece of bread as he replied. "The workers have a choice, too. If conditions are as bad as you say, they can work somewhere else."

"Work somewhere else?" Ozzie jumped in. "A nice idea. What if there's only one bread factory in town? What if there are two, but the owners run things the same way? They talk to each other in the barbershop, on the golf course. They work it out together, decide how they're going to handle things."

"I see your argument," Spencer said. "You make an interesting point."

Spencer's eyes were sharper than you might have noticed at first. You might have thought he was a windbag, the kind of man you can't take seriously—blustering his way through one argument after another, distracted by his own river of words. But if you really looked, you'd see that Spencer wasn't distracted, not one bit. He paid attention, not just to what was right in front of him, but off to the side, too. Talking to Effie but looking back and forth between Ozzie and Buddy and Sweetie—searching for something. A weak spot, maybe. A flaw in the argument, or a moment of doubt. When he found it, he would pounce, and show us the error of our ways. We *meant* well, Spencer would say, but we didn't understand the way things work. The complications of the system. He was just the one to set us straight!

As the conversation went on, I watched Spencer follow every point, and I noticed the reactions in his broad, fleshy face. A face as wide as a movie screen, with plenty of room to show expressions— and Spencer had a lot of them.

There were several categories of frowns—thoughtful, quizzical, doubtful. And each of these categories had variations, all kinds of subtleties, differences in tone. The eyebrows raised or lowered one degree at a time. Spencer could do a lot with those eyebrows.

And smiles—he had half smiles, quarter smiles, one-sixteenth smiles. Smiles in every fraction.

"So," said Spencer. He used up one of his doubtful frowns. "Would we be better off without bread? Or do you want everyone to make their *own* bread? Why not sew our own clothes, while we're at it? And every man can build his own house!"

"We don't have to bake our own bread," Mike said. "But tell me what's wrong with a real bakery. An ordinary place, a shop instead of a factory. A few ovens, a counter for the customers. Three or four people mixing dough, working side by side. Maybe they own the place together! Or if there is an owner, he knows all of his employees, he works right along with them."

Maybe Mike was thinking about Nancy when he talked about people mixing dough. I know I was.

"You realize," Spencer said, "that the owner is still in charge. What difference does it make if it's a shop and not a factory? Won't he still skimp on the ventilation? Or on the paychecks? It's more likely, even, because he's not making much of a profit. The expense of working on such a small scale. He might treat you more poorly than the factory owner!"

"Maybe he will," Mike said. "But if there is one factory, the workers have nowhere else to go. If there are ten bakeries, they have a choice."

Effie jumped in again. "*That's* the point," he said. "An owner might treat his workers badly, even in a small shop. The owner always has that choice. The point is to give the *workers* a choice."

Spencer's hand stopped, a slice of buttered bread halfway to his mouth. Of course he wouldn't agree—why should the workers have a choice? *They* didn't buy the ovens, pay rent on the store. They didn't put their money at risk. Why didn't they start their own bakery if they didn't like the bosses?

But he didn't say it. He looked unsure, for a moment—maybe he didn't want to offend Effie. Then he glanced at Mike, for a couple of seconds longer than you'd expect. As if he was trying to figure something out.

Effie chose this moment to clear his throat gently and ask, "Is there a Mrs. Spencer?"

Spencer put the bread back on his plate. He touched his wineglass but didn't pick it up.

"Beautiful as a spring flower." Looking at the wineglass, not at us.

Effie set down his own piece of bread. "What's her name?" he said.

"You can't depend on any one thing," Spencer said. His face looked tired at that moment, in the shadows of the gaslight. "It doesn't matter how tight your grip, how hard you try to hold on. It slips right through your fingers."

Buddy looked confused. "Are you married?" he said.

"You have to balance your investments," Spencer said. Still looking at his reflection in the wineglass. "You never know which ones will pan out."

"I'm sorry," Effie said, adding it up.

Spencer looked at him, then at Ozzie. He looked around the table, at eighteen plates of bread and butter. Eighteen wineglasses, empty or a quarter full. His face brightened a little.

"You can't live in the past," Spencer said. "But you can learn from it. No one will look out for you if you don't watch out for yourself." He nodded, as if we all agreed with him, although none of us had said a thing.

"No one will fill your pantry," Spencer went on, "if you let it run empty. No one will hand you their wallet when your bank account goes dry. When you come right down to it, it's every man for himself."

"I'm sorry you feel that way," Effie said, his voice steady. "I'm sure you have your reasons. But look at us." We all nodded, around the table, as Effie looked at Buddy Brodsky, at Ozzie, at Sweetie Malone.

"We *share* a pantry," Effie said. "And we all fill it. We may not be rich, but we don't starve. We have one wallet, and if you need something, you take from it. If you have something, you put it in. Why would you want to be on your own?"

"A nice idea," Spencer said. "But you're fighting nature. You're fighting the truth of who we are."

Ozzie raised his eyebrows. "Who, exactly, do you think we are?"

At that moment, the white-haired waiter returned from the kitchen, pushing a wooden serving cart. His back stooped as he made his way slowly toward the table. We listened to the squeak of the wheels as the cart approached, bearing a bowl heaped with salad, and stacks of china plates. The squeaking stopped behind Spencer's chair.

From a shelf inside the cart, the waiter picked up a pair of over-sized wooden spoons. Spoons so comically large that they might have come from another planet. Spoons that a giant might use to eat cereal.

"Wonderful!" said Spencer. "Time to eat!"

CHAPTER NINE

The waiter tossed the salad, working the wooden spoons like oars on a rowboat. He set a mound of lettuce on Spencer's plate, then moved down the table, rolling the cart as he went. At each man's left shoulder, he paused, trapped a perfectly sized portion of salad between the spoons, and lifted it gently to the plate. Not a shred of carrot dropped out of place, not a leaf of lettuce fell short of its destination.

We were starving, by then, and we stared at those spoons as if they were the hands of God.

Then we dug in. It's true that everything tastes good when you're hungry—but you've never had vegetables like that, I promise you. That fantastic crunch, that juicy snap. The lettuce practically gleaming, chlorophyll pulsing through the leaves. The radish slices shimmering, white as virgin snow, with brilliant scarlet edges. The carrots glowing with an inner light.

"I'm glad you're enjoying the salad," said Spencer.

He grinned as plates emptied around the table. The *tink* of forks against china. A good salad makes you hungrier as you eat, and Effie looked around to see if anyone wasn't going to finish theirs.

Spencer laid down his fork and wiped his mouth. "I want to apologize," he said. "I didn't mean to offend, before, with what I said about your path. You have chosen a hard course—but I know you have your reasons."

"That's right," Effie said. "We have our reasons."

"I appreciate the way you feel," Spencer said. "Who doesn't want to choose their own destiny? You don't want to live under someone else's power, to let them take advantage of you. Of course not!"

"I'm glad you understand," Effie said.

"I understand very well," Spencer said. "None of you want to be trapped on an assembly line. You won't leave yourselves at the mercy of the foreman. You won't let the bosses run your lives—that is not your path. You made a different choice." He picked up his glass and swirled the crimson wine. Then he raised his left eyebrow at Effie a quarter of the way, his expression thoughtful.

"I wonder, though," Spencer said, "what you really hope to accomplish. What you really expect to achieve, with this life of hardship."

"It's not about hardship—" Effie started to say.

"Oh, I know," Spencer said. "Not hardship for its own sake. But you live on a bus, for heaven's sake! Don't tell me it isn't a struggle. If a tire goes flat, I'll bet you have to skimp on dinner that night. I'll bet you sleep three or four to a room. Right? Does any one of you have fifty dollars in his pocket?"

We glanced at one another around the table. Of course we didn't have fifty dollars, but that had never bothered us before. Why should it now? Why should you judge your life by the cash in your hand?

"You don't want to be pampered," Spencer said. "Good for you! You don't believe in luxury. Fine! But why do you have to live like paupers when you could be stars? Every one of you—on the right team, I mean. With the right coaching, the right equipment. A modern ballpark. All the advantages you deserve!"

Effie put down his fork, pushed his salad plate away.

"We do just fine!" Effie said. "You have no idea what we are about."

"I know all about your ideals," Spencer said. "I know all about your principles. I know very well what you are trying to do. I told you, I'm your biggest fan!

"But tell me honestly. What does it accomplish? All this sacrifice. In the end, who is it going to help? Do you really think you can change anything, riding around in your little bus?"

"Yes!" said Ozzie, joining the argument. He threw his napkin on the table, and he fixed Spencer in his fierce catcher's glare. We all knew what he was going to say.

"We will *make* it change," Ozzie growled. There were nods, here and there. Of course we would make it change! Not on our own—we were realists, every one of us. We lived in the world, with our eyes open. We knew we couldn't bring Wall Street to its knees all by ourselves.

We didn't have to. We were part of something larger, part of an idea that was growing in the breadlines and the soup kitchens, the marches in Chicago and the picket lines of Akron and Flint. Hadn't friendly mayors been elected in Milwaukee and Reading and Bridgeport? Hadn't Eugene V. Debs won close to a million votes for president not so many years ago? Running on a platform that said, who is it all for, anyway? If the system does not serve the people, then who does it serve?

"People drive fifty miles to see us," Ozzie said. "They line up at the gate, they bring their friends and neighbors, more every day. Because they know what we are trying to do. The tide is coming in—do you really think you can stop it?"

"Oh, no," said Spencer. "You misunderstand me, you really do. Why would *I* try to stop you? I'm on your side!"

"For a man who's on our side, you argue an awful lot," Effie said.

"Only because I see what you're up against," said Spencer. "Isn't that an important thing to see? There are so few things you can count on in this world—but you can count on your enemies. Don't you want to know who they are?"

Spencer looked around the table, to make sure we were all listening.

"I'm not talking about a man who owns a bread factory," Spencer went on. "A single factory—it's not worth thinking about. Your enemies are more powerful than that!"

Spencer ripped off a chunk of bread and used it to mop his salad dressing.

"I'm talking about *giants*," Spencer said. "Bankers rich as Midas. Financiers as powerful as kings. I'm talking about men who build railroads, emperors of coal and steel. Men who couldn't count their money if they had a lifetime to do it. They buy senators, they sell judges. If the whim struck them, they could raise their finger and plunge a city into darkness."

Spencer's crust of bread paused halfway between his plate and his mouth as he kept talking.

"What makes you think you stand a chance?" Spencer said. "Against men who own governments, who could buy the very land you walk on. Why should they give you a moment's thought? What could possibly frighten them about a few baseball players on a bus?"

Ozzie looked evenly at Spencer, his expression perfectly calm—even nonchalant! As if he knew exactly what we were up against, who our enemies were, and it didn't concern him in the slightest.

"We'll take our chances," Ozzie said.

"Hear, hear!" said Sweetie Malone, raising his wineglass and grinning at Ozzie. And Effie said, "Hear, hear!" And the words echoed around the table as every man on the team repeated them. "Hear, hear!"

It didn't matter what we were up against. It might seem hopeless to Spencer—but doesn't everything start with an idea? Better to stand with the few, Effie would say, when the cause of the few is righteous.

Our enemies didn't matter! The carpenters and miners and railroad workers who filled those dusty ballparks would unite, would rise with one voice, would raise the banner of justice. We didn't think much about what would happen under that banner—we just knew that the powers-that-be would have to listen, that labor would stand head-to-head with capital, that our leaders would occupy the halls of power. And at long last, the country would belong to the people who built it.

We believed with all our hearts in our great victory—the victory that was still to come.

We raised our wineglasses again. The crystal sparkled in the gaslight.

"All right," Spencer said. He gave a little smile, and raised his glass to join the rest of us. "I'll toast your confidence. I'll toast your enthusiasm. I'll toast your unbreakable spirit!"

Spencer turned to his left and his right. He clinked glasses with us.

Mike looked at Spencer. "You should toast because we're right," he said.

"Hmmm," Spencer said. An eyebrow raised.

"We have enemies," Mike said. "We know that. We know they're strong—stronger than we are, at least for the moment, I won't deny that. But our *idea* is right! Isn't that what counts? In the long run, it's the idea that wins."

Exactly what people like Spencer can't stand. The notion that there's a better idea, another path. They want you to think there's no choice—that their system is the only way, so you have to give in. But here we were! We worked for no one, reaped the fruit of our own labor. We breathed the air of freedom, and if we earned more than we needed, the profits went to feed the hungry, to shelter the poor. Not to some millionaire in his mansion, with his limousine, his fat cigars.

We stood for something when we took the field. Everyone could see it—the fans who packed the stands, the boys who ran behind the bus as we pulled into Youngstown or Cedar Rapids. Who crowded around the door of our hotel, holding out a bat or a glove in one hand, a greasy pen in the other.

Everyone could see! No one ordered us around, no one controlled our fate.

People like Spencer can't stand it. Because if you can choose *our* path, why would you choose any other?

"Well," Spencer said. He looked at his wineglass, turning the idea around in his mind, thinking it over carefully. Finally, he set down the glass. "I admire the way you think," Spencer said. "I am an idealist myself, I find it refreshing! But you must realize that an idea does not win just because it's refreshing."

As Spencer said "refreshing," the kitchen door swung open. The waiter reentered the room, this time pushing a larger cart than before. Four shelves, each filled with plates of food, and the aroma was something you would have bought tickets for. The air thickened as the cart approached—a savory scent, juicy, with some smoke in it. A little spice. Something else, too—a deeper note, a flavor that was rich and dark. The way mahogany would taste, if mahogany were food.

The waiter whisked our empty salad plates off the table, and replaced each one with a heavy china platter, heaped with supper. Roast beef! We lived on meatloaf and peas, so you have to understand what that meant to us. Gleaming hot beef that stretched across the plate, glistening with juice. Mashed potatoes, silky as lingerie. Hot buttered carrots, so sweet a single bite could make you cry.

The knife sank easily into the beef. The kind of tenderness you might have heard about in a fairy tale, a legend passed down through the generations, so old you doubted its truth. Yet there it was!

Imagine—a square of beef slips onto your fork, you dab it in garnet-colored juices. You pop it into your mouth. It does something to you, the aroma of the beef mingled with the hot potatoes, the scent of buttered carrots and gravy and the smoke from the gas lights. All of them rising and swirling and blending together.

That kind of harmony wakes up something inside of you. A satisfaction so deep there should be another word for it. It made me think of a game we played in Iowa City—it was a blistering July day, and before the game we stood along the third-base line. The Iowa team trotted out of their dugout and lined up by first base. The crowd stood up, too, as a barbershop quartet gathered at home plate.

The quartet stood there in their red-and-white striped jackets, their handlebar mustaches, their spotless white shoes. They formed a little crescent to sing "America the Beautiful." We held our hats over our hearts, in that steaming Iowa air, as sunlight poured down like molten glass. Nothing moving, only a wisp of a breeze coming off the cornfields.

We listened to the quartet. Each voice keeping its own time, each rising and falling at its own pace. Blending like the colors of a sunset, four gorgeous songs flowing and melting into each other, until the melody built to a final note that was actually four notes, which flew in from different directions and landed on exactly the right spot. The music hung in the air like honey, and we stood like statues, holding on to the sound. Thinking it might last forever if only we were perfectly still.

Then it broke. A wave of applause from the grandstand, and the quartet walked off the field, their white shoes kicking up dust. The umpire cupped his hands around his mouth and shouted, "Play ball!"

That's what the roast beef was like.

"Well," Spencer said as he soaked up gravy with a heel of bread. He nodded in satisfaction as the waiter walked around the table refilling the wineglasses. Spencer raised his.

"Another toast," Spencer said. "To fine company!"

We lifted our glasses. It would be rude to turn down a compliment, wouldn't it? And we *felt* like toasting, with that roast beef on our plates. There was a glow inside, a feeling of satisfaction.

Only Ozzie was slow to raise his glass. From the look in his eye, I understood—and as I turned it around in my mind, I had to agree with him. This was not our kind of meal. There was something that just wasn't right—too much temptation in it.

We were working men. We lived on biscuits and chipped beef and creamed corn. We were sandwich men! Give us some bread and butter, some hard-boiled eggs, a slice of sharp cheese and we were happy as kings. If the bread was a little stale, so much the better.

Comfort was not the point. Luxury was dangerous, even if it was only a taste. It was a distraction, and could only get in our way.

So I agreed with Ozzie. On the other hand, we hadn't chosen the meal, had we? We had landed in the Rockefeller by chance, and we'd be leaving for Fort Wayne in the morning. We weren't going to make a habit of it.

"Let's put our quarrels behind us," Spencer said. "Any misunderstandings we may have had. I'm sure that we agree with each other more than we disagree."

A few nods, some of them skeptical. But it seemed wrong to argue just then, so we finished up our roast beef and drank our wine. We chatted about this and that, and swapped stories about life on the road.

Sweetie Malone remembered the hotel in Dayton that we shared with the Daughters of the American Revolution—the Southern Ohio chapter, holding their Fourth of July convention. Sweetie minding his own business, sitting in the restaurant with his newspaper and coffee. But every five minutes, the waiter would slip him a note:

Meet me in the garden at 10:30.

Meet me on the verandah.

Meet me behind the coatroom.

Each woman more frightening than the last. Of course, Sweetie ignored them all—because he already had an appointment, at nine o'clock, under the willow tree with the sweet blonde desk clerk.

Spencer told us about the time he shared a room with a traveling salesman. Through some combination of misjudgment and bad luck, the salesman was stuck with twelve crates of aging bananas. The perils of buying and selling. Five or six bananas have a nice scent, but twelve crates will knock you on your heels—especially when they are on the far edge of ripeness.

The salesman couldn't let those bananas go, because they had once been valuable. But the smell was strong enough to give Spencer nightmares. When he woke up in the morning, the fruit flies were so thick that you could have grabbed a handful out of a crate, squeezed them into the shape of a sausage, and fried them up for breakfast.

"When I went to the dining room to escape," Spencer said, "what do you think they were serving?"

Of course it was banana cream pie.

Spencer laughed. And Effie laughed. Then Mike, and the rest of us did, too. We had eaten well, the wine was delicious, and we felt like laughing with Spencer now. So what if we disagreed about one or two things? It didn't really matter, now that dinner was over. It was water under the bridge.

Finally, Spencer said, "It's been a real pleasure. But it's getting late."

"We thank you for the dinner," Effie said.

"It was nothing," Spencer said, brushing it aside. "I've enjoyed it more than you know."

He began to stand—then stopped himself.

"I almost forgot!" Spencer said. He looked at Mike. "Would you do me a favor?"

Mike looked puzzled. "A favor?"

Spencer reached into his jacket pocket and pulled out an envelope. He opened it slowly, with great care, and took out a photograph.

Touching only the edges, Spencer handed the picture to Mike.

"My daughter, Irene," Spencer said.

The photograph had been taken by a professional. Spencer's daughter sat in an armchair, composed and perfectly lit, the colors crisp and pure. Whatever he'd paid that man with the camera, it was worth it, because Irene was beautiful.

Her eyes caught you, first. Wide and clear, sea green, with a little bit of silver.

Her smooth cheeks, with a soft luster, like the inside of an oyster shell.

Then her lips. Not the color of roses—that would have been too ordinary for a woman like Irene. Too common. If you want to know the truth, it was hard to say what color they were. Not as obvious as red, more unusual than pink. Not far from the color of peaches, but they also had a sort of burnished glow you couldn't even name. Maybe the color of a rare tropical orchid, but none of us had seen anything like it.

Irene's hair flowed past her shoulders in goldenrod curls, gleaming in the gaslight.

Mike looked at the picture for a good long while.

"A pity Irene couldn't make it to dinner," Spencer said. "She was tired from the trip, she went upstairs to rest. But if I come back empty-handed, she'll never let me hear the end of it—sign her picture and you'll make her the happiest woman in the world."

Spencer reached into his pocket, and pulled out a fat black fountain pen. He took off the cap and handed the pen to Mike.

Ozzie scowled. Sweetie looked surprised and a little annoyed. Why Mike? But there was no reason to be jealous. We all had our fans. No reason to complain if Mike found one of his.

Mike felt the weight of the pen in his hand. He found a clean spot on the table, and carefully set down Irene's photograph. Then he signed his name, very slowly, across the bottom of the picture. The last few letters crawled across her feet.

"I can't tell you how much I appreciate this," Spencer said.

Effie looked at Mike. "I guess we'll be turning in," he said.

"An excellent idea," Spencer said. "We need a good night's sleep, after the day we've had!"

Spencer stood up, stretched, and patted his stomach. Chairs pushed back around the table.

But Spencer had one more thought. "Say, Mike," he said. "If I know Irene, she's sitting up reading a book. Let's give her a surprise—why don't you say hello in person? It will be the highlight of her trip!"

"It's late," Effie said. "We have a game tomorrow."

"We won't keep him up," Spencer said. "I promise. It's been so dull for Irene, tagging along on business. It will only take a minute to say hello."

Mike looked vaguely around the room, but he did not look Effie in the eye. Or Ozzie. Or me, for that matter.

Mike looked back at the photograph.

"Sure," he said to Spencer. "Just for a minute."

We watched Spencer and Mike leave the room together. They walked through the door and turned toward the stairs. Spencer's stride more confident than it should have been for a man of his bulk. Mike walking half a step behind.

Some of us were kind of mad.

CHAPTER TEN

Buddy Brodsky, Ned Kretzmann, and I climbed three flights of stairs to our attic room. The room was small to start with, and the ceiling slanted, so we had to duck as we walked in. A single window, with a wispy curtain. A bulb dangling on a chain. The light flickered as the wind blew.

We unpacked our toothbrushes and changed into our pajamas—flannels, because of the cold night. We shoved our suitcases under our beds, kicking up clouds of dust.

Mike's suitcase sat alone, unopened, on top of his mattress. He was off with Spencer and Irene.

The shamelessly beautiful Irene.

I sat down at an old, dented soft-pine desk that had been pushed to the back corner of the room, where there was not quite enough light. The chair wobbled on its uneven legs, and the desktop was bare and scuffed. The desk had been pushed as close as it could go to the wall, so when you sat down, you stared at cracked milk-white plaster.

I took out a sheet of paper and started writing a letter to Nancy. Did I mention that we met in Binghamton?

The Robins used to stop there, at the Chemung Cafe, whenever we swung through the eastern part of the league. It was just over the New York line from Scranton, on the way to Syracuse or Rochester.

The Chemung Cafe was on the way to a lot of places, as a matter of fact, and if it hadn't been, we would have stopped there anyway.

They had the best cinnamon rolls you have ever eaten. I'm not kidding, I don't care how many coffee shops you've been to, how many bakeries you've sampled. I don't care what kind of pastries you've tasted, you've never had anything like that, with raisins or without. The rest of the food wasn't bad either—you could be perfectly happy with your fried fish and peas, your roast chicken. Your mashed potatoes. Nothing fancy, but somehow, you couldn't get enough of it.

There was a real, honest cook back there in the kitchen. You could hear him humming to himself while he banged away with the pots and pans. His name was Virgil, and he had hair the color of a sandy beach, and forearms so thick it was absurd. How strong do you have to be to flip a grilled cheese sandwich? Virgil looked as though he could step outside and lift up the corner of the building if he had to. A tattoo of a mermaid rippled when he flexed his bicep.

Virgil had learned to cook in the Navy. Too well, for their liking, because word got around, and every sailor in the fleet wanted to be on his ship. They lobbied for transfers, they petitioned to leave their desk jobs, ready to cruise into battle for a taste of Virgil's Sunday dinners.

So we stopped at the Chemung Cafe whenever we could. Not just for the food—for the big, sunny windows overlooking the Susquehanna River. For the chairs with cushioned backs, which invited you to sit and relax. And for Regina, the gray-haired waitress, who had worked the counter since the dawn of time.

Regina was the first person you saw when you walked into the diner, standing by the cash register with her back rigid, her arms crossed. A permanent glare on her face. So rooted to the ground you might think she had been there for centuries, since prehistoric times—and maybe she had! Regina might have laid out her place settings as the glaciers retreated, as woolly mammoths strolled through the parking lot. Or even before. You could picture Regina on this very spot, back erect, eyes straight ahead, as the continent of North America thrust up from the Atlantic. Her head high, arms folded proudly across her chest. Her uniform dripping seawater.

"You again!" Regina would say when we walked in the door. She'd scowl then, as if she'd bitten a sour apple. But moments later she'd be bustling around, making a point of finding out how Mike was swinging the bat or whether Buddy's back was acting up. How Ned's mother was handling the farm, with all the rain they were having up in Syracuse. Although if you're going to settle down in Syracuse, you have to take what's coming to you.

Regina paid extra attention to Effie. She kept his coffee cup full, she put her hand on his shoulder. She slipped him cinnamon rolls on the house. There might have been something going on— although not what you think, something deeper than that. Sometimes two people just see the world through the same eyes.

So we had a lot of reasons to stop at the Chemung Cafe. Month after month, year after year.

Then all of a sudden, Regina was gone. The winter got cold, and Regina packed up her cats and her arthritic hip, sold her house, and moved in with her sister in Williams, Arizona. And Nancy was there, instead.

Nancy.

I heard her voice, first, before I saw her. From the kitchen—she was saying something about eggs, but with feeling.

Sometimes you hear a voice, and you *have* to know what's behind it. That's the way it was with Nancy—her voice had flavor in it, some earth. Not quite a purr, but heading in that direction. I thought of caramel when I heard it, if that makes any sense. Not those hard little candies. I'm talking about soft, buttery, spreadable caramel, right at the point of melting.

When Nancy swept out of the kitchen, she was still looking over her shoulder, still talking about eggs.

Her cheeks were not like cream. Her lips were not like rubies.

Nancy's hair was not like silk, and it didn't wave gently as she walked, like a field of wheat stirred by a gentle breeze.

She was better than that. She was real.

So what if her nose was a little on the flat side? Her chin—what can I tell you? It wasn't anything to write home about. So what if the dimple in Nancy's cheek was just the slightest bit off-center? She was the prettiest woman I had ever seen.

Those blue eyes, with a little ring of gold around the pupils. Hair the color of maple syrup, with a touch of copper stirred in. Falling in curls around her shoulders.

And her smile. Nancy had one of those smiles. I can't say anything more about it, but you know what I'm talking about. There wasn't a single thing you could have done to make it better.

I couldn't stop looking at her.

Nancy crossed in front of the big picture window, and I was spellbound by the swish of her dark pleated skirt. Her creamy-white blouse. The tap of her shoes on the linoleum.

Sunlight everywhere.

Nancy looked around, one of those looks that takes in everything. She checked to see that the cashier was at her post, that the customers were eating, that the empty plates had been picked up.

Nancy's eyes swept the length of the room.

A coffee cup needed filling at the end of the counter. It belonged to a redhead in a maid's uniform who must have had a long day. Her eyes looked tired, her uniform was rumpled. A little too much makeup, but that's none of my business.

She had a few bites left of grilled cheese, a little heap of fried potatoes. But her coffee cup was empty.

Nancy turned to pick up the coffeepot. Even as she was talking to the kitchen—"Over easy," she said. "Don't break the yolks." Even as she nodded to a customer coming in the door. Even as she carried a plate of French toast in one hand, a dish towel in the other.

Nancy reached for the coffee on the counter, deftly flipping the towel over her shoulder.

The plate of French toast shifted from her right hand to her left. So neatly, so effortlessly, that it was almost invisible. You couldn't tell how the plate had moved.

Nancy turned to pick up the coffee, and her hips swung precisely halfway around. Her skirt spun three-quarters of the way, then fell loosely back. Did I mention that Nancy's stockings were the color of eggshells?

She picked up the coffeepot and walked along the counter. Sliding the French toast in front of a grateful businessman. Scooping up a handful of change next to an empty plate, without breaking stride.

Nancy stretched out her arm at just the right moment—still a step or two away from the redheaded maid, but her timing was perfect, the angle exact. The coffeepot tilted, and a graceful stream bubbled into the center of the empty cup.

Again that swivel. The *swish* of Nancy's skirt, a glimpse of eggshell stockings, the curve of a gorgeous leg. Those wide, clear, deep, honest eyes.

Nancy carried the coffeepot back to the warmer and set it down with a hollow *tap*. The coffee responded with an infinitesimal quiver.

Nancy smiled.

I saw that smile a lot as Nancy walked around the diner, weaving through obstacles like a dancer. Steering around a fat man in overalls, who blocked the aisle like a truck hogging the highway.

Sidestepping a six-year-old sprinting for the bathroom. Toddlers streaking from booth to booth like unguided missiles.

She moved as though the laws of physics were on her side, gravity and friction not hindrances but loyal friends, doing everything they could to help. A step to the right, a glide to the left. Nancy wove this way and that without appearing to change course, as if she had planned that route all along. When she smiled, it was a smile of satisfaction.

Why shouldn't Nancy be satisfied? Her performance was a ballet—you could have sold tickets. It would have been the biggest thing in Binghamton, people would've lined up around the block for seats. Crowds of suitors packing the front row, jostling for a view, throwing armloads of flowers at her feet. But there was no place she'd rather be than in the diner.

To be graceful on a stage is one thing—to be graceful in the Chemung Cafe is something special.

* * *

So I stayed in my seat as my teammates drifted off. They finished their sandwiches and coffee, and two or three at a time wandered back to the rooming house. Meanwhile, I had five cups of coffee and four cups of tea while I waited for the diner to close.

Nine o'clock, Nancy had said. That was when she was done.

Even today, it's hard to believe that I talked to her. It's not what I usually do, in that kind of situation. I usually think for a while, maybe a very long while, ponder over what to say until it's too late. But not this time. We were in Binghamton for one night—and I knew, as well as I have ever known anything, that I would not be able to climb the steps of that Crown Coach Company bus until I had spoken with Nancy. I simply would not have been able to do it.

Nine o'clock, Nancy had said.

I didn't mind waiting.

For one thing, there were those cinnamon rolls. I ate them one after another—I'm ashamed to tell you how many. That melting dough, that sugary crust.

There was music, too—an old Philco radio on a table in the corner, playing music with some swing to it. The melody coming through a tin speaker, with crackles and hisses, the buzz of static. What can you expect, from a signal that makes such a long, complicated journey? That climbs over hills, dips into valleys. That picks up errors as it passes through storms, as it detours around buildings. A signal distorted by the shape of the landscape.

The way memory itself can be distorted, as it passes through the hills and valleys of time.

I try to listen to those songs now, that old music, but it doesn't sound right. The equipment is too fancy nowadays, whatever sort of disk they're using at the moment. The music is clear as a bell, and who wants to listen to that? It's unnatural. If you're going to hear music, you need that background of static, the nicks and scratches of life.

So I sat at the counter, and listened to the radio, and did the only thing in the world I wanted to do. I watched Nancy.

She was pretty in a way that was hard to explain. Not like Ella—I've already told you that Ella was pretty, and I'm not going to take that back. But Ella was attractive in a general kind of way, if that makes any sense. Her prettiness was right on the surface, for anyone to see. That pearly skin, glossy dark hair. Those big dark eyes. Of *course* people noticed Ella. What I'm trying to say—and I hope I don't sound selfish—is that Ella's type of beauty was not meant specifically for *me*.

It was different with Nancy. Some people wouldn't understand if I said that Nancy was beautiful. They'd ask me what I saw, they'd wonder what I was talking about. Sure, they'd say, she has nice curls. Yes, it doesn't hurt to look into those blue eyes. But they wouldn't see what I did.

When I looked at Nancy, it was like opening a menu in a restaurant, and finding that every single dish had been chosen from my personal list of favorites.

A perfect omelet. Crisp green peppers and onions, ripe tomatoes, juicy mushrooms. An invisible sprinkle of salt.

A roast chicken, the skin crackling and dark. Garlicky steam when you cut it open, the meat tender on your fork.

A hot-from-the-oven pie—let's say peach melba. A buttery crust. Fruit like golden velvet. Here and there a fat blueberry, ready to burst with pride.

Every dish prepared exactly the way I liked it, down to the sprinkle of paprika on the omelet, the squeeze of lemon juice over the chicken. A scoop of strawberry ice cream next to the pie.

When I looked at Nancy, I knew—she was made exactly for me.

So I waited.

At eight forty-five Virgil turned off the grill. Nancy stood at the register sorting coins, slipping rubber bands around packets of bills. She stacked them in a lockbox under the counter.

"You want dough for tomorrow?" Virgil called from the back.

"I'll take care of it, Virgil," Nancy said. "Go home early, give Claire a surprise. Cook her something nice."

"See you in the morning." Virgil nodded at Nancy on his way out the door.

Nancy and I were alone.

"Come back here," Nancy said. "I'm going to show you my secrets."

CHAPTER ELEVEN

I had always wanted to go behind the counter in a diner. To walk through that little swinging gate, into the waitresses' private territory, to see what they kept out of sight.

A lot of silverware, it turns out. Napkins. Condiments. Little bottles of maple syrup. No big surprises. Even so, I was happy to see it.

Nancy waved at me to follow her, and she pushed her way into the kitchen through a wooden half-door, her dark skirt swinging as she turned.

A small room, but they had packed a lot into it. Cabinets up to the ceiling. Countertops squeezed against the wall. Canisters and boxes lining the counters, and shelves jammed in wherever there was space. One whole wall was a grill, blackened from years of service, still hot from Virgil's cooking and shiny with oil. A pair of ovens below.

A refrigerator with a white enamel front, a deep porcelain sink. A huge mixing machine on the floor in the corner, battleship gray, the size of a catcher in his crouch.

"Ever do any baking?" Nancy dragged a sack of flour from a low cupboard. She pointed to the bowl of the mixing machine.

I shook my head.

"Eight pounds of flour," Nancy said.

There was a ladle to scoop the flour, and an old kitchen scale to weigh it on. I began to scoop into a bucket on the scale. Nancy sniffed the contents of a blue ceramic bowl on the counter, where it sat between a rack of knives and a box of onions—then she motioned me over to sniff it, too. There were a couple of inches of froth in the bottom of the bowl. Nutty, with a tiny bit of sweetness.

"The yeast is ready," she said.

"Yeast?"

"It's been growing since this morning. That's the first secret." She took a wooden spoon and stirred. The nutty scent grew a little stronger.

"What are you making?" I said.

"Cinnamon rolls."

My eyebrows went up.

"You know the ones I'm talking about," Nancy said. "The ones you've been eating without a break for the last four hours."

I was surprised. "I thought Virgil made them."

"Another secret. Virgil is a great cook, but the cinnamon rolls are mine."

Nancy opened the icebox and took out four quart bottles. Their contents were thicker than milk, but not as thick as cream. She set the bottles on the counter.

"I've been eating these rolls for years," I said. "Who used to make them?"

"So you're a detective," Nancy said. "But not a good one. The cinnamon rolls have always been mine. You would have known if you'd looked in the kitchen."

"You were here?" I said. Thinking about all the times I had sat at the counter with my teammates, with Nancy just a few feet away. Only a half-door between us. The years we had wasted!

I missed her retroactively, if that is possible.

"You can learn a lot about a person by looking," Nancy said. "When they don't know they are being watched."

"You watched me?"

"Don't get a big head," she said.

I blushed. I am not sure that I had ever blushed before. Because she had been watching *me*. Not Sweetie Malone, not Buddy Brodsky. Not Mike, with his blue eyes, his dark curls. The smile that made everyone want to talk to him.

She'd been watching *me*.

I said, "What did you learn, when you were watching?"

"It's time to mix the dough," Nancy said. "Come on, I'm going to show you the rest of my secrets."

*　*　*

She pried the caps off the milk bottles as we talked. We were born just a few days apart, we discovered. I had arrived on the fourth of March, and Nancy three days later.

"So I'm older and wiser," I said.

"We'll see," Nancy said.

Nancy was Regina's granddaughter, it turned out, and she told me the whole family story. About Regina's parents, who came on a steamer from Greece. About Regina's four brothers, the chickens in the backyard.

About the scandal when Regina was caught with a rose, at sixteen years old. The shame of it! A rose that had been given to her, with infinite shyness, by a Lebanese boy named Rami, who was helping his mechanic father install a furnace in her parents' house. Of course the mechanic was fired. And the son was banished from the neighborhood—along with his shy smile and coffee-colored eyes, which Regina found she couldn't forget.

"Did she see him again?" I said.

"She told her mother she was going to the store to buy canning jars. Instead she went downtown, to the mechanics' union, and they told her where he lived.

"He had twenty-five dollars in his sock, so they eloped to Elmira. It was a year and a half before they dared to come home."

"They eloped at sixteen?"

"They were in love. When her parents saw the baby, they couldn't help themselves, everything was forgiven. The baby had my grandmother's face and my grandfather's eyes, so what were they going to say? The baby was my mother."

We tipped the bottles into the bowl of yeast.

"Buttermilk," Nancy said. "To soften the dough."

I stirred the buttermilk with a wooden spoon. Then Nancy handed me a pot of cold oatmeal porridge, which looked about as edible as clay.

"Oatmeal makes them chewy." Nancy's smile was shaded a little to the left, the slightest bit off-center—and I couldn't stop looking at her. Her flat little nose, the crinkles around her eyes. I didn't want to do anything else in life except wait for Nancy to smile. I swear that if I could have packed up all my belongings and moved into that kitchen, I would have. I'd have spent the rest of my life in there, watching Nancy mix dough.

Her mother loved animals, Nancy said. Not the way everyone does, but more than that. When her mother was a girl, she walked around the neighborhood hugging every dog she could find. When she got older, she earned her spending money by walking and feeding and brushing everyone else's pets, and then she broke every rule of the family by going to veterinary school. She had to travel upstate, the only woman in her class. When she came back, she opened an office in the front of her house, so when Nancy was a girl, there were always animals in the living room.

The doorbell would ring in the middle of the night, and Nancy would get up to help. She'd pull on her clothes, run downstairs. Then she'd sit on the living room floor, holding a dog with a broken leg while her mother gathered what she needed. The dog panting in fear, his heartbeat racing against Nancy's chest.

As I stirred the oatmeal into the yeast, Nancy told me about her great-uncles—three policemen and a mechanic. One of the policemen had turned in his badge a few years before to open a lunch counter. The mechanic had worked in Rami's father's shop, then bought it from him. The others retired and moved south. Who wants winter in Binghamton once your arthritis kicks in?

I heard about Nancy's cousins, and her nephews, and who knows what other relatives. So many people, it was hard to keep their names straight. But I tried to pay attention.

Nancy was happy working at the Chemung Cafe. She knew the routines of the customers—the man who ordered coffee and never drank it, the woman who brought her own salt, the couple who had the same argument every single day.

"Don't order the potatoes, you don't like them."

"I *want* the potatoes, don't tell me what to order."

"You don't like them. They have the skins on."

"I *like* skins."

"Stubborn as a mule. . . ."

She told me all about her life, and I didn't know what to tell her in return. Nancy already knew about the team. My friends were my teammates—what was so interesting about them? There was nothing to say about my family. I was an only child, and so were my parents. I didn't have aunts or uncles.

My life was full of empty spaces.

But Nancy could grip onto the smallest piece of information. I could mention a great-aunt, a distant cousin, and she'd want to hear everything I knew. She'd dredge up things I barely remembered—what was this person like, and that one? What happened at this event or that? Who said what, and why, and what happened afterward?

Where did she get all those questions? Nancy was like Mike that way, wanting to know every little thing. It never occurred to me to do that kind of poking and prodding—but as I watched Nancy take it all in, I realized that she was interested, in a way I'd never imagined anyone *could* be interested. Not just in what I said, but what was behind it, what it meant to me. How I felt about it.

I might not even know that I was feeling a certain way, but Nancy knew—I could see it in her face. And then a strange thing happened. As I saw the way Nancy felt, my own feelings became more clear to me. They took on weight, became a little deeper.

"Pass me the salt," Nancy said.

She stood at the mixer, looking at eight pounds of flour in the bottom of the bowl. I took a box of salt from the cupboard.

"A quarter of a cup."

I measured it out. There wasn't much room by the mixer—as we stood there, our hips almost touched.

Nancy shook the salt over the flour.

"Now the blue bowl."

I carried the ceramic bowl from the counter to the mixer, a foamy slush of oatmeal, buttermilk, and yeast. Nancy tipped the bowl over the rim of the mixer, and I backed up to give her room. The buttermilk sloshed into the flour. A plume of white dust rose into the air.

"Now it's the machine's turn to work," Nancy said. She flipped a switch, and the paddle of the mixer began to turn. The ingredients came together, first in a batter, then a lumpy dough.

Nancy watched me as the machine stirred. There was an undertone of red in her hair, a bronze shine at the edge of her maple-syrup curls, where they caught the light. She reached out and touched my hand.

"Thanks for helping," she said.

Nancy let the mixer spin while she led me out of the kitchen. Lights shone on the empty tables, and our reflections stared at us from the dark windows. She opened a drawer next to the cash register and pulled out an old book, bound in leather and heavy as a doorstop. *The Collected Works of William Shakespeare.* The pages were thin, but there were a great many of them—Shakespeare had a lot to say, apparently.

I didn't know much about Shakespeare. I'd read as little as I could get away with in school, and honestly I'd never had much use for him. I don't see the point in making everything so complicated. Why make people dig for all those symbols and themes, those hidden meanings? Why didn't Shakespeare just lay it on the table? He should have told it straight, given us a story we could follow. Why try to hide the inner workings?

But Nancy had a thing about Shakespeare. Her grandfather Rami had given her the book when she was five years old and couldn't read a word. So Nancy had curled up on his lap in a big armchair, snug in the soft cushions while he read to her. He let her touch the leather binding, which always felt warm, let her run her fingers along the gilt at the edge of the pages. Nancy listened to the sound of Lebanon in her grandfather's voice and smelled the mint tea on his breath. There was a force to the words that she couldn't explain—a rhythm that drew her in, that put her under a spell.

It wouldn't be the first time someone fell in love with an idea before knowing what it meant.

Nancy set the book on the counter. I opened to the middle and heard the crackle of the onionskin pages. The type was minuscule, to squash in as much as possible. Even so, the lines sometimes overflowed their columns—although the typesetter had worked hard to prevent this, squeezing the letters closer together, shrinking the space between words. Sometimes, if a line was especially long, you couldn't see a break at all. How did you make sense out of "Whereforewashemock'd"? *Forewash*? *Shemock*?

Sometimes the only way to fit a line was to chop off the end. "To be, or not to be, that is the"—and then a blank wall. Your mind went into free fall before you remembered to look up, above the line, where the typesetter had stowed the missing "question."

In eleventh grade, Nancy had a teacher, Mr. Elman, just out of college, who was on such good terms with Shakespeare that he'd written a thesis on *The Taming of the Shrew*. In class, he took it slowly and talked about every line, not just the words but what was *behind* the words, and Nancy sat in the front row and soaked it up. Maybe you need Shakespeare if you're going to live in Binghamton.

And Nancy talked about Mr. Elman's eyes. You could learn a lot by watching those eyes—about what Shakespeare meant, what made his world the way it was, dark one minute and comical the next. Nancy also loved the rhythm of Mr. Elman's voice. Maybe she liked Mr. Elman a little too much, although of course nothing happened.

"He was a lot like you," Nancy told me. "A dreamer."

I don't know what Nancy meant by that. I was the last person in the world to sit around dreaming, to wish and hope, to imagine that things will get better. Our team was all about *doing* things. What could be more sensible, more practical, than rolling up your sleeves, setting out into the world, and making things better with your own hands?

But I didn't want to argue with Nancy. I liked hearing her talk about Shakespeare, about things I had never understood. I liked that Nancy could see the hidden meanings, the symbols and themes I would miss. It didn't matter whether it was a poem or a play or any kind of novel—Nancy could see through the mystery, and she could explain it to me in a way that made it interesting. The only person I've ever met who could do that.

Mr. Elman was the drama teacher, too, so of course he put on *The Taming of the Shrew*. Nancy wanted to play the lead, but it went to someone older and taller. Nancy was a servant named Grumio, and she had some snappy lines—she recited a few for me, and it made me laugh to picture her prancing around the stage, wrapped in a man's cloak, her hair tucked under a cap.

When Mr. Elman saw how good Nancy was, he made her the understudy for Kate, and that's where she put her heart. Nancy worked at it for hours, reading all those lines with her grandfather until she knew them forward and back. You could start her cold on any page, and she could pick it up without a flaw. If the regular Kate had taken ill onstage, Nancy could have thrown off her servant's cloak, tossed her long hair out of her cap, and stepped right into the starring role.

She turned off the mixer.

"Feel the dough," Nancy said.

I reached into the bowl. The dough was wet and shiny, heavier than I expected. I had to work to get my hands under it. It was a little sticky, and cold from the buttermilk.

"A cold rise takes longer. It lets the dough build character. Put it on the counter."

Nancy divided the dough into eighths. She showed me how to shape a piece into a ball, then press from the center with the heels of my palms. There was a satisfying resistance. With the weight of my shoulders, I made the dough give way, I gathered up the edges and pushed down again. Nancy worked beside me, on another piece of dough. We built up a rhythm: press down, gather up, press down, gather up.

It felt good to work.

"Not as sticky?" Nancy asked after a few minutes.

"Yes." The dough had developed a soft, pleasant feel, as though it had matured. Elastic and satin-smooth.

"The machine does most of the work," Nancy said, "but you have to finish by hand. It needs the human touch."

I felt the work in my arms and shoulders. It was starting to get warm, back there in the kitchen. Nancy rolled up her sleeves—her forearms were sleek and muscled.

"It's faster with you here," she said.

We kneaded all eight pieces, then laid the dough in stainless-steel trays. We draped wax paper across the top, we covered the paper with towels. The trays were just the right size to slide into the icebox.

"It rests there for the night," Nancy said, and swung the door shut. "In the morning we'll warm it up, we'll roll it out. Eight pounds of flour is a hundred and sixty rolls, enough for one day, unless *you* show up again."

I don't know how we decided to stay up all night. But neither of us wanted to leave.

Nancy made a pot of Lebanese tea. She boiled water, threw in a handful of mint leaves. She strained the water into cups, and added fresh sprigs of mint. Tea fragrant as a meadow.

We sat at the counter and sipped our tea and talked about whatever came into our heads. I told Nancy about the hotel in Buffalo where Sweetie Malone got stuck in a dumbwaiter. The rooming house in Cedar Rapids, where the backyard was lined with pens of turkeys, and a confused rooster who started crowing when the moon rose.

A police car pulled up to check on things, and Nancy waved him away.

We picked apart some cold chicken. Nancy made a second pot of tea.

We talked about Regina's life in Arizona. She had written to Nancy about her snug little house, the perfect weather, warm and sunny every day. It was unnatural, Regina said. She could barely stand it.

We talked about Nancy's nephew, and the collection of jelly jars that filled half of his garage. Why would anyone collect jelly jars?

We talked about the time Nancy's great-uncle stopped Lou Gehrig for running a red light. Her great-uncle had the ticket framed, and when he opened his lunch counter, he hung it on the wall, and called the place Lou's.

At four o'clock in the morning, we looked in on the dough, and Nancy showed me how well it was rising.

As I walked her home, the edge of the sky was beginning to freshen up—not exactly light, but a softer kind of darkness. The outlines of hills were emerging on the horizon, and it gave you the impression that some things were ending, as others were about to begin.

* * *

I wrote to Nancy every day. She couldn't write back, because the mail can't find a moving target. So I had to keep up the conversation on my own.

I told her about the cities we visited, the teams we played. The places we stopped for lunch. Anything I could think of—the funny things people yelled from the stands, the odd facts Effie revealed over meatloaf.

I told her about the bus rides. The rumble of the engine, the slippery leather of the seats. Teammates sprawled across the benches, using their warm-up jackets as pillows. The kind of *time* we had on the bus. Enough to lean back and relax, to gaze out those dusty windows as the empty landscape rolled by, to listen to your own quiet breath, to let thoughts drift through your mind. I told Nancy how much I used to love those bus rides—that delicious solitude. Now, they just made me miss her.

I saw her again the next time we stopped in Binghamton. And again, a few weeks after that. I saw Nancy whenever I could, and when I walked in the door, she would take off her apron. She'd leave the diner to whoever was helping that day, and the two of us would walk to the park across the street. We'd follow a path through the trees, to a little clearing at the top of the riverbank.

Nancy and I would stand at a cast-iron railing, and look out over the river. We'd watch the fishermen as they stood in the water in their hip boots, casting their lines. And we'd talk for hours, bringing each other up to date, sharing every detail, everything that happened while I was away. Trying to make up for the time we had missed.

The fishermen never caught anything.

When it got dark, we would walk down the street together, stopping at the bakery for bread, at the grocer's for lettuce. My arms would fill with packages.

We would climb the steps to Nancy's porch. We'd walk into her living room. Her kitchen. Her pantry.

Her bedroom.

The truth is I saw Nancy whenever I could, but it wasn't enough. We were apart for weeks at a time, and all I could do was think about her. Kneading cinnamon rolls in the diner, the muscles in her forearms gleaming as she pressed and pulled on the dough.

Picking up plates full of breakfast from the grill. Taking orders behind the counter.

The pleats of Nancy's dark skirt moving with her, her white blouse gleaming in the light from the picture window.

I pictured Nancy chatting with the customers. She had a way with people, the same as Mike did. She could cheer you up if you were grumpy. She'd prod you right through it, she'd bring you around bit by bit until finally, against your better judgment, you would smile. You just had to! Still complaining—but smiling at the same time.

I knew that when business was slow, Nancy would pull out her book of Shakespeare and browse the tissue-thin pages. She still knew all of Kate's lines, from *The Taming of the Shrew,* which she was happy to prove by reciting them. So I had a feeling that I knew what was in Nancy's mind as she moved around the diner.

There was a particular speech she liked from that play, something about not having to listen if you don't like what you're hearing. Something about sticking cotton in your ears, only more poetic.

I memorized a couple of lines myself—*My tongue will tell the anger of my heart; or else my heart, concealing it, will break.* I wanted to impress her, to tell the truth, although I don't think it worked. I couldn't get the rhythm right. My Shakespeare had no music. But when Nancy recited that speech, it was really something.

I sat on the bus as we rattled past empty hayfields, picturing Nancy with Shakespeare in her head as she carried plates and cups around the diner. *He that is giddy thinks the world turns round.* The rhythm of her walk reflecting the rhythm of the lines in her head.

Nancy held a glass of juice in one hand, glowing brilliant orange. A fat muffin in the other, a crust of crackling gold, cranberries scattered across the top like garnets. She set the glass of juice on the table, and the muffin floated down next to it, like a dove settling on a branch.

She smiled.

Can you see why I fell in love?

CHAPTER TWELVE

We waited for Mike until a quarter past eleven, up in our little room on the fourth floor of the Rockefeller. Buddy, Ned, and I. The three of us in flannel pajamas—Ned and I in red, Buddy in pastel blue.

I sat at the ancient desk, with its nicks and scratches, and worked on my letter to Nancy. I rocked a little in the wobbly desk chair.

Buddy did toe touches while Ned sat with his legs crossed on the bed, drinking a glass of hot milk he'd begged from the kitchen. Ned couldn't go to bed without his hot milk—he was twenty-two but looked younger, the wide eyes of a kid who's just left Syracuse for the first time, who misses his mother on the dairy farm. His face the very definition of apple-cheeked. Ned looked too young to play first base, if you want to know the truth, especially in red pajamas. But when he swung the bat, you didn't notice those apple cheeks anymore.

None of us wanted to go to sleep before Mike got back. But we were tired. You couldn't be a night owl on our team—not the way we worked. We started the day early and ran our hearts out. Other teams had their trainers, their clubhouses, all kinds of fancy equipment. They had people to give them massages, people who stretched the players' legs *for* them.

All we had was determination.

We worked hard. We did push-ups, sit-ups, pull-ups. We ran until our legs felt like rubber. We lifted weights. We didn't have our own, of course—that Crown Coach Company bus didn't have the strength to drag them around. So everywhere we went, we kept an eye out for heavy things. Cinder blocks. Sandbags. A chunk of lead pipe.

We loved to play in Harrisburg, because a train had derailed not far from the ball field, and you could scrounge in the weeds for lengths of broken track. A two-foot piece is as heavy as you need, unless you're Ozzie Gadlin. So why bother with fancy weights? An hour with a piece of railroad track will do you a world of good.

We worked hard, we gave it everything we had. At the end of the day, if you had enough strength to brush your teeth, you felt as though you hadn't done your job.

We were drowsy by nine o'clock.

By ten, we couldn't stop yawning. We rubbed our eyes to keep them open.

At ten thirty, if we weren't in bed, we were dreaming that we were. Who stays up past ten thirty?

It's a different story in the morning. I'm sharp as a tack at five o'clock—I jump out of bed with the sun. And why not? The world is freshly washed, nothing has been decided yet. Everywhere you look there are possibilities.

Mike and I used to run at that hour. We'd jog to the edge of whatever town we were in, past stores that were shuttered for the night, houses still dark. Offices with hours left to sleep. Only the diners and coffee shops had lights on—someone coming in to turn on the ovens, to scramble the eggs. To heat water for coffee.

Mike and I would jog out of town, looking for a country road. We'd find a path through open fields, a trail at the edge of a forest.

The grass a little dewy under our feet. Our breath steaming in the dawn light.

Do you know that feeling? Your stride is long and easy. You have that strength in your legs, your muscles glad to be working, happy to make themselves useful. Your lungs not straining, but working just hard enough, matched to your partner's pace. You hear his breath as your legs move in rhythm. The sun is just coming up—your shadows trail behind, and the shadows are also in rhythm.

You glide along the road, and you don't have to say a word. You both see the same pink light at the horizon, the same mist rising from the meadow. Your footsteps crunch the same gravel, you match each other step for step. His blood is pounding, the same as yours. Your foreheads are glazed with sweat. Clean, sweet air in your lungs.

The greatest feeling in the world!

I don't run anymore. Don't think that I couldn't—I could lace up my shoes if I wanted to. Reach for my toes, limber up my legs. Jog around a little, to get the juices moving, then head for the open road. The spirit is strong!

But there are no more bases to steal.

Even so, I like to get up early. I like to see the sun rise. It doesn't matter how old you are, if you're moving around when the day is young, you *feel* young. At least, you remember what it feels like.

Although—if you want to know the truth—once in a while, I stay in bed. Not every day! Not every other day. I'm talking about once in a while.

All right, maybe every other day.

I stay in bed, not because I have to. I could bounce to my feet if I wanted—I'm old but not decrepit, and I don't need help to get up. Any more than I need those safety bars in the bathroom, that ridiculous contraption for my ankle. Or, God help me, that alumi-num cane.

I could walk out of here tomorrow, if I had a place to go.

But I don't walk out. I stay in bed, hoping to hear the footsteps of my blonde-haired nurse. I never know for sure, but four or five days a week, I'll hear the familiar *tap* of her shoes. I'll keep my eyes closed as she opens the door, walks into the room, sits down on the edge of the mattress. I won't move a muscle.

I'll feel the warmth of my nurse's hand, right through the sheet. The pressure of her palm as she rubs my back a little, as she smooths the sheet around my shoulders. Grazes her fingers against my spine. A couple of long strokes, from the base of my neck to the small of my back. She gives the muscles a little squeeze.

You can't imagine how good that feels.

* * *

But we were talking about Wisconsin. I had filled three pages of that letter to Nancy, and was thinking about starting a fourth, when Mike walked through the door.

He was smiling.

The day had been too long—we had gone from drowsy to wea-ry, from weary to fatigued. Ned and Buddy and I didn't feel like smiling, and not just because we were tired. But Mike didn't notice, he was in such a good mood.

"You should have seen it," he said. "The way she looked at me."

It was no surprise that Irene would be drawn to Mike. Those blue eyes, that dark curly hair. That way he had of looking at wom-en, right in their eyes, that said he was interested in *them*.

Almost like Sweetie Malone—although Mike was choosier. Sweetie could wind up with anyone: the desk clerk, the chambermaid, the cashier's daughter. Whoever had a fresh smile, skin like the petals of a lily. Of course they had to be pretty—Sweetie had an artist's sense of balance, an obligation to match his good looks to theirs. To tell you the truth, it could be almost too much, watching Sweetie with one of his girlfriends. Seeing his prettiness next to hers felt like eating too much sugar.

I hate to be unkind, but sometimes, with Sweetie's women, prettiness was all there was. I don't mean to judge, but I'm talking about women without the slightest bit of substance, their good looks a veneer, hiding the empty space behind their sparkling eyes. It's unnatural, to see that kind of beauty with nothing behind it. Like a flower without a scent.

It was different with Mike. If Mike was with a woman, you knew she was going to have depth, she was going to have layers. All the substance you could want, and then some—personality would burst out of her like feathers from an overstuffed pillow. A woman who was a handful, to be honest. And every bit as pretty as Sweetie's. More so, even, because it went all the way through.

Here is the odd part. Mike liked spending time with these women, he liked getting to know them. But he never let things get serious.

You wouldn't have expected that from Mike—because he was a serious person. But it happened every time. Things would be on the right path, headed in just the right direction. You'd look at Mike, at the two of them together, and you could see how well it was going, how much sense it made. How happy they were! Everything Mike wanted was right in front of him—and then, at the critical moment, he would back away.

You knew exactly when it was going to happen. It was right after you'd gotten used to seeing them together—but just before you *expected* to see them together.

Mike told me, once, that he let women go because he felt guilty. Not because he had done anything wrong. Of course he hadn't! Mike would never hurt anyone, not on purpose. He started to feel guilty, he said, because something *might* go wrong.

I don't know if that was the whole story. But it's the part Mike told me.

I suppose it made sense. The world is a complicated place— things can get out of control, even when you have the best intentions. You might lose perspective, for a moment, you might get distracted, and miss what's really important. You might hurt someone—even by accident. Even if you didn't mean it.

I wish I had understood that back then. I had to learn the hard way, when it was too late.

So Mike would let things end, and I was always disappointed, because I liked the women who were drawn to him. They were the kind of women *I* might have been drawn to, if the circumstances had been different. Why not? They were interesting women, women with substance, and it didn't hurt that they were pretty, too. Women who might, possibly, have been interested in me, with a little work, a little maneuvering on my part.

If they hadn't been with Mike.

But I never made the slightest move in that direction, because they *were* with Mike, and he was my best friend. I would see them together, I'd watch things blossom and wilt. The last thing I could do when it ended was step in on my own, no matter how much interest I felt. No matter how much I liked her.

It's surprising that I never felt jealous, at least not that I can remember.

* * *

"You should have seen the way she looked at me," Mike said.

He stood in the doorway of our little room.

You know how it feels—that jolt of electricity when things begin, the way you float, for a little while, above your ordinary life. But I could tell that this was different. There was something in Mike's voice that said he was really in it this time. Deeper than usual. Was Irene that much prettier? Or was it something else?

"You've got to be kidding," Buddy Brodsky said. "*Her?* The one in the picture?"

When Buddy was irritated, there was a sound in his voice like gravel. His eyes got sharp when he didn't like what he saw.

Mike's smile lost half its altitude.

"Why not her?" Mike said.

"She's pretty," Buddy said. "I'll give you that. I'm sure it doesn't hurt to look at her."

"*Really* pretty," Ned said. Sipping his cup of milk.

Mike nodded at Ned. "You should see her in person," he said. "The picture is nothing."

"She's pretty," Buddy said. "But she's still that blowhard's daughter. His *daughter*. What do you think, she's going to leave his side and come over to ours?"

"I'm not talking about her father," Mike said. "And this doesn't have anything to do with sides. I'm talking about *her.*"

"Did you hear him at dinner?" Buddy said. "'Why did we choose this life?' 'Why do we live with this hardship?' She's not going to think any differently—it doesn't work that way."

I nodded in agreement as Buddy paced in his pastel-blue pajamas.

"There are plenty of women out there," Buddy said. "Don't waste your time on one you can't have. Don't waste *our* time."

I watched Buddy's irritation climb. Ozzie had the team's quickest temper—he was the one person you didn't want mad at you. But Buddy was in second place.

Mike didn't notice. He shook his head.

"I don't care who her father is," Mike said. "I like talking to her, I like looking at her. She is worth looking at."

Ned tried to jump in. "I know someone in Syracuse . . ."

Mike wasn't listening. He pointed at Buddy. "You're right," he said. "There are plenty of women in the world, I know that. But when I talk to Irene—it's *different*."

I must have turned my head when he said that, because Mike looked over at me. He looked a little angry. I wasn't going to argue—I really wasn't! I was Mike's friend, and I could see it had meant something, to him, to sit with Irene. To relax on the couch with her, and ease into a conversation. I could picture exactly how it went, because Mike had that way about him, that gift of making you comfortable. Of starting things off on the right foot.

There was a man who sold apples outside our hotel in Madison. Mike went to buy an apple, and wound up spending an hour. He found out everything! How long that man had been selling apples, why that spot was better than the other corners, why apples were the best fruit to sell. Before long, Mike knew where you could buy apples a bushel at a time, and how to get the best price, and what profit you could make on the corner. He knew how to set up the cart, and the best times to open and close. He knew how to spot who would buy and who was going to walk right past. He could have gone into the business, if he wanted to.

Mike was that way with everyone! The hot-dog vendor in the ballpark, the counterman in the diner. Anyone could be his friend. I don't have that gift—it always feels a little awkward to me, because

I don't know how to read people, I never know what to say next. Especially in the beginning, that bantering back and forth.

All kinds of things can go wrong.

It's different on the team, because you have time to get comfortable, time to settle in with your teammates. You don't have to worry about first impressions, you're there for a good long while. There's nothing but time, as a matter of fact. All those hours on the bus, one endless conversation, spilling over from town to town, from one dusty highway to another. You learn everything there is to know about your teammates, and they know all about you.

You do everything together. You train, you drill, you sleep under the same roof. Your next meal comes from the same place as theirs. You win and lose together, and it doesn't matter if you go into a slump—when you step up to the plate, your teammates will stand in the dugout and cheer. So relax—say what you want, or keep quiet, if you'd rather. Your teammates will understand, they've seen all your moods. They can tell that you have different *kinds* of quiet, that's how well they know you.

Something occurred to me then, in that cramped room on the fourth floor of the Rockefeller. I thought about the way Mike warmed right up to people, pumped them with endless questions. He wasn't just being polite—Mike listened to every answer as if he were about to hear some vital secret, some critical piece of information that no one else could reveal, like the directions to buried treasure.

I thought about the way Mike talked to women. All the things he had to know about them, the details of their lives, the particulars of their personal histories. Their opinions about this and that, what they thought about *everything*. Mike had been that way for all the years I had known him—but as we stood there on the fourth floor of the Rockefeller, I realized for the first time that Mike was looking for something.

Sometimes you don't notice. It's right in front of you, and you don't see it—the most important thing.

Mike was looking for something he was missing, something he really wanted. I should have realized that sooner, because I was looking for something, too.

Nancy and I used to walk around Binghamton when I was in town. We'd pass through one neighborhood after another as dusk turned into night, watching men come home from work, the lights go on in people's houses. We'd smell meatloaf cooking, roast beef, baked chicken. We'd hear music from the radio drifting out of the windows.

"You think you have it all figured out," Nancy said one night. We had been walking for a while, and stars were coming out in the deepest parts of the sky.

"What have I figured out?" I said.

"You go off to play your game. You travel through all those states, you and your teammates. All those cheering crowds—you're a big hero. Then you come back here and look me in the eye and tell me how much you missed me."

I stopped. Nancy stopped, too, and looked at me, her eyes dark in the starlight. She had a look, sometimes, that I couldn't quite figure out. Not upset with me, exactly, because I hadn't done anything wrong. Had I? Disappointed wasn't the right word—I hadn't broken any promises, after all. But it was something *like* that, and I was not sure why.

"I *did* miss you," I said.

"I know," she said. "I know you did."

We started to walk again. It was the truth—I had missed Nancy, a lot! But there was work to be done, she knew that as well as I did.

There were problems in the world, things that had to be changed. They *had* to be. I wanted to see Nancy more often—but what was I supposed to do?

"Tell me something," Nancy said. We were on her block now. We had reached the steps of her porch.

"What?" I said.

"When you are all done," Nancy said. "When you've fixed it all, when you've solved the world's problems—are you going to come back and stay?"

I said yes. I said it without hesitating, even for a second. I said it with so much feeling that Nancy smiled.

It was going to take a while. I didn't have any illusions—the job was big, the problems were fundamental. But the team was strong, and we had the force of our ideas. Our opponents might be powerful, but crowds cheered us in those dusty ballparks. Boys chased the bus in every town. We swung the bat with all our hearts—and justice was on our side. Weren't we bound to win in the end?

"Yes," I said. "I will come back." I said it with such conviction that Nancy's confusing, almost disappointed, look went away.

We kissed right there in front of her house. She stood on the porch, and I stood one or two steps below her, to even out our heights. The air was sweet, and Nancy's cheeks were warm, and everything was soft, soft, soft.

I would come back, I said. There was nothing I wanted more, I told Nancy, and she knew that I meant it.

We went inside.

The darkness was thick as velvet in Nancy's living room, and her warm skin felt good because the night was cool. We kissed for a good long while, and I was sure that Nancy could feel my heartbeat.

She stepped back. There was moonlight, just a little, enough to see Nancy's eyes. Her lips. Her hands at her sides.

Nancy looked at me.

All kinds of things can happen at a moment like that.

Nancy reached for the top of her blouse, her hands gleaming in the moonlight. Her fingers at the top button.

She watched my face, looking at me as I watched her. She stared into my eyes, as her fingers moved to the second button.

Her lips, her cheek, the softness of her neck. I kissed the pale skin at Nancy's collar, and I can still feel it, the fabric of her blouse against my cheek. Nancy's fingers in my hair. The warmth of her skin against my lips. The kind of warmth that makes you want more, to be closer than touching, if that's possible.

I stepped back.

Then *I* reached for the third button.

I watched Nancy's face, and at that exact moment, I realized: *this* is what I was looking for. I had missed it my entire life, it had slipped by entirely. I hadn't given it a moment's thought.

Sometimes you know yourself least of all.

This is what I had always wanted—to look in someone's eyes the way I was looking in Nancy's. To see exactly how she was feeling. I mean, *exactly*—as sharp as if it were your own feeling bubbling up inside. To feel it so completely that you didn't care about anything else, because she was a part of you, or you were a part of her, or maybe both—it was all mixed up. You looked in Nancy's eyes, and you knew for an absolute fact that the way she felt was the only thing that mattered in the world.

Is *anything* better than that?

So as I stood with Buddy and Ned in the attic of the Rockefeller, I understood that Mike was looking for something, too. And he seemed to think he had found it.

CHAPTER THIRTEEN

She's all wrong for you, Mike," Buddy said. "You think it isn't complicated. But it is."

"What's so complicated?" Mike said.

"You don't know her yet," Buddy said. "You don't see all of the difficulties. Her father is only the start. What about that dress in the picture? That pearl necklace! Where are you going to buy those kinds of things? She's the kind of person who gets what she wants, believe me. Tell me it isn't true."

Mike walked quietly over to his bed and opened his suitcase. He rummaged through his clothes until he found his flannel pajamas, then sat on the edge of the bed, holding the pajamas in his lap. Still thinking.

Ned broke the silence, his tone softer, more soothing, maybe from the hot milk he'd been drinking.

"Listen, Mike," he said. "You met her by chance. It came out of nowhere. You had a nice evening, right?"

Mike fingered a button on his pajamas and nodded.

"You talked to her."

Mike nodded again.

"You held her hand."

Another nod.

"You kissed her?"

Mike blushed.

Ned smiled. "Good for you! Everyone deserves a night like that, once in a while. Even if it doesn't last."

Buddy broke in again. "Ned's right. We've had a long trip—it's nice to have a little bonus. Now put it behind you. Tomorrow we'll be back on the road, where we belong."

Mike looked at Buddy and opened his mouth, then thought better of it. He shook his head. He frowned at the pajamas in his lap.

Finally, he said, "I can see what you're getting at."

That was Mike all over. Seeing an argument from every angle, looking at it from your side, if you saw it differently. Trying to understand your point of view, whether he agreed or not. Even with people like Spencer—he would test their ideas, weigh them in his head, even when they didn't deserve to be weighed. Even when they were so obviously wrong.

I can't live that way. It's one thing to be open-minded, to think things through. I have nothing against pondering, when you really don't know the answer. But once you've figured it out, you don't need to agonize, you don't need to know everyone else's opinion. Once you know what's right—you just do it!

"I see what you're thinking," Mike said. "A businessman's daughter, how is that going to work? Although she isn't like him, not at all. Some people are *nothing* like their parents. But still, I see your point. She's his daughter—that means something. They *are* different from us."

"That's all I'm saying," Buddy replied.

"Maybe I could look at it your way," Mike said. "Just a meeting by chance, a little bonus, like you said. A fun evening. Even though it feels like more."

Mike smoothed the pajamas in his lap. Still thinking.

"But I know what it felt like," Mike said. "I was *supposed* to be with Irene, that's what it was like. We were *meant* to be together. Maybe she was the reason we stopped here."

Buddy's eyebrows went up, and he spread his arms in disbelief, as if he were questioning an umpire's call.

"You think we were meant to get caught in this storm?" Buddy said. "Are you trying to tell me this was *fate*?"

"I'm just saying there might have been a reason for Irene and me to meet," Mike said.

"Don't say it," Buddy said. "Don't even *start* to think that way. Because you know where that goes. Pretty soon everything happens for a reason, it's not up to you anymore. It's not your responsibility!"

"That's not what I'm saying." Mike shook his head. "I'm just saying it feels right with Irene. It feels *simple*. Maybe fate has nothing to do with it—but still, it was meant to be, even if we're only here by chance."

"We'll be gone tomorrow," Buddy said. "We'll be in Indiana by nightfall. You can write her a letter, explain the whole thing. Tell her all about the team, the way we live our lives. See if she writes back."

Buddy was making sense, but something bothered me. It bothered me a lot. Something about how sudden Mike's feelings were. Only a few hours ago, we had never heard of Irene, we had never dreamed of her blonde curls, her sea-green eyes. As far as we were concerned, Irene didn't exist! But now she was the only thing we could think about.

That wasn't right. Irene wasn't *supposed* to be the most important thing. The important thing was our team, wasn't it?

There are major characters in life, just like in a book. The ones the story is really about, who play the important parts. Who are right in the middle of the action.

There are minor characters, too, people in the background. They also have a purpose, but they are not the center of the story. They are not the *point* of the story. The Robins were the point of our story, and Mike and I were the major characters, along with Buddy and Ned and Sweetie. Ozzie, of course. And Effie. The theme of the story was our great cause. The cause that was the very purpose of our lives.

The minor characters were the people we met as we traveled around in our Crown Coach Company bus. People not important in themselves, who are only there to flesh out the picture. To add color to the story. They're necessary in their own way—what would life be without minor characters? But the story was not *about* them. It was about us.

Wasn't it?

As I listened to Mike in our room in the Rockefeller, I had a terrible fear. Maybe I had been wrong all along about the story. Maybe the story was not about Mike and me. Not about our team, our great cause. What if the story was about Mike and *Irene*?

Maybe the story was just getting started. Everything that had happened so far was just background, setting the stage. Sometimes a story has a long introduction.

Maybe *I* was a minor character—one of those people who aren't important by themselves but are only there to flesh out the picture. To add color! What if our entire team only turned out to be a detail in Mike's history? A detail that one day he would barely remember. Could it be that Mike's real story was just beginning?

I felt a moment of panic.

How do you know which is the real story?

Was the real story about men and ideals—the battle for justice, the struggle for a lofty goal? Or was it about the triumph of the system, the victory of the powers-that-be? Maybe Spencer was the major character. Maybe Spencer was the hero!

What if the story was about someone I'd never even met? That girl in Green Bay, for instance, at the union rally. Sitting at her father's feet, eating peanuts out of a paper bag. Why *shouldn't* it be about her? She might grow into an adult and have all kinds of adventures, travel the globe, see the wonders of the world. Have experiences you can barely imagine. But somewhere in the back of her mind, there'd be a scrap of memory—the faintest impression, a fragment of an image—of a baseball player standing at the back of the stage at a union rally. Was *that* my part in the story?

"I'm going to brush my teeth," Buddy said. He and Ned took out their bathroom kits and headed down the hall.

Mike and I were alone in the room, the wind still gusting outside, the snow driving against the sides of the building.

"I *like* Irene," Mike said. "It feels so nice, to be with her."

"I know," I said. "You don't have to explain."

I saw the look in his eyes. Sometimes these things bowl you over—you know what I mean. Someone knocks you back on your heels, and all of a sudden you don't care about anything else, you can't stand to be without her, you need her more than air.

That was the way Sweetie lived, every day of the week. Each new woman took his breath away, each gorgeous redhead was a fresh thought, each soft blonde a simple, beautiful idea. Her warm hand, the spark of gold in her sweet brown eyes. You know how it goes. All of a sudden you've found the secret of life. The problems of the world evaporate like mist. But in the morning she wants to know what's for breakfast, and you're not ready for breakfast yet, for the specifics of it—the when and where and what—and you think, how did things get there so quickly? What about *after* breakfast, what happens then? You don't even want to think about it, the tangle of details, the blizzard of complications.

What happened to that simple, beautiful idea?

Maybe it would be that way for Mike. At some point you take a second look, and you realize you made a mistake, you can't believe how wrong you were. All of a sudden! You look again and she's not anything like you thought, you can't imagine why she took your breath away. The second look might come in a week, or a month. Or a year. All I could do was hope.

"We'd better get ready for bed," I said. "We'll need an early start in the morning."

Mike put on his pajamas, but he was thinking about something else. He tugged up his flannel pants, then broke into a little smile.

"Let me show you something," he said. "Let me show you what she did."

I shrugged.

"Hold out your arm," Mike said.

I held out my arm. Mike rolled up the sleeve of my pajamas.

"She held my hand," Mike said. "Like this." Mike held my hand.

"Then she took her finger, and she went like *this*."

Mike put his fingernail on the very softest part of my forearm, just at the elbow. It almost tickled. Then he began to trace, very slowly, down my arm. The edge of his nail dragged ever so lightly along my skin.

"Do you feel that?" Mike said. "She barely touched my arm, but it was like a flame—a *good* flame. I never felt anything like it— it was better than kissing."

Mike ran his fingernail along my skin. Very slowly, all the way down to my wrist. "Do you feel it?" he said.

Mike showed me what Irene had done. If I live another five hundred years, I will never forget the way it felt.

CHAPTER FOURTEEN

Spencer was the most cheerful man you could imagine as he walked into the lobby the next morning. He practically pranced into the room, his eyes sparkling, his smile impossibly broad. You took one look at that smile, and you thought—this is a man who knows exactly what he wants to do next.

He wore a nifty sky-blue suit, which looked as though it had been pressed that very instant.

A starched white shirt, crisp as a cracker. A blue silk tie, to match the suit.

Spencer had scrubbed his face until it gleamed. His cheeks shone as if they'd been rubbed with butter.

"Beautiful morning!" he said to the five of us. Ozzie Gadlin and Buddy Brodsky. Effie, of course, and Ned Kretzmann. And me. The early risers.

Mike was still asleep. Sweetie, too.

"Beautiful?" Effie said. "If you say so."

The wind howled outside. The shades were drawn to hide the falling snow, as if the hotel were ashamed of the weather.

I admit that I felt a touch of gloom myself, and not just because of the weather. We'd been driving around the Midwest for three long weeks. Three weeks without Nancy!

It's one thing to write letters. To picture Nancy sitting across the table, her wide blue eyes looking at you over her cup of tea.

Almost smiling—but not quite! You know what she's waiting for, what it will take to make her smile. So you move closer, so close you can see the threads of her blouse, feel her breath on your cheek. You reach for her imaginary hand, and you *almost* touch.

It's another thing entirely to drive into the parking lot of the Chemung Cafe. Gravel crunching under the tires of the bus, the plate-glass window all lit up. You pull in and look through that window, and catch a glimpse of Nancy, just as *she* looks up and sees the bus. Her blue eyes widen in surprise. She sets aside the coffeepot. She calls something over her shoulder.

Nancy walks toward the door, handing a stack of orders to the teenager who is helping out that night, a well-meaning girl with rosy cheeks, blonde hair tied in a ponytail. Trying as hard as she can, but she can never be Nancy.

When you step off the bus, Nancy is already there. She throws her arms around you—you forgot how strong she was—and you practically lift each other off the ground.

Her cheeks are warm.

Her lips are salty.

You can't do *that* in Wisconsin.

I'd been three long weeks without Nancy, and now I was trapped with Spencer. It didn't bother him, of course! He was happy as a clam to be stuck in the John D. Rockefeller, the sky dark, snow piling up around us. He beamed as though it were a sunny summer morning.

"Mind if I join you for breakfast?" Spencer said.

"Well—" said Effie.

"I'm hungry," Spencer said. "And I'm buying!"

"I don't think—" Effie began.

"We can pay for our own breakfast," Ozzie said.

"I insist! It will be my pleasure," Spencer said. "I enjoy the conversation. And after all, it's on the expense account."

Effie was still shaking his head. Spencer walked over to him and spoke in a low tone.

"It would be a favor to me," Spencer said. "I feel badly about last night, I know how strongly you feel about your team, your ideals. It's not my place to raise questions!" He looked almost mournful. "The least I can do is buy you breakfast."

Ozzie scowled, but Effie thought it over. We were spending more than we should to stay at the Rockefeller, and it would be nice to make it up on meals. We had a long trip ahead of us, the bus burned a lot of gas. Whatever we saved would go to the cause.

"All right," Effie said. "As a favor to you."

So we walked back into the dining room. The dark paneling, the gas lights. A shorter rectangular table, this time, with Effie and Spencer at opposite ends, Buddy and Ozzie along one side, Ned and I on the other.

We recognized the waiter from the night before, arranging silverware on the far side of the room. That mop of white hair, if anything more untidy than we remembered, and in the light you could see how deeply his face was wrinkled. But his gaze was sharp enough to slice bread.

When he saw us, the waiter stopped.

You couldn't tell what he was thinking, but he was thinking *something*. The waiter's expression didn't change—he might have been carved from wax, for all you could read in his face. But there were wheels turning inside. There was something in his eyes that you couldn't decode.

"Come here!" Spencer said. "Over here. We're hungry as ditch-diggers!"

Spencer motioned with his arm, a broad sweeping wave. It was a theatrical gesture, the kind you might use to catch the attention of a slow-witted animal, to direct its ponderous movements. To back an elephant into its cage.

The waiter set down his tray of silverware, and walked toward us reluctantly, as if he were wading through deep water.

"It's wonderful to see you again," Spencer said. Smiling as though he really meant it. "What's your name?"

The waiter's frown was the mirror image of Spencer's smile. "Burgess," he said.

"I had a neighbor named Burgess," Spencer said. "An odd fellow. His wife drank too much."

The waiter's eyebrows went up, if only by a fraction of an inch.

"No offense," Spencer said. "I didn't mean anything by that—you're nothing like my neighbor! He was bald as an egg, and I'm sure your wife doesn't drink."

Burgess's expression remained frozen.

"At any rate," Spencer said, "we are hungry men. I hope you'll take good care of us."

Spencer extended his hand. Between two fingers was a neatly folded bill. The paper was crisp—the money must have been brand-new. We couldn't see the denomination.

Burgess didn't look at it. It seemed, in fact, as if the last thing in the world he wanted to do was touch that money.

His blue eyes stared into the distance.

Spencer continued to hold out his hand. I swear that Burgess didn't move a muscle, and yet somehow, the bill managed to pass into his palm. You couldn't quite make out how it happened—it was almost as if the paper didn't make contact with his fingers. As if it traveled entirely under its own power. But the money wound up in Burgess's hand.

"Why don't we start with coffee?" Spencer said.

Burgess gave the tiniest of nods. He retreated to the kitchen for the coffeepot.

As the kitchen door closed, Spencer looked around the table. "I don't know about the rest of you," he said, "but I'm starving! I might clean out the pantry in this place, if I'm not careful."

I took a drink of water. I was hungry, too. But what I really wanted was one of Nancy's cinnamon rolls—or maybe five or six of them.

Almost as much as I wanted her.

"I have to warn you," Spencer said. He raised an eyebrow at Effie. "Don't try to keep up with me. You won't be able to! Not that it's a competition, I don't mean it that way. It's no fault of yours if you can't match my pace. There aren't many men who can."

Effie looked at Spencer. He didn't react at all, he didn't move a muscle. But Ned glanced over at me. Buddy Brodsky nudged Ozzie. I knew what that nudge meant. It meant that Spencer had no idea who he was talking to.

Because Effie Mendez could eat.

It might have surprised you, because Effie wasn't the slightest bit plump. If you went by appearances, you would have pegged him for a salad man, someone who'd be happy with vegetables and a glass of water, maybe a cup of soup. But you'd be wrong.

Because Effie Mendez could *eat.*

Second helpings, thirds, fourths. It didn't matter what you put on his plate, Effie would polish it off and ask for more.

If you had a roast, Effie would cut slice after slice, until there was nothing left but a film of grease. Then he'd wipe that up with a heel of bread.

If you had two or three broiled chickens, Effie would pick every last scrap of meat from the bones, then shovel down a platterful of biscuits.

I'd seen Effie eat eight baked potatoes. I'd seen him eat three loaves of bread. I'd seen him take a five-pound sack of cookies on an afternoon bus trip, and by dinnertime have nothing left but crumbs.

It wasn't just quantity—Effie had endurance *and* speed. Once, at a ballpark, he swallowed half a dozen hot dogs during the seventh-inning stretch. With mustard and onions! And he had time to wipe his chin before the umpire called for the batter.

Effie didn't know what it meant to be full. He only stopped eating out of boredom, or because everyone else had left the table. Or if all the food was gone, and he didn't see a practical way to get more.

Like any true champion, Effie was modest about his talent. So all he said to Spencer was, "I'm hungry, too."

"Splendid!" Spencer replied. "We'll have ourselves a good meal."

He looked at Burgess, pouring cups of coffee around the table.

"What do you recommend?" Spencer asked.

"Take your pick," Burgess answered. "We can make anything you like."

"Eggs, then," Spencer said. "Eggs all around. Scrambled, with some of that good Wisconsin cheese. And toast, with plenty of butter. Strawberry jam if you have it. Agreed?"

Spencer looked around the table. He saw nods.

Burgess took the coffeepot back to the kitchen.

Spencer unfolded his napkin in his lap. He said, "Twice in one weekend! I can't tell you what a treat this is for me."

We sipped our coffee, nice and hot. It felt good going down.

"I'm not surprised your center fielder is still asleep," Spencer went on. "So is Irene. The two of them really hit it off last night! Staying up to all hours. They must have had a good time."

Around the table, we shifted uncomfortably in our chairs. All of a sudden, it was a little awkward.

Mike was free to do as he liked, of course. Why not? He was a grown man. Sweetie Malone stayed out with women all the time. Ned Kretzmann had a sweetheart in Syracuse.

I told you about Nancy, didn't I?

But something didn't sit right about Mike and Irene. It was hard to put a finger on it, but it didn't sit right at all.

Effie looked at Spencer. "I don't know whether they had a good time or not," he said. "I'm in bed at that hour. I don't carouse in the middle of the night, like certain people who should know better. People who have a game to rest up for. People who might need a good talking to."

"I know exactly what you mean," Spencer said. "But young people will do what they want these days. We can talk, but they don't have to listen!"

Effie set down his coffee cup.

"Listen or not," Effie said, "it ends this morning. We'll pack up the bus, we'll be on our way to Fort Wayne."

"If the storm allows!" Spencer said. "Have you looked out the window? Fate may have thrown a monkey wrench in your plans."

It might have been a perfectly nice breakfast. We might have enjoyed the food, gossiped about baseball, complained about the storm. But Spencer had to go and ruin it.

He saw the expressions on our faces. He should have known, from our dinner the night before, how we might react—but Spencer looked puzzled, or at least he pretended to be. "What did I say?" he asked.

It was Ozzie who answered.

"Fate!" Ozzie said. The way he spat the word made it clear that Spencer had committed a grievous sin, that he had made an embarrassing social blunder.

That he should be ashamed of himself.

Ozzie was right.

Let's say I'm standing on the pitcher's mound, with the ball in my hand. The crowd cheering, my teammates looking on as I stare in at the batter. Turning the ball in my palm as I sort through the considerations. The kind of pitch he likes to hit, the day he's had so far. The pitch I threw him last time, and what he did with it. What *he* thinks I'm going to throw.

I weigh all the angles—then make my choice. I tighten my grip, set my shoulders. I reach back and put every last ounce of strength into the pitch.

Let me ask you a question. Why would I bother with all that, if I believed in fate? What's the point of weighing the pros and cons if the ball is going to go wherever it goes? If its path is already set? Why worry about the possibilities—I might as well just give in, if it's all determined by fate.

That's exactly what they want. The people running things, the ones in control. It's exactly what they want us to believe.

There's nothing you can do about it.

It's just the way things are.

It's meant *to be that way.*

Ninety-nine times out of a hundred, when someone talks about fate, they're on the side of the bosses. They want you to lie down, throw in the towel, let the powers-that-be have their way.

"Fate!" Ozzie repeated. He was right to have contempt in his voice. We couldn't take what Spencer said lightly, we couldn't forgive it as a figure of speech. It hit right at the center, the core, the beating heart of what we believed.

The whole point was to change things. The point of *everything*. Our team, our cause, our very lives. To change things that were not right, things that had gone off course. Things that had become a little unjust.

Or more than a little.

The point was to fix those things, to straighten them out. To make them the way they *should* be. What could be more right, more honest, more natural than that?

It never fails to surprise me, that some people consider this a radical idea. But if you believe in fate, it is.

Spencer looked at Ozzie with his eyebrows raised. "You have to admit," Spencer said, "that *something* has set an obstacle in your path. Just look out the window."

Ozzie scowled. "When I look out the window," he said, "I see snow. Not fate! And so what if it snows? We'll dig it out, we'll clear a path. We'll move a mountain of snow if we have to.

"*You* might stop dead in your tracks, the minute something gets in your way." He glared at Spencer. "Go ahead, give up and call it fate. That's your privilege! But when we see an obstacle, we go over it. We go around. We move it.

"We don't believe in fate," Ozzie said. "We believe in shovels!"

It made you want to stand up and cheer.

Effie waded in to help. "You're not *really* telling us that fate sets our path," he said to Spencer. "You can't really believe in some mysterious power."

"I'm only pointing out the obvious," Spencer said. "You think you set your own course, yet here you are in Wisconsin."

Effie shook his head. "Anyone can run into bad weather," he said. "Anyone can have a flat tire. All kinds of things can happen."

Effie put down his coffee. "I've been on the road a long time," he said. "I'm the last one to question bad luck, I've seen plenty of it! But bad luck is not the same thing as fate."

"And here's our breakfast!" Spencer said. Burgess pushed open the swinging kitchen door, his arms loaded with plates of scrambled eggs and thick toast slathered with butter.

It was time to eat.

CHAPTER FIFTEEN

Burgess set down our plates, and we dug in. The food was a relief—not just because we were hungry. We needed something to distract us, we didn't want to listen to Spencer anymore. We'd rather sink our teeth into eggs that were fluffy and creamy at the same time, with just a tang of Wisconsin cheddar. Enough on each plate for three men.

But the quiet didn't last. "Let me explain," Spencer said after a few minutes, as his fork slowed down. Buddy Brodsky rolled his eyes, but there was no way around it—Spencer was going to talk again. His plate was nearly empty, while the rest of us still mined mountains of eggs.

"You're absolutely right, there's a difference between fate and luck," Spencer said, chewing his last mouthful of eggs. "I agree with you! There is no invisible hand putting snowstorms in your path. We don't believe that, we are modern men."

Spencer pointed his fork at Effie.

"But my point remains," Spencer said.

We waited to hear his point. But Burgess had noticed that Spencer's plate was empty, and he hurried over, waiting for instructions. Spencer looked up at Burgess, then around the table. "Who's ready for the second course?" he asked.

Those eggs were heavy, and most of us were still chewing. The slices of toast were thick, and we had eaten a big dinner the night before. We didn't really need a second course.

Except Effie. Effie had eaten everything on his plate, and a slice of Buddy Brodsky's toast, and now he was taking spoonfuls of strawberry jam. Spencer looked at Effie directly, and said, "Your choice, this time. If you want to keep going, that is. If you feel you're up to it."

There was a look in Spencer's eye. A certain kind of challenge.

But Effie wasn't ruffled—it didn't bother him at all. A challenge from Spencer was of no concern to him, Effie's expression said. It was beneath his dignity to notice.

"By all means," Effie said. "Let's order."

Spencer smiled. "Two more plates," he said to Burgess. Then to Effie: "What shall we have?"

"Pancakes," Effie said. Looking at Burgess instead of Spencer. "Buckwheat, if you have them. Thick ones, in a stack, with honey on the side. And a couple of sausages."

"Right away," Burgess said, and disappeared into the kitchen.

"I hope you're *up* to it," Effie said to Spencer.

Spencer laughed. "I like it!" he said. "You won't give in without a fight!"

Spencer adjusted the napkin in his lap.

"Now," he said, "where were we?"

"We are modern men," said Buddy Brodsky. Buddy didn't miss a thing.

"That's right," Spencer said. "We are modern men, men of science. We don't believe in magic. We know that everything that happens has a cause."

Spencer nodded his head, for emphasis.

"Take a fly ball," Spencer said. "You can calculate where it's going to land, if you work it through. You look at the speed of the bat, the angle of impact, the exact point where it strikes the ball. Dead on, or off-center? With an uppercut, or flat out? If you want to know where the ball is going—just look at the way it is hit."

Spencer traced an arc with his fork, to show the path of a batted ball.

Effie frowned. "There are too many things you don't know," he said. "What if the ball is hit on a seam? What if there's a little dimple on the bat? Some rough spot, that puts just enough spin on the ball to change its path. Maybe a gust of wind blows through, just as the ball clears the infield."

"Of course you have to account for the complications," Spencer said. "The direction of the wind. You have to look at humidity— the ball travels farther when the air is dry, doesn't it? Or is it the other way around? There's the spin on the ball *before* it hits the bat. But if you track down all the causes, and add them up, you will know exactly where that ball is going. It's a matter of physics."

Spencer folded his hands over his stomach. "My point," he said, "is that once you *do* know how it works, it's predictable. Like a machine! If you know how the parts work, then you know exactly what the machine is going to do."

"I don't know what kind of machine you're thinking of," Effie said, "but the ones I know break down, they wear out. They act one way on Monday and another way on Tuesday. Drive our bus for a week—then tell me machines are predictable!"

"Of course there are imperfections," Spencer said. "You have to take them into account. Maybe there's a loose wire, a spring so finely tuned that if you jostle the machine—even breathe on it—you will upset a delicate balance. You will set in motion a chain of events. It may *seem* unpredictable, but if you truly understand the machine, you will know exactly how it happened. And you will know that it couldn't possibly have happened any other way. Sausage!"

Burgess set down two plates of pancakes and sausages, and Spencer and Effie tore in right away. Four pancakes on a plate, and Spencer ripped through the stack like a buzz saw tearing up kindling. Sparks practically flying from his knife and fork. He speared his sausage like a man who hadn't eaten meat in years—and within minutes, he'd gobbled down the last piece. Nothing was left but the droplets of fat sparkling on his empty plate.

Effie was not far behind, mopping up the last bits of his own food. Butter, pancake, honey, sausage. The rest of us sipped our coffee.

"You've left something out," Effie said as he set down his fork. He couldn't let Spencer's comment sit. "Your idea that the world is predictable, like a machine. You've left out the fact that *we* are not machines."

Spencer's expression did not change. He looked at Effie without raising an eyebrow. Ned Kretzmann stirred sugar into his coffee, looking confused. This wasn't breakfast table conversation in Syracuse.

"Maybe *your* world runs like some complicated piece of equipment," Effie said. "I don't know, I'll give you the benefit of the doubt. But we have brains to think things through, to weigh one thing against another. We decide things in our own minds. And our *minds* are not machines."

"I understand," Spencer said. "Who wants to admit they are only a piece of machinery? We are flesh and blood! We want to feel that we are in charge. And yet—"

He was interrupted by Burgess reaching for the empty plates. Spencer picked up his fork from his plate, wiped it with his napkin, and set it down on the table.

"Would you like anything else?" Burgess said.

"I'm beginning to work up an appetite!" Spencer said. "Fire up the griddle—we'll have plates of French toast. And don't skimp on the portions, this time. Bacon on the side, and a couple of biscuits.

"Unless . . ." Spencer turned to Effie, who was leaning back in his chair. He looked Effie in the eye. "Unless you've had enough?"

"Plenty of butter for the biscuits!" Effie said to Burgess.

Spencer smiled. "That's the spirit," he said. "Make me work for it!" He pointed at Effie while looking around the table. "You wouldn't guess he could put it away like that. He doesn't carry his bulk the way I do. But you can't go by appearances. At the table, I fear the thin man!"

Burgess raised an eyebrow as he returned to the kitchen, but Spencer didn't notice. He turned back to Effie.

"Now let's settle this," he said. "You are right that we have minds of our own. Of course we do! We don't like to think of ourselves as machines." Spencer patted his stomach, looking satisfied. "And yet, aren't we like machines, in a way? Complicated, to be sure. We are very, very complicated! But we are made up of parts, and every part has a job to do. If you understand the way the pieces work together—then you know what the *whole* is going to do."

Spencer looked curiously at Effie, as if he really wanted to know what Effie thought about this argument.

Effie looked at Spencer for a long moment. "You can say what you want," Effie said, still holding his coffee cup. "But I make up my own mind, and my mind is not a machine."

Spencer shook his head. He looked a little disappointed.

"Your brain is made up of parts, too," Spencer said. "And those parts follow rules. Chemical rules, electrical rules. The rules of physics. That's all there is! Like clockwork. If you know how the parts work, you can figure out exactly what the clock will do."

"We are *thinking* about things," Effie said. "We are *deciding*. It is not the same as clockwork."

"It is *exactly* the same thing," Spencer said. "It is a *complicated* clockwork."

Whatever line of work Spencer was in, I hoped it didn't require common sense. I imagined what Nancy would have said, about brains working like clocks. She would have laughed, would have said it was too silly to talk about. What kind of clock falls in love?

I would have given anything to see Nancy at that moment, to look in her clear blue eyes. To walk out of the dining room, and leave Spencer behind.

Effie took a drink of coffee, then set down his cup. There were coffee grounds in the bottom, and Effie looked into the cup, staring at the pattern of the grounds.

"You are wrong," Effie said. "Our minds are not clockwork at all."

Again, here came Burgess. This time he carried plates heaped with slabs of French toast, stacks of bread so heavy with egg you could have used them as ballast on a freighter. Side plates heaped with rickety mounds of bacon. A biscuit wider than a hockey puck, split through the middle and slathered with butter.

Spencer picked up his fork.

Effie cut into his French toast.

Spencer popped a piece of bacon into his mouth.

"I had a feeling you'd be stubborn," Spencer said as he chewed. "But that's all right—let's try something."

Spencer swallowed his bacon and reached into the pocket of his sky-blue suit. A suit that was now a bit worse for wear, biscuit crumbs scattered on his lapel, a drop of maple syrup on his sleeve. His white shirt was not as crisp as it had been either. The meal had taken its toll—Spencer was not exactly sweating, but his face was pink, and there was an atmosphere of moisture about him. A steaminess, as if he had been lightly poached.

Spencer pulled an index card out of his pocket. He handed it to Effie. There was a handwritten sentence, in block letters, on one side of the card.

"Read it," Spencer said.

Effie finished chewing a bite of French toast. Then he read the card.

> AT TEN O'CLOCK ON WEDNESDAY
> MORNING, EFFIE MENDEZ WILL
> ROB THE FIRST NATIONAL BANK.

Effie's eyebrows went up. He couldn't decide whether to be shocked or offended. Or angry. Or all three.

Spencer stared right back. "Don't be upset," Spencer said. "I'm only making a point. I don't know you very well—I have no idea whether you're going to rob a bank. The point is that the card is either true or false. Right? There is no other choice."

"Well, obviously, it's false," Effie said.

"I'll take you at your word," Spencer said. "The real point is that it has to be one or the other. If it's true, then you *will* rob the bank. Don't get excited—we're only speaking hypothetically."

Spencer crunched a piece of bacon before going on. He looked as though he thoroughly enjoyed it. Effie chewed his French toast slowly, with less appetite than before.

"Your motives would be pure, I'm sure about that," Spencer said. "Like Robin Hood. You'd be stealing back the people's money, you'd return it to its rightful owners. And think of the thrill! You'd wave a pistol around, wear a bandanna over your face. Trade in your bus for a getaway car, some black sedan with enormous fenders, headlights the size of dinner plates."

"This is ridiculous," Effie said. "I'm not going to rob a bank!" Effie speared another chunk of French toast. The fork looked heavy in his hand.

"If the card is right, then you *will* rob the bank," Spencer said. "You have no choice, there's no way to avoid it. That's the *meaning* of truth."

Spencer chomped on his biscuit. God help us, he was still hungry. He stuffed a slice of bacon in his mouth, to chase down the biscuit.

"I am not a thief," Effie said.

"Well, then, the card must be wrong," Spencer said. "In that case, you won't rob the bank. Not only that—you *can't*! You can get yourself to just the right place, at the right time, with all the right equipment. But it won't happen! Your car will stall, your gun will jam. The street will be closed for repairs.

"If the card is false, then you can't *possibly* rob the bank. It's out of your control!"

Why did Spencer care so much? Some people love a good argument, but was there something more than that? Spencer looked eagerly at Effie, who frowned as he picked up his last slice of bacon. He chewed it with some effort.

"You're wrong," Effie said. "You're wrong about all of this."

"You try so hard to change things," Spencer said. "You give up so much for your great cause. A cause I admire!" He looked thoughtfully at Effie.

"But what will it get you, in the end? Whatever is going to happen *will* happen. It's fate, and there is nothing you can do to change it."

Spencer popped the last piece of French toast into his mouth and sat back with a satisfied smile. Satisfied with his logic, with the points he had made. Satisfied with his French toast and bacon, his biscuits and his creamy Wisconsin butter. Satisfied to be warm and cozy in the dining room of the Rockefeller, while the wind whistled outside, while snow piled in mountainous drifts.

Never mind that so many things were wrong in the world—Spencer was perfectly content. That's the problem with people like Spencer. They drive around in fancy cars, wallets stuffed with twenty-dollar bills, while men are out of work. While children cry in hunger. While the poor fight over scraps. Spencer was satisfied—everything was fine, according to him, just the way it should be. The way it *had* to be.

Effie set down his fork and reached down with a grimace to loosen his belt. Burgess walked over to fill the coffee cups.

"Will there be anything else?" Burgess said.

Spencer looked at Effie.

"If you've had enough," Spencer said, "you can stop here. No need to be embarrassed. As I say, few men can keep up with me!"

We knew what was coming next, because we knew Effie. "Steak and potatoes," Effie growled. We rarely heard him sound angry.

Burgess turned to Effie, his eyebrows raised. He might have been a bit concerned. "How would you like it cooked?"

"Broil the steak. A nice thick one. And fry the potatoes. Do you have gravy?" Effie said. "All right, then, a pot of gravy, and another one of those biscuits."

There was a touch of bravado in Effie's voice. He turned to Spencer, and said, "You *do* want another biscuit, don't you?"

"Make it two apiece!" Spencer said.

Burgess hurried away. Effie took a long drink of coffee, then leaned back and crossed his arms.

"You're wrong," Effie said. "Wrong about the bank, wrong about all of it! What it says on that card can't possibly make a difference."

"But it does," Spencer said. "The future is already written."

"I'll prove it to you," Effie said. "Let's say I'm standing in the batter's box. Ninth inning, tie game, a runner on second base. I step in, ready to swing—and the crowd gets to their feet, everyone holding their breath. Waiting to see what happens."

Effie locked eyes with Spencer, to make sure he was getting through.

"It depends on me!" Effie said. "You can't possibly know what's going to happen, you can't see it in advance. I might strike out, I might hit a home run. It's up to me and my bat—but according to you, I have nothing to do with it. It's already decided."

"Isn't that obvious?" Spencer said over the rim of his coffee cup. He dabbed his lips with a napkin. "Either it's *true* that you're going to hit a home run, or it's *false*. It has to be one or the other, right? If it's true—then you will hit one, there's no way around it. If it's false, then you won't. Either way, the outcome is set. I can write it out on a card, if you'd like."

"Let's say you're right," Effie said. "For the sake of argument, let's say I'm going to hit a home run. By your way of thinking, there's nothing I can do to stop it. Right?"

"How could you?" Spencer said. "It's already decided."

"What if I miss on purpose?" Effie said.

"Miss on purpose?"

"What if it's a high fastball, and I swing low? Just to prove you wrong. Just to go against what's written on the card."

"You can't," Spencer said. "If it's *true* that you're going to hit a home run, then it's also true that you will hit the ball. You'll take your swing, and the bat *will* hit it."

"What if I don't swing, then? What if I leave the bat on my shoulder?"

"You're not making any sense," Spencer said. "If it's true that you're going to hit the ball, then it's also true that you will swing the bat. It's just a matter of logic. You *will* climb out of the dugout. You *will* walk to the batter's box. You'll look at that pitch, and take a nice fat swing. The bat will connect with the ball, and you'll watch it sail out over the fence."

"*I* decide whether to step out of the dugout," Effie said. "I only walk to the batter's box if I tell my feet to take me there. I only swing if I want to."

"You have to follow the logic," Spencer said. "If you're going to hit a home run, then all the steps are going to happen. If it's true, you can't do anything to stop it."

"And I'm not just talking about the home run," Spencer went on. "I'm talking about everything. The entire future! Things are *going* to happen, or they are not. Either way, there's nothing you can do about it. So why work so hard? Why sacrifice so much? Sit back and enjoy the ride!"

Spencer's argument was a game of words. I couldn't put my finger on where he had gone wrong—but I knew that his logic was tangled, even if I couldn't quite pick out where the kinks were. I had to give Spencer one thing, though. He was sincere. He truly believed the path was set, and you can see how it would be comforting to believe that. To see the road stretching in front of you, a road you know you are meant to follow. Maybe you *want* to follow it. There's a job, a house, some money. You need money, don't you? A car, some furniture. A pantry stocked with food. There might even be a woman who loves you. Isn't that what you want?

All you have to do is follow the path.

Spencer picked up his coffee cup, saw that it was empty, and set it back down. Effie opened his mouth to speak—but once again, Burgess was at the table.

This time the plates were oval, more like serving platters. As wide as they could be and still fit on the table. The plates had to be that big, because of the steaks.

Steaks? More like continents, if you want to know the truth. "Big" doesn't do them justice. "Gigantic" falls pitifully short. The steaks were exhibits from some museum of butchery, trophies from a cattlemen's hall of fame. So juicy you could have squeezed them into a glass. So thick you could have used them as the foundation of a house. The aroma just about knocked you over—temptation in its purest form.

Spencer sliced open his steak. Steam rising from the cut. All our eyes on Spencer's knife and fork as he lifted that fantastic meat to his mouth.

"Incredible!" Spencer said. His face lit up slowly as he began to chew. A smile that began with his chin, somehow, then moved up to his lips, his cheeks, his eyes. Pure delight traveling north, like sunlight climbing the wall of a cliff.

Spencer pointed his fork at Effie. "Admit it," Spencer said. "This is living."

Effie didn't say anything. He didn't want to agree.

"I can tell that you're not convinced," Spencer said. "After everything I've told you. All of my logic. After everything I have explained—you still think you can change things."

Effie's fork had slowed down. His jaw worked steadily but without enthusiasm—heaping plates of eggs and biscuits and butter had taken their toll. It even looked, for a moment, as if he meant to stop eating. But then he cut another piece of steak.

"Logic," Effie said, his knife paused, "means that things happen in a logical order. A logical order is that *first*, you think things over. *Second*, you make your decision. *Third*, you act on that decision. And your action makes something happen! That is logic. There is no room for fate in the picture."

Spencer ate steadily until he was down to the last part of his steak, a strip that had once been the western coast of the continent. He cut that piece in thirds, and put one of them in his mouth.

He watched Effie patiently, as he chewed. Effie seemed reluctant as he cut another piece of his own steak.

"All the work you do for your team," Spencer said. He looked serious, choosing his words carefully. "All the sacrifices. Everything you do, to try to change things. And for what?"

Spencer speared the second piece of steak. He raised it to his wide lips as we stared at him. It was almost casual, the way he slipped that piece of meat into his mouth. As if the sausage, pancakes, scrambled eggs, French toast, and bacon had never existed. As if Spencer had not already eaten his way through a truckload of groceries.

Effie stared at his own knife and fork, trusted weapons that had lost their power. A lesser man might have laid them down—but Effie had trained for the battlefield, for the struggle that is bigger than any single man. A cause not his to surrender.

An aging gunfighter making one last stand.

Effie cut a tiny piece from his steak. He chewed it slowly.

"You think you can steer things a certain way," Spencer said. "You think you can make things better."

God help him, Spencer reached down with his fork and stabbed the last piece of steak. He lifted it to his mouth, he slid it off the fork with his teeth. And he began to chew.

Easily, naturally, happily. As if he were just getting started.

"I wish you were right!" Spencer said. "I wish you could snap your fingers, and make it happen. I wish you could bring those beautiful ideals of yours into existence. But it doesn't matter how hard you try. That world exists only in your imagination."

Spencer patted his mouth with his napkin and leaned back in his chair.

"Try what you will to change things—our path is chosen, our fate is set. It is written on the card!"

There were a lot of things Effie might have said to Spencer at that moment.

He might have said it was all trickery, this talk about fate. Predictions on index cards, the mind working like a machine. The twists and turns of logic.

He might have said none of it mattered, that Spencer could believe in fate or not, it was all the same to Effie. That Spencer was welcome to twist common sense into a pretzel, if that's what he wanted to do. It was all beside the point.

The point, Effie might have said, is that we had power in our arms. We had the strength of our ideals. We could see—not just what was wrong with the world, but the way it *should* be. So didn't we have to try? When you see what's wrong, don't you have to charge onto the field—bat in hand, glove poised—ready to give it your all? Ready to battle with everything you have?

How else would you want to live?

But Effie didn't say anything.

He gripped his fork, maybe a little harder than necessary. His face had a tinge of white.

Effie's eyes were focused inward, as if there were some kind of struggle going on. Some internal matter that needed his full attention. I realized that I was seeing something I had never witnessed before.

Effie had a stomachache.

I looked at Spencer as he sat back in his chair, hands clasped over his satisfied belly. I realized that I was seeing another first. Effie had never met his match—until now.

Effie opened his mouth. I don't know what he meant to do. Maybe he was going to pick up the argument, give it one more try to show Spencer where he had gone wrong. Or maybe, as Effie's face continued to pale, he was going to tell us that he didn't feel very well.

Or maybe—knowing Effie and his determination, his fighting spirit, knowing the size of his heart—maybe he meant to take one more valiant bite.

We never found out, because Sweetie Malone burst into the dining room. He looked at the six of us around the table, and said, "He's not with you?"

"Who?" said Ozzie.

"He's gone!" Sweetie said. "I can't find Mike!"

CHAPTER SIXTEEN

Mike was not in bed, not in the shower, not on the stairs—Sweetie told us that much.

We didn't find him in the lobby. The glass-eyed elk presided over an empty court.

Mike wasn't in the corridors or the bathrooms. His suitcase was still under his bed—not that we needed to check, because where was he going to go in this weather? Where would he *want* to go?

We were family.

When Ned Kretzmann chased a fly ball, didn't we all feel our own legs churning? Our own arms stretching for the ball? When Buddy Brodsky hit a double into the corner, I might as well have swung the bat myself.

You could trust Effie Mendez with your life. Ozzie Gadlin would give you his last nickel. Sweetie Malone would drop his latest blonde in a heartbeat if you needed him. When the bus drove out of Topeka, or Bloomington, or South Bend, we knew one thing for sure—win or lose, we played the game together.

There were times when we couldn't afford a hot meal, when all we had was bread and coffee. Maybe a slice of cheese, an apple or two. We drove from Harrisburg to Kenosha with nothing but a sack of radishes. You try it sometime!

If anyone felt like complaining, Mike was the one who'd settle down next to them, on that cast-iron bench. He'd look them in the eye and remind them what it was for. All those months on the road, sleeping on lumpy mattresses, freezing in unheated rooms. The jolt of potholes through the seat, day after day on that empty highway. Sure, a hot meal is nice, Mike would say, but a cause is something you can hold on to. That you stick with. A cause is what you live by.

Who would change the world, if not us?

We were family, and it was unthinkable that Mike would want to leave. So we didn't think it.

Not even for a moment.

There had to be an explanation. Mike must have found some private corner with Irene, a hidden spot where something nice was going on, something warm and delicious. Was that so hard to understand? The cause is the important thing, but once in a while, you need something you can touch. That you can *feel*. Changing the world is well and good, but sometimes you need that warmth right next to you, a warmth you can curl up against, wrap your arms around. As it wraps itself around *you*.

Why did I always think of Nancy? The curve of her back as she snuggled into my side. She would nestle against me on the couch, I would pull her close, her soft hair would brush against my cheek. Nancy would let out her breath, I would feel her relax.

Why shouldn't I think about Nancy? What else was there to think about?

I would have understood if that's what Mike was doing. I wouldn't begrudge him a moment like that. I wanted it myself.

We split up to find him, a search party for each floor. Buddy Brodsky and I went to check the back stairway, and we were two-thirds of the way down when we heard a voice.

"Looking for your friend?"

We peered down the stairwell. On the first-floor landing we saw an angular figure, a sheaf of white hair. The sharp blue eyes of Burgess, the waiter.

"Have you seen him?" Buddy asked.

"It isn't right," Burgess said. "The way they push everyone around."

"What?" Buddy said.

"People like Spencer. They think they can buy everything."

Buddy and I walked down the stairs. There was a landing at the bottom, maybe ten feet square—a space the Rockefeller used for storage—nearly filled with stacks of wooden folding chairs. From the stairwell to the door, there was a narrow path between the chairs.

Burgess stood in the middle of that path.

"You've seen Mike?" Buddy asked.

"They think they can buy everything, with their money," Burgess said.

He took a step toward us, his hip brushing against a tower of chairs. Eyes electric blue, hair like whitecaps on a stormy sea.

"They think the world is made for them," Burgess said. "The way they order us around, as if they were kings. Who's going to do something about it?"

Burgess glared at us, as if we were the ones responsible. His eyebrows were overgrown and menacing, like hedges that had not been clipped in many seasons.

"Don't look at me that way," Burgess said. "I used to wear a uniform, just like you! I was young then, and strong as an ox. The best curveball in Milwaukee, and where did it get me?"

"I'm sorry," Buddy said. "We're looking for—"

"They think they can buy everything!"

Burgess looked contemptuously around the stairway landing, as if Spencer might be hiding behind a stack of chairs. "Who is going to stop them?" Burgess said. "No one pays attention, no one takes the time to think. They don't want to see what's going on."

We moved in the direction of the door. But Burgess stood his ground, blocked our path.

"You couldn't touch my fastball," Burgess said. "You couldn't even see it! At the end of the day, my catcher had to soak his hand in ice water. But what good did it do me?"

Burgess looked at Buddy, then at me, then back at Buddy. To make sure it was sinking in.

"I was in love once," Burgess said.

"Well, that's hard luck—" Buddy started to say. But Burgess wasn't listening.

"I worked in a hardware store. That's real work, let me tell you! Up and down the aisles carrying cans of paint, tubs of plaster. Finding odds and ends for the customers, a certain diameter of pipe, the right type of nail. At the end of the day, you're dead tired. You add up the cash and lock the register. You sweep the floor."

Buddy and I nodded in sympathy. We fidgeted, looking for a way to edge past Burgess. But he wasn't moving.

"The store had one of those steel cabinets, the wide kind, with stacks of thin drawers. You know the one I mean? It holds screws and bolts, nuts and washers. All the little parts. The drawers are divided into compartments, so you can sort things by size."

Buddy and I nodded. We knew what Burgess meant.

"Every day I stocked those drawers. After all the other work was done! Dark outside, of course, and everyone else was home eating dinner, but I stood in front of that cabinet. Sixteen drawers, thirty-two compartments in each. That's five hundred and twelve compartments! I went through every one of them, every day. I made sure each part was stocked up."

"Sounds like hard work," Buddy said. "But we're trying to—"

"Would the *owner* of the store do that? Stand there in front of those five hundred and twelve compartments? Why should he, when he can pay me thirty cents an hour! While he sits home eating steak and pockets all the profits.

"I stocked the cabinet every night, so when customers came in the store they would find what they needed."

Burgess scowled at the stacks of chairs.

"One day, a woman leaned over the counter and asked me where the hinges were. What did she need a hinge for? It's forty years later, and I still don't know. But when she came back for a picture hook, I asked her to go with me for coffee. A quarter of the way through the cup—that's when I fell in love."

"I'm sorry," Buddy said. "But we're looking for—"

"She fell in love with me, too! I couldn't believe my luck. It didn't matter that I earned thirty cents an hour—I'd go to her apartment after work and she'd throw her arms around me. The kind of thing you hear about, but it only happens to other people."

Burgess stared at us with those sharp eyes. The look of a man who was going to have his say.

"She didn't care if I lived in a room over the store. That you don't get rich in the hardware business. We made all kinds of plans—we would paint the room, put in a hot plate. A flowering plant. A real bed.

"One day she came into the store. She wore her yellow dress with white polka dots, because she knew it was my favorite. We leaned on a counter, looking at colors of paint. She let her head rest on my shoulder. A strand of her hair fell into my eyes, and I didn't want to move it.

"You know what's coming next. The bell jingled—a man walked into the store. Taller than me, and good-looking in that casual way, one of those people who takes it for granted. Who is so used to having everything, he doesn't even know he has it.

"He smiled at her. She looked annoyed and squeezed my hand. But in that very instant, I knew what was going to happen. I knew from the *way* she looked annoyed. The way she squeezed my hand.

"He bought a box of thumbtacks, and paid with a ten-dollar bill. He closed the door behind him and got in his sedan, chocolate brown with cream-colored fenders, so shiny you could see the reflections of clouds. A car that would have cost me five years' salary."

Burgess spread out his arms, as if imploring Buddy and me for our sympathy.

"He looked back at us, through the store window, and touched the brim of his cap. He drove off—but I knew he'd be back. There was nothing in the world I could do. Forty years later and I still can't think of a single thing I could have changed. For all I know, they're happy." Burgess took a step toward us, still blocking the path to the door.

"Did you ever work in a place like this?" Burgess waved to indicate the John D. Rockefeller. But he wasn't looking for an answer.

"I'll bet you know the score," Burgess said. "You do what they tell you, you jump for a living and don't fuss about it. If you want your paycheck, you follow the rules.

"Then a man like Spencer comes in. He snaps his fingers, and people come running. He points at what he wants, and it flies to his hand, even if it belongs to you.

"Who are we, that we let him do it? Who *are* we?"

Burgess stared at us, his bright-blue eyes glittering. Making sure it sank in.

"Your friend is in the piano room."

CHAPTER SEVENTEEN

How could we have known there was a piano room? Buddy and I walked the way Burgess had pointed, down a hallway lined with clocks, picking up Effie and Ozzie along the way. Effie not quite as pale, after taking a little time to digest. Although he still didn't move like a champion shortstop.

The four of us stepped back into the lobby and found a door we hadn't noticed before, hiding in plain sight next to a bookcase. A small and unassuming entrance that should have led to a broom closet, but in fact opened into a large, square, nicely furnished room. Red velvet couches, draperies on the wall. Fancy plaster moldings. In the center of the room, a gleaming grand piano.

Mike stood next to the piano, the wood glossy with black lacquer. Mike stared at the keys, as if they might be able to answer some difficult question.

"Did you know she can sing?" Mike said.

"What?" said Ozzie.

"She plays the piano, and she sings. You've never heard a voice like that."

"Irene was in here with you?" Effie said.

"What do you think? *I* don't know how to sing."

Ozzie looked at the couch, the red velvet cushions. "What else was she doing? Besides singing."

There was a tone in Ozzie's voice, and you could tell that Mike heard it.

"We talked," Mike said. There was a tone in *his* voice.

"About what?" Ozzie said. He scowled at the draperies, the plaster moldings. The carved oaken mantel. The room was overdone, Ozzie's look said. He took in the silver candelabra on the mantel, a crystal vase on the piano. Not just expensive, but *wrong*.

"What are you so suspicious about?" Mike said. "What do you want to know?"

"You tell us," Ozzie said. "What do we *need* to know?"

It was time for Effie to come to the rescue. That soothing tone.

"No one is suspicious, Mike," Effie said. "If you like Irene, then *we* like her."

"All I wanted to do was talk to her again," Mike said. You could tell from his eyes, though, that he was thinking about other things besides talking.

"Get her address," Ozzie said. "You can write to her from the road."

"You can't judge people by their fathers!" Mike said. He glared at Ozzie. "Like I said last night, Irene is different. She is not the enemy."

"We know that," Effie said, his voice smooth. "No one thinks Irene is the enemy."

"She's on our side," Mike said. "She went on and on about the team, all the good things we do. She thinks we could do even more."

"What does that mean, *even more?*" Ozzie said. "What are we not doing, according to her?"

"She had a couple of suggestions," Mike said.

"Such as what?" Ozzie demanded.

"What if we charged a little more for tickets?" Mike said. "I'm not saying a *lot* more—it wouldn't be for ourselves, at least not most of it. But sometimes we don't even cover expenses. If we charged more, we'd have more to give, wouldn't we? Just as an example.

"We could play in a higher league, in bigger cities. We could be a little more professional! I'm not complaining—but don't you get tired of Akron? Couldn't we do more at a higher level? For the cause, I mean."

"We're doing just fine," Ozzie said. "Plenty of people are better off because of us."

"We do our little part," Mike said. "We go from town to town, fifty dollars here and a hundred there. It's something—I know it is. But we have so much talent. Couldn't we think a little bigger?"

"We should charge more for tickets?" Ozzie said. "That's her big idea?"

"Well," Mike said. "That's not all. She said something else."

Effie's eyebrows went up. "What did she say?"

We all watched Mike, waiting for the answer. But we knew.

We knew what Irene had said, because all of a sudden, Mike looked nervous. We never saw him nervous.

We knew, because Mike wasn't looking at us head-on. He wasn't really looking at us at all.

We knew, because temptation was always with us. It hung above our heads, like a poisonous cloud. It's not always easy to resist, if I'm going to be honest. If you want to know the truth.

"I'm not saying she's right," Mike went on, talking to the piano. "I'm not saying I agree with her. But haven't you ever thought about it?"

"No," Effie said.

"Never!" Buddy said.

"Not for a second," Ozzie chimed in.

But we knew exactly what Irene was talking about. You could trade hardship for luxury. Poverty for comfort. Obscurity for fame and fortune.

The major leagues!

Not a single one of us would admit it. Not one of us would entertain the thought. We would never concede, even for a moment, the slightest bit of doubt. But we knew what was going through Mike's head. The idea hovered at the door, like an uninvited guest. It leaned on the doorbell, it rapped on the windows. It tried to sneak in through the basement.

You couldn't blame Mike for a moment of weakness. Could you?

Any one of us could make the leap—we knew that. So how did you *not* think about it? The riches that called you by name, the glittering prize that dangled in front of your nose.

The major leagues!

Who wouldn't want a little comfort, after all those years on the road? You can't play the game forever. Why not plan for the future? Think about your own security? And what's so bad about a little pampering, when it comes right down to it? Something for yourself, after all you've given to the team.

You might as well sell your soul.

"You don't understand," Mike said, avoiding Ozzie's glare. "It wouldn't be for me. It would be for the cause."

"You'd use the money to do good, right?" Ozzie said. Ozzie knew how this argument went—we all did. An argument each one of us had been through, in our own heads.

"You're not looking for luxury, for your own comfort. All you want to do is help people."

"Yes, but—"

"They'd be grateful," Ozzie went on, his voice a little sharp. "People would give you awards, hold banquets in your name. A big philanthropist! They'd pin a medal on your chest."

"It was just an idea," Mike said. "Irene was just talking. You know me, I'm as much a part of the team as you!"

Mike stood next to the grand piano. His fingers rested on the keys for a moment, although he had no idea how to play.

"If I *did* have money," Mike said, "I'd do a lot of good with it. Irene and I would only need a little for ourselves, a house somewhere warm in the off-season. A cabin on a lake. That's all we were talking about."

Mike looked at me, hoping. And why wouldn't I understand? Didn't I face the same temptation, every time I saw Nancy?

But Ozzie scowled. He saw the picture that was taking shape in Mike's mind, and he knew how that picture could pull on you. He knew what you have to do when you face temptation.

"Forget Irene," Ozzie said. "Forget her father. Put it out of your mind! You can't fix the world's problems by turning into one of *them.*"

Ozzie folded his arms. He glared at the piano as if it were his mortal enemy.

Mike looked impatient. "You're so sure of how it would go," he said. "But maybe it would work the other way around. Maybe *I* would change *them.*"

Ozzie's scowl only deepened. "It's their game," he said. "You play on their field, and they make the rules. You'll never change it from the inside."

"What if I could?" Mike said. "What if you *have* to change it from the inside? What if that's the only way?"

A debate so old we knew it by heart. How do you attack the system? A system that has all kinds of defenses, alert for the slightest threat. Hit it, and it hits right back. Ask the autoworkers in Toledo—they can tell you all about the National Guard, about tear gas and fire hoses and machine guns. Let them show you their scars. The system hits hard! Ask the strikers at Republic Steel.

So people hesitate. Maybe attacking from outside is not the answer, they think. Why not go *inside*? Sneak behind the walls, slip in, find a comfortable spot. Make a place for yourself, where you can start to maneuver. Not too fast! You have to gauge the pressure—there's delicacy involved, you have to be smart about the timing. But little by little, you can start to push, to gently steer, to slowly change the course.

How much can one person do? It doesn't matter, you're not alone. People around you will pay attention—they'll see what you are doing and join in. Not everyone! But there are reasonable people in the world, who just haven't seen the right path. The way things *should* be. You can show them.

Minor improvements will add up, small gains become larger. Doors will begin to open as momentum builds. Openings will be pushed even wider, new possibilities revealed. The world will change, and you won't even have to fight a battle!

Mike must have run all this through his mind as he thought about Irene. All the good he could do from the inside. And why not? It's one of those things that sounds reasonable, that seems like a good idea when you paint the picture in your mind.

But show me where it has worked!

Effie put his hand on Mike's shoulder. "You had a good time with Irene," he said. "That's all right, no reason you shouldn't have. But she doesn't understand our business, does she? What it means when the boys chase our bus down the street. When everyone in town lines up at the ballpark, every last farmer and mechanic and shop clerk. When they get on their feet in the bleachers, clapping and stomping and cheering as if old Eugene V. Debs himself were on the mound. You think the major leagues can match that?"

I chose this moment to jump in. "Effie's right," I said. "And you can't argue with nine and two. This is the year we've dreamed about—we have everything we wanted!"

Mike stared at me. "*You* have Nancy," he said.

He said this loudly, and there was a certain tone in his voice. A tone I had never heard before. I might have imagined it, to tell the truth—but for a moment, I thought Mike was angry at me.

Why would Mike be angry?

Effie stepped back in.

"There's a long way to go," Effie said. "A lot of work to come. But we're doing our part. We can hold our heads high."

"She met Carnegie," Mike said. "He cut the ribbon at a library, and Irene shook his hand. He gave half a million dollars to have it built. Half a million! It would take us fifty years to do that."

"*Carnegie*," Ozzie said. He looked like he was ready to spit. "Let's drive to Pennsylvania. We'll visit the steel mill in Homestead. We'll talk to a few people there about Carnegie. Let's go ask the steelworkers—all they wanted was an honest wage, and he gave them the National Guard. Did you forget about the Pinkertons? About the rifles and bayonets? Come on, let's go to Homestead. We'll talk to some of the widows." Ozzie scowled at the floor. He shook his head. "Carnegie is your hero, now? Sure, he built libraries—with the blood of his workers."

"I only said we could charge a little more for tickets," Mike said. "I'm not talking about the National Guard!"

Mike glared at Ozzie. He pointed his finger at him. "I know what's wrong with Carnegie," Mike said. "You don't have to tell me. I know what's wrong with people like Spencer. But the world is complicated—what makes you so sure you've figured it all out? There's more than one way to do things!"

Effie walked over and put his arm around Mike's shoulder. He massaged it a little. He gave it a squeeze. He winked at Ozzie and me, to tell us that we didn't need to worry, that everything was going to be fine. Reminding us that you could count on Effie in a difficult situation—he knew how to manage things, how to handle the delicacies.

"You make some good points, Mike," Effie said. "You're smart to ask those kinds of questions."

Mike's glare softened a little. Effie knew what he was doing.

"No one doubts you," Effie said. "We know you're a team man. No one thinks you're on the side of the Pinkertons."

Mike nodded. Still frowning, but listening.

"It sounds good, doesn't it, to have all that money," Effie said. "You think about all the things you could do with it, all the good you could do for the world. Right?"

Mike nodded again.

"But ask yourself one thing," Effie said. "Where does that money come from? If the owner gives you a sack of gold, where does he get it? By honest work? Does he roll up his sleeves to pitch in? Are his muscles sore? Does he have blisters at the end of the day? You tell me, Mike. How does the system work?"

Effie paused, but he didn't expect an answer. "You know as well as I do where the money comes from," he said. "The owner grinds it out of his factory. A can of beans costs fifteen cents, but the man on the canning line gets a penny, even though it's his arms that are scalded, his fingers that blister to the bone. It doesn't go to the farmer either, the farmer is *lucky* to get a penny. It goes to the bosses, sitting in their fancy offices, lounging in armchairs. Sipping whiskey and living off the work of honest men."

Effie shook his head. "You might do some good with the money," he said. "But look how much harm was done getting it."

"I know," Mike said. "But—"

"Think about the crowd in Madison yesterday," Effie said. "And in Fort Wayne tomorrow. What it means to them, when they see you at the plate. When you swing the bat. You stand up there, and you swing it for *them*."

"I know!" Mike said. We all knew what it meant when we took the field, mechanics and farmers and railroad workers filling the bleachers. When we sprinted across the grass in uniforms no owner had paid for, to positions no manager had assigned.

We knew where the dimes and quarters came from when we looked up at the stands. We knew where they were going, too—back to the people, where they belonged. Wherever they were needed most. Why should it be any other way?

How *much* money was not the point. The point was that we took on the teams of the bosses, teams of hired hands. Teams that would use a man like a piece of machinery, then toss him on the rubbish heap. Teams whose soul was profit and loss.

We took on the bosses—and *won*. What is Carnegie, compared to that?

"I know what it means," Mike said. He looked a little embarrassed, sorry he had made us worry. "I'm only saying that I like Irene. I *really* like her. It feels good to hold her."

That was something I understood. I knew exactly what Mike was talking about. Because I felt that way about Nancy.

* * *

You know what it's like to have a woman lean her head against your shoulder? You're sitting on the couch together, talking, and there's a pause in the conversation. She sets down her cup on the coffee table and gives you a certain look as she leans back into the cushions. That look! You could spend your whole life on the couch, watching her, and you wouldn't get tired of it.

She leans back on the couch and slides close. She snuggles against your side, and you feel her soft hair, her warm cheek, the weight of her head against your shoulder. She curls up against you, and lets out a contented breath.

How can you live without that?

We'd sit that way on Nancy's couch, and talk about people on the team. Nancy told me things I hadn't noticed. That Effie and Ozzie never sat together in the diner, for example. They took different tables, but they kept looking over at each other, Nancy said. The kind of look parents exchange when they're watching their children.

She noticed that Buddy Brodsky glared at his food, as if it were trying to trick him.

She told me that Sweetie Malone wouldn't notice a pretty woman unless she looked at him first.

"It's not that he ignores her," Nancy said. "He doesn't even *see* her, until she looks over at him. Why do you think that is?"

I had no idea. But Nancy had her own opinion. Something complicated, about Sweetie being interested in women not because of what he saw in *them*, but for what they saw in *him*.

See if you can make any sense out of that.

It was odd that Nancy could tell me so many things about my teammates, people I knew so much better than she did. At least, I *should* have known them better. To be honest, though, I don't know what good it would have done for me to know all the details— because you can't solve anyone else's problems. Try as hard as you want to understand, even with the best of intentions, all you can do is make a mess. But Nancy was interested anyway. She loved the details and the complications, and whether there was any use for the information didn't seem to be the point.

We would sit on Nancy's couch, and she'd tell me the latest news in her family.

Most of the stories didn't stick in my head, but I remember the time her great-aunt ended up with bees in her walls. She found out when a little stream of honey seeped from the baseboard. When the bees started to eat the wiring, her aunt needed an electrician—and electricians cost money. Not too much, but more than she had.

The great-aunt asked her sister-in-law for a loan, the one whose husband owned the lunch counter. Money wasn't a problem for them—everyone in Binghamton wanted to eat lunch. But the sister-in-law made it a problem. Her answer was yes, but she said it slowly, and with conditions. She said it in a way that offended Nancy's aunt, but what was the aunt going to do? The lights were flickering.

Nancy went on and on about it, why it happened, what it meant. Who said what and why. It was open-and-shut to me. The aunt needed money, the sister-in-law had more than she needed. There was nothing even to think about—it was a matter of principle. The sister-in-law was wrong. What else was there to say?

But Nancy wanted to talk it all through. It was almost as if the principle didn't matter. Instead, she had a hundred questions—what was going through the sister-in-law's mind? What else had happened between the two of them that made the sister-in-law react that way? What did the sister-in-law's husband think, and what did that say about him? What about the rest of the family? What did it mean for this or that relationship?

I remember talking it all over as we sat on Nancy's couch. A pot of tea, a plate of cookies. Every little detail and motive. To be honest, it's not the kind of conversation I'm good at.

It's easier to talk about something concrete, something specific. A particular idea, for example. An idea has shape—you can see the surfaces and angles. You can pick it up, turn it around, feel its weight in your hand. You can't do that with a feeling, because it's hard to see the shape, if there even is one. A feeling has a vagueness to it, a softness. Try to hold on to a feeling, and you see how fluid it is—it trickles right through your fingers.

When you have an idea, you have something specific—you know what you're dealing with. Feelings are more diffuse, like clouds, or fog. What are you going to do with fog?

But Nancy wanted to know how I felt about things. She was interested, I don't know why. And somehow, that made *me* a little more interested.

Once in a while, as we sat on the couch, Nancy would get out her book of Shakespeare and we'd read aloud—Nancy playing the women while I filled in the parts of the men. I tried different voices for each character, and it made her laugh. I admit that I wasn't very good. But I tried!

I did sound effects. Hoofbeats, church bells. I put on a Scottish accent for *Macbeth*, and Nancy giggled her head off.

"Good thing you can pitch!" she said. "You won't make your living on the stage."

Now and then, we would listen to the radio, and Nancy would rest her head on my shoulder, and I thought, *This is the kind of thing I could get used to.* The feeling that we were meant to be together. That we would always be together.

At least whenever I was in Binghamton.

And that was the problem.

I saw Nancy twice a month—three times if I was lucky. Sometimes only once. What kind of life was that?

If we played in Buffalo, Nancy would come to watch. She'd stay with her cousin, and we'd have two or three days together, every hour a precious gem. But then we'd be apart again.

When the off-season came, Nancy's uncle gave me work in his lunch counter. For three months I slept on his porch and washed dishes in the back of the store. Nancy worked all morning, and I worked at night. But we had the afternoons together! It was a luxury, to see Nancy every day, the first luxury I ever cared about.

I thought I was in heaven—at least the part of heaven where people wash dishes.

But three months flies by, and then it was spring training, and back on the road. Back to endless weeks apart.

Naturally, it became a question. Neither of us asked it—but we didn't have to. The question was there anyway, hovering above us like a cloud.

Could I stay?

A lot of questions went with that one. What would I do if I stayed? Get a job? What kind of job? Where would I live? Would we live *together*? How would that work?

I had never thought about questions like that. I never had to, because I knew where I belonged. My place was with the team! I never had to worry about the other parts of life, the practicalities of it. We had a cause, and the cause was more important.

But now the question was here. We talked about it without talking about it.

Nancy knew what the team stood for. And she cared! She cared as much as I did. But she thought you could fix things where you were, that you could make things better by staying in one place, by solving the problems closest to you.

When Nancy closed the Chemung Cafe at the end of the day, she packed up the leftovers for a soup kitchen. She made sure there *were* leftovers. She helped out if a neighbor was sick, if a cousin needed money. She raffled off pies to fix the library roof.

If you walked up to the counter flat broke, Nancy would feed you. She knew who needed help and who didn't, and what kind of help would work—how much sympathy and how much of a push. If you needed a job, you could sweep the parking lot, you could wash dishes.

I could see how people could admire that. I admired it, too. But there was a problem.

It was the *system* that needed to be fixed.

It was one thing to feed a hungry man—it was another thing to understand why the system *wanted* him hungry. And to change that system. Wasn't it obvious which was more important?

Nancy and I didn't argue about it. The truth is, we didn't exactly disagree. Nancy understood the problems with the system, she knew they had to be fixed. But she wasn't going to hold her breath waiting, she said. There was plenty of work to do in the meantime, you could do a lot of good right where you were, and what's wrong with that? Why not settle down, live your life? Why not be with the people you love?

That's what Nancy said—the people you love.

I could have done it!

The Robins could have gone on without me. Was I the only pitcher in the world? Was any one of us so important? Let's say Sweetie Malone fell in love. It was bound to happen, just by the law of averages. Sweetie would get down on his knee, put a ring on some brunette's finger, move back home to Sioux Falls. And the world wouldn't end! We'd find a replacement—second basemen are a dime a dozen. So why couldn't I settle down with Nancy?

Didn't I deserve a little happiness?

Didn't *Nancy* deserve a little happiness?

I thought about it. I thought long and hard. It was true, what Nancy said, there was a lot of good work to be done right there in Binghamton. Maybe I was just the man to do it! And I would be with Nancy every day.

But I hesitated. There was a problem—of course there was! Once you start thinking that way, you're asking for trouble. You lose sight of what's important when you make your own life the most important thing. When you let *yourself* come first.

The first compromise may not seem like much—but it opens the door. You start to feel comfortable, and you like it! What's wrong with feeling comfortable? Enjoying life a little. You find yourself settling in, owning things you never thought you would own. But you like those things, it turns out, and pretty soon you want more. Maybe even *need* more.

One thing leads to another. You do things you didn't plan to do in the beginning. That you might not even believe in. Nothing terrible! Little adjustments here and there—no one lives a perfect life. But it's one decision after another, and after a while, you get used to it. It stops bothering you. You stop admitting to yourself that you don't believe in it.

Or maybe you don't even remember.

You're doing all right, and if other people have problems, maybe it's their own fault. Maybe they *deserve* their bad luck. If they tried harder, they could have avoided it. Your own good fortune is more than luck, isn't it? Haven't you worked for what you have? Don't you deserve to relax a little, after all you've been through? Not that you are blind to the troubles of others—of course there are problems in the world, and they need to be addressed. But it doesn't have to be *your* job, does it? Not every minute of the day.

I couldn't do it.

I couldn't live that way.

All my life, I had been headed in one direction—I wasn't about to turn around. I wasn't about to compromise.

Nancy hadn't asked me to stay—not directly. But it was only fair to tell her. To explain, once I had made my decision.

I knew that Nancy would argue. She'd tell me that the things I called compromises weren't hurting anyone, that people have to find a way to live their lives. What's wrong with living your life?

I'd say that if you are really going to change things, you can't *only* live your life. The problems in the world are deep, they are fundamental. How can you fix them unless you make deep and fundamental changes?

Nancy would have an answer to that, and we would go back and forth. In the end, she would understand. She might not agree, but she would know how I felt—that I loved her, even if I had other things to do. Things I *had* to do. We would see each other when we could, and that would make it all right.

* * *

I told her.

I stood in the door of Nancy's kitchen while she was at the sink, washing a bowl of berries. It was late afternoon, and you could see clouds through the window.

I explained to Nancy that I *wanted* to stay with her. I wanted it as much as she did. Maybe more!

I heard the water splash over the berries. They might have been gooseberries, from a bush in Nancy's backyard. Green and shiny and hard.

My feelings were strong, I said to Nancy. No one could ever love her more than I did—it was impossible! But I had responsibilities.

It wouldn't be right to run away, to turn my back on the team. She could see how important that was.

I paused for a moment, so Nancy could tell me there were a lot of ways to do good, a lot of ways to serve the cause. You don't have to drive all over the country, she would say. You don't have to spend your life on the road, away from the people who love you.

The water ran over the berries.

She didn't say anything.

Nancy was supposed to give me that look—the one that told me I was making a mistake, that I had it all wrong, she couldn't even *believe* how wrong I was. A sharp look, but at the same time there would be a light in Nancy's eyes, because she enjoyed the argument. The back-and-forth between us. I enjoyed it, too!

She would give me that look, and start to set me straight. We would talk it over, argue it out. We'd find some way to work it through. I'd come back whenever I could, and Nancy would meet me on the road, in Wilkes-Barre or Rochester. Maybe come down south for spring training. We'd figure it out—and everything would be all right.

But Nancy didn't give me that look. She stared into the sink as water gurgled from the faucet, the berries bobbing in their overflowing bowl.

There was some kind of noise from the plumbing, a low moan from a pipe in the basement.

I kept talking. What else was I supposed to do?

It was hard for both of us, I said. But we all have to sacrifice sometimes. To give things up for the greater good. I loved her! But she couldn't deny there were problems to fix, injustices to correct. Things I had to do.

Nancy turned her head to look at me as I spoke. Not her whole body, just her head.

Nancy looked at me with those wide eyes—the deepest, most genuine shade of blue possible. Sunlight distilled in the purest water.

Nancy didn't say a word. She shut off the faucet, and a pit began to open in my stomach.

I will never, in my entire life, forget the look in Nancy's eyes as she watched me say those things.

* * *

I knew how hard it must have been for Mike, to think about losing Irene. Of course he hadn't known her very long, not nearly as long as I had been with Nancy. But can't these things come on fast? Does that make them any less real?

It's the hardest thing in the world, to tell someone that your place is somewhere else. That you can't stay with them, even if that's all you want to do. It's hard! But after all those years, can you really abandon your ideals? Your great cause? How can you compromise when you know where compromise leads?

The team has to come first.

Doesn't it?

CHAPTER EIGHTEEN

My nurse knows I don't like to wake up alone. When I do, a strange thing happens—as I struggle out of sleep, I feel weightless, unmoored. Uncertain of where I am. I don't know what I'll see when I open my eyes. It could be any of the cities I drifted into over the years, any of a hundred boardinghouses or cheap hotels. An empty highway in the old Midwest.

The playground of my old school.

The window of Ella's favorite coffee shop.

The parking lot at the Chemung Cafe.

I might wake up in the vacant lot behind Mike's house. Throwing fastballs until my arm is sore, as Mike knocks one pitch after another into the outfield weeds.

On the Crown Coach Company bus, settling into that crackling crimson leather as we head out of town at the end of the day. The sun setting over the hayfields. Shadows growing longer across those dry Wisconsin fields.

Leaving Nancy's house, the day I explained things to her. When I laid it all out, when I said the things I had to say.

Those terrible things.

But if my nurse *is* there, I feel her hand on my shoulder. That warm pressure tells me right away where I am—the soft bed, crisp sheets. Sunlight streaming through the open window.

My nurse will have the morning paper, because she knows I like to grumble over the headlines. She'll bring a glass of water, because she knows I'm going to be thirsty.

She sits on the edge of my bed and gives my shoulder a little squeeze. Not enough to startle me. Just enough to let me know it's morning.

*   *   *

We stayed a little longer with Mike in the piano room, but there was nothing really left to say. We had all been in a spot like this, one time or another, and we knew how it worked—the team would move on, life would get back to normal. Mike just needed a moment to get used to the idea, to figure out how to tell Irene good-bye.

We left him sitting on the piano bench, fingering the keys, while the rest of us went back to the lobby. Outside, the wind still howled, but the snow wasn't quite as thick, and the clouds were finally pulling off to the east. You couldn't exactly see light on the horizon—but there was the *feeling* of light, you could tell it was on the way.

The desk clerk found us a few rusty shovels, and we set out to work.

It's one thing to shovel when you're equipped for it. Coats and scarves, boots and gloves, a nice wool sweater. Long underwear, if you have it. You know it's going to be cold, the wind will be raw, the snow wet and heavy—but at least you're prepared.

We were not prepared! It was April, and what we were ready for was baseball. We didn't have coats and scarves, we didn't have wool hats. Forget about boots! But we were working men, and we knew the snow wasn't going to shovel itself. People were counting on us in Fort Wayne, rain or shine. We were tired of the Rockefeller.

And it wouldn't hurt to get Mike back on the road, back where he belonged.

So we made the best of it. We pulled on extra shirts, wrapped ourselves in warm-up jackets. Flannel pajamas, if we had them, a bathrobe here and there. Towels pressed into service as scarves. Socks for mittens—it wasn't pretty, but it would have to do.

We were ready for battle.

It was a struggle to open the front door of the Rockefeller, because a great snowdrift had piled against it. We gave up and went out the back—the sheltered side of the hotel, although even there the storm had a punch. Wind racing across frozen dunes, squalls whipping in our faces, so we had to lower our heads like explorers ready to tackle the North Pole. We pushed into the snow as well as we could, groping along the side of the building, through drifts up to our hips in some places, to our chest in others. Buddy Brodsky and Ned Kretzmann led the way, blazing a trail toward the parking lot.

We took it as a good sign that the snow was coming at us sideways, for the most part. Windblown from the piles on the ground, rather than falling from the sky.

We rounded the corner of the Rockefeller and squinted through the blustering wind. And there it was—an impossible job. A line of drifts up to our shoulders. Another ridge behind that, and then another. Snow in every direction. We would need a hundred men, with a hundred shovels!

And the bus! We could barely see it through the swirling snow, and when we did, we rubbed our eyes, hoping it was a mirage.

The wind had blown up a Himalayan drift that climbed to the roof and beyond. A mammoth tidal surge, frozen at the moment of breaking—as if the snow meant to swallow the bus alive. As if it planned to digest it.

The bus had become Mount Everest. To reach the top you'd have to plan an expedition, hire a team of guides, lay in supplies. Fit yourself with pitons and gear.

What do you do when you're faced with an impossible job?

You get started.

The snow was wet and thick. You had to slam your shovel in, then lift hard, with all your strength. You almost buckled under that heavy load, as if you were lifting all of the world's problems at once. You grabbed a load of snow, then tossed it into the wind.

We worked in shifts, three at a time, because the lifting was so hard, and anyway we only had three shovels. After five minutes, you'd feel it in your shoulders and your arms. In ten minutes, your legs would be sore. In fifteen minutes, your fingers would start to freeze, and you'd hand your shovel off to the next man. Everything hurt—but slowly, we cleared a path.

Between shifts, we warmed up in Effie's room. He had the best heating grate, a cast-iron rectangle, black as coal, with a filigreed design too fancy for its purpose. Why do people do that? Turn something useful into an ornament, one more unnecessary luxury.

But I have to admit it was warm. When you came in from outside, you could kneel around the grate and thaw your fingers. Enjoy a steady blast of hot air, a straight connection to the furnace.

Buddy, Ned, and I trudged up the stairs to Effie's room after our shift. We shook snow out of our jackets, pulled off our wet shoes, and settled down next to the grate.

Effie brought up a pot of coffee from the kitchen.

We warmed our hands, then our feet, and as everything thawed, we drank mugs of coffee. The heat of the steaming mug felt good against our curled fingers.

We were startled by Spencer's voice, filtering through the grate.

"Think about what I've said." A little muffled, but you could tell it was Spencer. His room must have been directly below.

We set down our mugs of coffee. We bent our heads close to the grate, as if we were huddled around a radio.

"I *have* thought about it. I've thought about it a lot."

There was no doubt about that voice—it was Mike! What was he doing, down there with Spencer, when the rest of us were shoveling snow? We frowned at each other. Irene was one thing—those green eyes, those goldenrod curls. You could understand why Mike would be interested, why anyone would be.

But *Spencer*!

A look came into Effie's eye. Not worried, exactly, because Effie knew his players. He was confident in Mike—and why shouldn't he be? Mike was the same man, whatever had happened with Irene. Still a person you could count on, the kind you want on your team.

But Effie bent his head down to listen, too.

"So many opportunities!" Spencer's voice again. He sounded different somehow, when you couldn't see him. There was something stronger in his voice, more deliberate. As if you could hear his purpose more clearly when you weren't looking right at him.

We didn't need to see Spencer—we could picture the scene. Spencer standing there in his blue suit, his carefully knotted tie. Looking right at Mike, with that buttery smile. A politician's smile!

I thought about the mayor of Bloomington, the year we played there on the Fourth of July. A stifling hot day, clouds smothering the cornfields. Thunder in the distance, but the crowd turned out anyway, full of Indiana optimism, counting on the rain to hold off.

The Elks served up a barbecue before the game. Hot juicy chicken, glittering ribs, sausages on sticks. People walked around drinking root beer and eating buttered corn, while the mayor worked the crowd.

The mayor of Bloomington was a thick-necked man whose face was precisely square except where his chin stuck out like a low porch. He knew everyone in town and exactly two things about them—he would shake your hand and ask how your daughter in Chicago was doing, if the engine in that old truck was still running. Then the mayor would smile that broad politician's smile, and pat you on the shoulder as he looked past your ear, his attention already on the next target.

The mayor's son followed him around, a pudgy twelve-year-old with cornflower-blue eyes and a smile so insincere you could only stare in wonder. The boy had apparently taken a break from setting the tails of cats on fire to come down to the barbecue and eat an appalling number of sausages.

"Hello," the boy would say, trailing his father through the crowd, sticking his hand out to each citizen of Bloomington. "Hello, my name is Stanford. It's a pleasure to meet you." Sausage fat gleaming on his chin. A younger, greasier version of the politician's smile.

The mayor worked his way over to the team. He looked each one of us in the eye, shook our hands, made a comment—something different for each person, because *we* were each different. Listening to our reply with a look that said he was interested, that he genuinely cared. Smiling that politician's smile. A hand on a uniformed shoulder, and off to the next person.

Once you've seen that smile, you can recognize it anywhere. At least, some of us could.

Spencer was talking again, through the grate. "Any team would want you," Spencer said. "They'd snap you up, they'd pay a fortune!"

"I don't know," Mike said. "Maybe they would."

Behind us, the door opened. Ozzie Gadlin and Sweetie Malone looked surprised to see the four of us crouched on the floor.

"What the—" Ozzie started to say. But Effie put his finger to his lips. Again, the voice came through the grate.

"They'd grab you in a second," Spencer said. "With your talent— just pick the right team, and they'll make you a star!"

Ozzie tilted his head to the side, as if he couldn't believe what he was hearing. "Isn't that—"

But Effie shushed him again, and pointed to the floor. Sweetie and Ozzie knelt down behind us, leaning over our backs, to get their heads close to the grate.

"You've never dreamed of so much money. Think what you could do with it! You'll be like a king, Mike."

Ozzie practically leaped out of his skin. "*Mike* is down there?" he said to Effie. "With Spencer? *Alone?*"

Effie put his hand on Ozzie's arm, to keep him from jumping up, from bolting out of the room.

"He's all right," Effie said. "Just listen."

Silence for a moment, from down below. Then Mike's voice again. "Maybe it's true," he said, his voice a bit muffled, through the grate. "They'd give me a nice fat check. Maybe you're right!"

We heard footsteps. Mike liked to walk around when he was thinking.

"But I know why I play. And it's not for the money."

The footsteps stopped. We gave a silent cheer.

"I play for people who don't have food to eat," Mike said. "For children who don't have clothes to wear. A roof to sleep under."

Effie beamed at Ozzie with satisfaction. As if to say, "I told you so."

"I play for the cause!" Mike went on. He was building up a head of steam—we could feel it right through the grate. "I play to change things that are wrong, to fix things that are broken. I play for people who work hard, but don't get a fair shake. People who do their best but never get a chance, because that's the way the system works. I play for them!"

"Yes, but—" We heard Spencer try to get in a word. But Mike had built up his momentum, and he was going to speak his piece.

"It's not about money," Mike said, his voice rising. "It's about rolling up your sleeves, doing your share. Pitching in, to make things better with your own hands. What is money compared to that?"

Effie and Ozzie and Buddy and Ned and I looked at one another, our hearts full to bursting. Mike was all right! It was only natural to be tempted—to wonder about things you don't have, to think about what you might be missing. It was only natural to imagine what it might be like on the path you didn't take. That so many others *have* taken.

Temptation was always there. We faced it every day!

But Mike would keep his balance, we knew, as we heard the way he talked to Spencer. We'd pack our bags and get back on the bus, Mike in his familiar seat across the aisle from mine. He'd settle back into that cracked red leather. He'd lean against those hard metal arms, through the highways of Illinois, the back roads of Ohio.

We would travel from ballpark to ballpark. Mike would sit in the dugout, Ozzie on his right side, and me on the left. When the inning changed, Mike would grab his glove and run out onto the field.

He might wonder about other paths. We all would once in a while! But Mike was going to be all right, because he knew what he had.

He had *us*.

We huddled around the heating grate, Ned and Buddy and I on our knees, ears almost to the floor. Sweetie hovering just behind us. Effie bending over my back, his face a few inches behind my head, while Ozzie scowled.

"Hmmm," Spencer said. We could picture his broad face working, his mouth shifting through its inventory of smiles. Trying to find the right arrangement. He had lost, but he wasn't giving up.

"You are loyal to your team," Spencer said. "Of course you are! But think for a minute."

A couple of footsteps. I imagined Spencer moving closer to Mike, fixing him with a stare. Mike backing away but still listening.

"You say you want to make things better," Spencer said. "Then why don't you do it! Find a team that knows your value, and make them pay. Take advantage of your talent. Put yourself in a spot where you can *really* help, if that's what you want to do. I'm not talking about pocket change—I'm talking about the kind of money that can change *everything*.

"People don't have food? Feed a townful! You want to give children a roof over their heads? Put a roof over the whole state! Give every cent away, if that's what you want. But you have to *have* something before you can give it away.

"Here's your chance to have something. Why wouldn't you take it?"

A pause. An argument like that can be confusing. People throwing all kinds of complications at you, a blizzard of logic, words piling up like snow. Feed a townful of children! Of course you had to think about that—it's why we were in this business in the first place. Could you pass up that kind of chance? To help more people than we ever dreamed of? Wouldn't it be selfish *not* to? Spencer knew just what to say, to tangle things up in your mind, and I heard Mike pace around the room, trying to find the right way to answer. To push Spencer back.

I listened at the heating grate, my toes still cold in wet socks.

"I understand your point," Mike said. No longer pacing. "You could do a lot of good with all that money. I know that!"

Ozzie began to get to his feet. Effie put his hand on Ozzie's arm again.

"It would feel good," Mike said. "All the people you could help. But there's a price."

Effie nodded his head, and Ozzie settled back down.

"You'd feel like you were helping," Mike said. "Of course you would! People would thank you for all that money, they'd call you a hero.

"But you'd know where the money came from. You'd be working for the people who *cause* the problem in the first place! You'd be *part* of the problem.

"All that money you'd give away? It comes from the owners. And everyone knows where the owners get it—they take it away from the people."

The sound of a chair being pushed aside.

"It's the wrong side," Mike said. "It doesn't matter how much good you do with the money—it's the wrong side, and it's not for me!"

Footsteps. Mike was going to walk out of there.

But we heard Spencer's heavier footsteps, too.

"You make some good points," Spencer said. "I understand perfectly. I might feel the same way in your position."

He paused.

"I only want what's best for you!" Spencer said. "Whatever you think is right. But you are missing something."

The footsteps stopped.

"What exactly?" Mike said. "What do you think I'm missing?"

"These are modern times!" Spencer said. "You need to come up to date a little. Your ideas are old-fashioned, putting owners on one side, workers on the other. It's yesterday's news!"

Heavier footsteps started again—this time, Spencer was pacing.

"Listen to me, Mike. The world is changing, the old battles don't make sense. We have science now. We have machinery! We don't need drudgework, we don't need men standing on the assembly line, slaving for pennies. Working their fingers to the bone. It's a whole new world.

"The workers don't need to fight the owners. That's the old way of thinking! We'll build new factories, where machines do the work. Workers will sit in offices, they'll lean back and prop their feet on a desk. They'll drink coffee, they'll chat with the secretary while the mechanism hums beneath them.

"Everyone will prosper, everyone will be better off. Why should workers battle the owners? That's yesterday's fight! We want the same thing—we want the wheels of commerce to turn, so that everyone gains.

"You can *help* make this happen. You can bring us together, help us work in the same direction. For the greater good!"

Spencer turned everything around. He muddied up the issues, so it was hard to tell where the mistake was. He left you all tangled, so what you thought was bad turned out to be good, wrong changed places with right. Your enemies became your best friends.

People like Spencer always have an argument—and if you disagree, they tell you there is something you overlooked, some mistake in your point of view. Some complicated reason why you should see things their way.

But it's actually very simple.

* * *

We played a game in Erie, Pennsylvania. One of those drawn-out battles, the score tied in the tenth inning when Buddy Brodsky came to the plate, with Sweetie Malone on third. Buddy stood in the box, he waited for his pitch. Then he swung, just a little bit too high. He tapped a grounder toward first base.

Sweetie didn't hesitate an instant. The ball hit the bat and he bolted for home.

The first baseman charged in, without a second to lose. He saw that play right in front of him, he raced at the ball, he made a beautiful scoop. The ball rolled right into his mitt.

And froze there.

The first baseman's arm came back to throw—but his hand was empty, the ball still nestled in the webbing of the glove. The first baseman looked at that empty throwing hand, and his eyes widened in disbelief. While Sweetie streaked home with the winning run.

The crowd roared. The pitcher stamped his feet.

The catcher stood with his arms raised to the sky, as if questioning the existence of God.

We ran off the field, shouting and laughing with the thrill of it all, the taste of victory. The joy of being alive. The crowd was cheering, one of the best we'd had in a while. The stands were packed, so even after setting aside gas money, we'd be able to stock up a soup kitchen for a good couple of months. And eight or nine families would get their rent paid.

It felt good.

We stopped at a barbecue shack a couple of miles out of town. The sun had gone down, but it was still warm, and we sat outside at picnic tables. Chatting and joking, stretching out our legs. Happy with our chicken and lemonade.

Effie stood up.

"Boys, I want to tell you something," Effie said. The barbecue shack had a picture window, and Effie stood in front of it, lit from behind by the yellow light of the store.

The dark heavens spread overhead, the horizon glowing silver as the moon began to rise.

"We were in our place today," Effie said. His arms folded across his chest. He looked tall in the twilight, and heads nodded as we ate. We knew in our bones that Effie was right.

"When the battle comes," Effie said, "some people stand on the sidelines. Some people sit at home. But not us."

Effie paced in front of the window. Smoke from the barbecue swirled above the grill. A sign spelled HOT in red neon.

"Our place is on the field," Effie said.

The barbecue had a nice warm tang. It felt good to sit there in the twilight, eating our chicken, drinking our lemonade. Crickets chirping in the bushes.

"We may not always win," Effie said. "You all know that. Some days, the odds will be against us. Some days, things won't come out the way we want."

"Not if *I* can help it!" yelled Ned Kretzmann, a chicken leg in his hand, barbecue sauce dribbling down his chin.

"Hear, hear!" said Sweetie Malone. We all mumbled our support, mouths full.

"Obstacles will block our path," Effie said. "Enemies will stand in our way. The world may line up against us. It doesn't matter!"

Effie looked all around at the team, neon lighting up the back of his head. He knew what he was talking about, there in the twilight.

"We may not always win," Effie said. "But we will *always* be in our place."

* * *

Isn't that the point, when you come right down to it? You can make things as complicated as you want. You can go back and forth with Spencer or people like him, arguing about this or that. But in the end, the important thing is to be in your place.

Our place was on the field!

We huddled around the heating grate. There was a pause downstairs, and then Spencer said, "Look in this envelope."

A moment's silence. Another moment. Then the sound of paper being slowly, carefully torn open.

The six of us crouched there holding our breath. Listening to the ripping envelope.

We heard a door open, then a woman's voice. A voice like warm honey. The sound silk would make if silk made a sound.

"We could be together."

Suddenly Effie's voice, sharp as nails: "Let's go!"

We were already jumping to our feet, scrambling out of the room. Squeezing through that little door, sprinting down the hall in our socks, into the stairwell, taking the stairs three and four at a time.

I don't know how we missed it. I don't know why we didn't see it before, why we couldn't put the pieces together. But we saw it then—clear as day, the second we heard Irene's voice.

We burst into the hallway below. We raced at top speed to Spencer's open door. And there they were.

Spencer with a grin on his face, as wide as the Atlantic Ocean.

Mike with an envelope in his hand. A fat envelope! The bills were crisp and green, and they weren't singles. It must have been a fortune.

Irene. We saw her for the first time, just as Mike must have seen her. Eyes so green they startled you. Hair a blaze of gold. She stood right there, next to Mike.

In her hands—there it was, in Irene's hands.

She held it up, like a terrible flag. Unfolded to its full length.

She held it in front of Mike's chest, and it stretched to the floor, in all its shameful glory.

The sparkling pinstripes of the New York Yankees.

CHAPTER NINETEEN

Even now—after all these years—I remember what it felt like, to run onto the field with my teammates. I'll hear a game on the radio, a cheering crowd, the announcer's voice, and the memories will feel close enough to touch. A breeze will come up, and I'll catch a scent of fresh-cut grass. A whiff of old leather.

Or a bus will drive by, and I'll suddenly be back on my cast-iron bench, feeling the rumble of the engine, the heat of the exhaust. I'll be back on the road—rolling down those dusty highways with the team. Tingling with anticipation as we drive into a new city. As we pull up to the ballpark, driving past carts selling hot dogs, roasted nuts, cotton candy. We step out of the bus, our shoes crunching gravel as we head for the players' entrance, the rusty iron gate that takes us to the visitors' locker room. Dark and cool inside, even though the day is hot. Every locker room feels like home, with hooks to hang up our clothes, a wooden bench where we pull on our uniforms, lace up our shoes. A bench that is probably older than we are—the varnish has flaked away, the wood worn smooth as satin by all the people who have sat there before us. The same in every ballpark.

We grab our gloves and head for the tunnel, even darker and cooler than the locker room. A couple of flickering bulbs, but it's mostly shadows. The walls used to be white, but that's only a memory now, buried under layers of grime, because who bothers to repaint a tunnel? We don't care about the walls anyway. Our eyes are straight ahead, on the tunnel's silver mouth, our footsteps echoing as the outside world grows larger and brighter. We move a little faster near the end—and as we take that last step into the dugout, a blast of light makes our blood rush. We hear cheering now as we walk past racks of bats and boxes of baseballs. It puts a bounce in our stride. I give my cap a little tug and pound my glove with my fist, because they're cheering for *us*. We pick up speed as we climb the dugout steps—the field spreads out in front of us, and we sprint into the roar of the crowd.

A few years ago, I drove past a junkyard. They hadn't taken away my license yet. I wasn't living in this ridiculous place, which they have no business calling a "home"—what kind of home has nurses around every corner? Nurses I don't need, because there's nothing wrong with me except that I've lived so many years. I'd walk out the door tomorrow if I had any idea where to go.

Anyway, I drove past a junkyard, and I couldn't help myself. I stopped, turned the car around, and pulled into the little parking lot. Because there, at the edge of the lot, next to the rusty trailer they used for an office—parked in a place of honor—was a Crown Coach Company bus.

Not the same model as ours, but almost the same. Not in bad shape either, for its age. A couple of broken windows, the tires flat, but otherwise in one piece.

I got out of my car.

I walked over to the bus.

The door was open a crack, so I grabbed the edge and pulled. The hinges creaked, the door swung open the rest of the way, and I climbed the steps. A musty smell, but I didn't mind. After all those years, it felt like home! The cast-iron seats, the cracked red leather. The chipped enamel arms we grabbed when the bus went around a corner. I might never have left—that's the way it felt. I walked slowly past the benches, past windows caked with dust, and stopped next to my old seat. I looked across the aisle at the bench that would have been Mike's.

"Sad old dinosaur, isn't she?"

I turned around. A man stood just outside the door. Fat belly, oil stains on his T-shirt. Thin black hair, with eyebrows that had already gone gray. He drank something slowly, from a paper cup.

"I used to sit right here," I said. "Right in this seat."

He ignored me. "Can you believe this thing was still in service? Came in a year ago. What a relic! It belongs in a junkyard, that's for sure."

I nodded. I didn't know what else to do. My hand was resting on top of the bench—*my* bench—and I held on to that hard cast iron. That ancient leather.

These days, it's all about comfort. Cushions and headrests, fabric that feels plush to the touch. They curve the seat to fit the shape of your own back. You can tilt your seat if you want, just press a button and stretch your legs. Don't worry about the man behind you—he'll find a way to make do. He'll bend his back somehow, twist his legs into a pretzel. It doesn't matter, as long as *you* are comfortable.

I've heard that you can even watch television!

Where are the people who understand what luxury can do to your character? Who just want a place to sit, not a cushioned recliner but an honest bench, solid and firm? A bench that is there to serve its purpose—nothing fancy, just a place to rest.

Where are those people now?

"Take it off my hands," said the man in the greasy shirt. "I'll give her to you cheap." I smelled liquor on his breath. Some people throw away their lives.

I'll tell you something—I didn't want to get off that bus. I had a little of the old feeling, if you want to know the truth. More than a little!

I could have put on my uniform, rubbed oil into my glove. I might be old, but I had an inning or two left in my arm, I was sure of it. Just show me the way to the mound.

My legs might have slowed down. When I bend at the hip, I feel a little twinge. But isn't it your heart that counts?

I could have settled down on that cast-iron bench. I could have listened to the hum of the motor, felt it throb through the stuffing of the seats. I'd grip those chipped enamel arms as we set out for the highway, out on the open road. A basket of sandwiches on the front seat, my uniform hanging in the back. The transmission would growl, and off we'd go—to the next ballpark, and the next, and the next. The dusty fields, the cheering crowds. I'd head off to change the world!

But there was no one to go with me.

* * *

Nancy would have tried to see Mike's side. To understand his point of view.

He's in love, Nancy would have said. But that doesn't make any sense. Mike was a thinker, the kind of person who worked things through. He didn't jump to conclusions, he wouldn't just change his mind—about *everything*—on a whim.

How is it even possible? How can you fall in love in less than a day?

And what if Mike *were* in love? He would have talked it over with his teammates, he would have kicked it back and forth. He would have puzzled it through. Sure, love can make your head fuzzy, but love or not, Mike would have taken his time. He would have given it plenty of thought, the way he did with everything else.

He's looking for something, Nancy would have said. Some kind of balance, a way to even things out. A cause is well and good—but everyone needs room for their own life.

But that doesn't make sense either. What kind of balance is it to throw out your ideals? To give it all up, the work you've done, everything you've fought for. An entire lifetime!

Just for the sake of argument—let's say that Mike really was in love. Irene was pretty, I'll give you that. Those green eyes, those blonde curls. If you like that obvious kind of prettiness.

Let's say Irene was the only woman in the world for Mike. The one he was meant to spend the rest of his life with. Even then—the *Yankees*!

You know what I'm talking about. Everyone knew about the Yankees, their fabulous wealth, their magical stadium. The aristocracy of the diamond, the monarchs of the field, prancing around the base paths in their pinstripes. They were lords, and the rest of the league were their subjects.

The Yankees!

You know how we played the game. We had what we needed, our bats and gloves, our uniforms. A few changes of clothing, whatever we could stow under the seats of the bus. The strength of our arms and legs—that was enough!

We didn't need fancy equipment. The Yankees could have their gymnasium, all kinds of modern contraptions, machines with weights and pulleys. Dumbbells in every size. Their steam rooms and whirlpool baths.

We'd heard what the Yankees did in their clubhouse—you could lie on a cushioned bench, and someone would bring you a glass of water. A stranger would rub down your back, work oil into your hamstrings. While you talked on the phone with your stock-broker.

The Yankees had hot showers, and you could use as many tow-els as you wanted.

We didn't need luxury. We didn't need cushioned benches. We were working men!

The Yankees could have their coaches, their managers, their scouts and statisticians. All kinds of people telling you what to do. What did we need coaches for? We knew how to play the game, and we played it with our hearts, the way it was meant to be played. If we had a question, we could ask Effie.

The Yankees could have their trainers—people who had gone to college to learn how to exercise, if you can believe that. They took classes in stretching your legs!

We didn't need any of that. We knew what we stood for, and that was enough.

Who wanted to stay in hotels with chandeliers? With push-button elevators, feather pillows, satin sheets. Champagne in buckets of ice. Hotels where the bellhops brought anything you needed—and things you didn't.

The Yankees rode in trains that barreled down the tracks, as if nothing else in the world mattered. As if no one could get in their way. Trains that had beds and showers, dining cars where they gave you real silverware. Where you could get a mug of cold beer. Porters who bowed and scraped for tips.

The Yankees!

The darlings of Wall Street. The toast of Fifth Avenue.

Titans of industry sat in the box seats of Yankee Stadium, look-ing down like kings from their thrones. They snapped their fingers, summoning serving boys to bring them hot dogs, candy, peanuts.

Stooping, for a few moments, to eat the food of commoners, pretending to be part of the crowd.

But that night, they'd go back to their filet mignon. Their plates heaped with lobster, with prime rib. A bottle of wine with a price tag that could support a family for a month. They might not even drink it! They'd fill their glass, take a sip, and let the rest go to waste.

They opened that wine because they could. It was their privilege, their right. They might even have felt that it was their obligation, as sovereigns of the world. Everyone has to hold up their end.

If you looked around the stands at our games, you wouldn't find titans of industry. You'd find people who worked with their hands, who lived from week to week and had never seen a plate heaped with lobster. They had never stuck their fork into a filet mignon. They had never even heard of Fifth Avenue.

If you looked in the crowd at our games, you didn't see kings on their thrones. You saw people who had nothing, who had no one to stand up for them. So that's what we did.

We stood up.

The Yankees bought and sold players like cattle. Politicians bowed and scraped for tickets. The press ate out of their hands. They could have bought and paid for Creation itself, if they wanted to.

The Yankees were the ruling class.

So we looked at Irene as she stood in Spencer's hotel room. Holding up that uniform, crisp and pressed, glowing brilliant white in the incandescent light.

Irene held the uniform in her hand, she draped it in front of Mike. She held those pinstripes right to his chest.

I looked him in the eye.

Mike didn't look back.

CHAPTER TWENTY

Maybe Nancy was right. Maybe balance was the most important thing.

Sure, principles meant something—but could you live your whole life for an idea? Couldn't Mike find a way to hold on to his principles in the major leagues? He'd have plenty of chances to do good if he looked for them, and plenty of money to do it with. And he could have his life with Irene.

He could have his life!

What about the bigger picture? What about the things that needed to be changed, the fundamental problems with the system?

Nancy would tell me I was missing the point, if I started to talk about the system. She'd say it isn't real, you can't touch it, you can't sit next to it on the couch. So what good does it do you? You get lost in complications, she'd say, when you try to solve the fundamental problems. You get all tangled up. Why not keep it simple—live your life, and help the people around you.

I thought about that on the bus, after I left Nancy's house. After I left her standing at the sink. I thought for a long time—about what it meant to live your life.

I pictured the water running over Nancy's bowl of berries. I saw the look in her eyes.

I remembered the feeling I used to have on Nancy's couch as we sat together, as I felt her warmth against my side. Her hair against my cheek. She would relax, she would lean into my arms, I'd feel her heartbeat against my chest. And then I said those things!

I had plenty of time to think about it, because we were away for a solid month. I saw those berries as we drove through the hills of Michigan, the back roads of Illinois. The empty cornfields of Iowa. I thought about that look in Nancy's eyes as we drove from Youngstown to Dayton to Battle Creek. I saw her standing at the sink, and I remembered that feeling in my stomach. I knew exactly what had happened.

I had lost everything.

* * *

I remembered a day in Binghamton when my teammates had gone to an orphanage and I stayed behind at the Chemung Cafe. I sat at the counter watching Nancy work, talking to her between customers.

"No orphanage for you?" Nancy said.

"They don't need me," I said. "I'd rather be here with you."

I dipped my cinnamon roll in a cup of coffee, the dough steaming as I took a bite.

"You like the *idea* of helping," Nancy said. "More than the helping itself."

That was not a nice thing to say. I told Nancy she was wrong— of course I want to help! It's true I didn't visit the orphanage. But isn't it enough that we played our hearts out on that hot August afternoon? That we raised a hundred and fifty dollars so the orphanage could buy a new stove? I didn't have to see all those children in person. What difference would that have made? I don't have to know about each person's problems.

It's true that I am more interested in the fundamental issues, the root causes. What's wrong with that? There *are* deeper issues.

Problems you can't see or feel or touch, but you know they are there. Someone has to deal with the fundamentals, don't they? The flaws in the system. Isn't that the most important thing?

Nancy used to tease me, if she thought I went too far. If I got too serious.

"You're right," she would say. "The world is a mess! And you're the *only one* who can fix it!"

I'd get worked up about the latest grievance. I'd complain about one injustice or another. I'd build up a head of steam.

"Good thing you're on the job!" Nancy would say. "The whole place would fall apart if it weren't for you."

Of course Nancy was exaggerating. I never said I could solve the world's problems, not by myself. I have ideals, but I'm a realist— I can see what's happening around me, how far we have to go. Our team could only do so much, even with all of our energy, our good intentions. Even with the crowds behind us. They loved us in Pennsylvania and Illinois. They threw flowers in our path in Wisconsin. But the most we could hope for was to tip the scales a little.

What's wrong with that? If all you can do is tip the scales, don't you want to tip them in the right direction?

Nancy might have teased me, but she teased me in good spirit. She saw what had to be changed, she knew how important it was. But if I went too far, Nancy would let me know. She'd tell me to shake it off, take the load off my shoulders, let someone else worry about it for a little while.

"Forget the world's problems," Nancy would say. "You can fix them tomorrow! Take care of things right here where you are."

She was better at it than I was, I admit. I'd sit there on the couch as she talked about the details of the day, something that happened to her at the diner, some complication with a customer, or a supplier. Maybe a visit from her aunt. A visit where not much happened, on the surface—but if you thought about it, there were all kinds of implications. If you really picked it apart.

My mind would start to wander. I wouldn't realize, at first, that I was following a train of thought, because it would start innocently enough. I'd stop for a moment to think about something, a fragment of an idea. At first it was related to something Nancy had just said, but then the path would take me in its own direction. I only meant to follow it a little way, I didn't plan to lose my focus, but the path has a mind of its own—it turns one corner and then another, connecting one idea to the next. I'd lose sight of where I started as I followed those turns, as the path bent and looped. All kinds of distractions! I'd come across a detour and leave the trail entirely, truly lost in thought.

Then I would look up, see Nancy right in front of me—and be surprised.

Nancy's mind didn't wander. She was always *right there,* looking me straight in the eye when we talked. She took it all in and asked all kinds of questions, digging in as deep as she had to until she understood. It could be a bit much, to tell you the truth. It's nice when someone pays attention, when they really listen, when you know it's important to them. But do they really need to know *everything*?

As the bus drove through the empty fields of the Midwest, I thought about that day when Nancy stood at the sink, when I told her what I had decided.

There was a moment when she turned away, to look back at her berries, and I kept talking even though I couldn't see her face. I looked at the muscles of Nancy's back, the movements of her shoulders. Shoulders so familiar, so comfortable. It felt so good to put my arm around them as we walked over to the park, as we looked across the Susquehanna River. As we stood on Nancy's porch watching the sun go down behind the houses.

I watched Nancy's shoulders from across the kitchen as I explained things to her. As I patiently laid it out. As I talked, I saw Nancy's shoulders move a little. I saw them change their angle so they looked harder in a way. Nancy didn't say a word, but her shoulders told me what she was thinking—they had set themselves against me.

As though I were a stranger.

She was supposed to argue! We would have gone back and forth, in her kitchen. I would have said the things I had to say, and in the end, Nancy would have understood—that I had things to do, *important* things, but it would work out in the end, because I loved her. The cause was important, but Nancy had my heart. Ninety percent of it, at least. Ninety percent!

What more could she want?

Then Nancy turned to look at me one last time. I will never forget the way she stared at me, as her bowl overflowed. The berries abandoned, floating loose in the sink.

She looked at me as though I were selfish.

Can you imagine? How can it be selfish to dedicate your life to others? To give up every minute of your time, every ounce of comfort, every chance at personal happiness, for the sake of the common good?

How can it be selfish, to take on a great responsibility? The most important responsibility there is—to make the world a better place!

I had given my entire life to a principle.

How can that be selfish?

* * *

I had plenty of time to think about it, on that Crown Coach Company bus. I mulled it over for weeks, as we drove down those empty highways. I thought about the look in Nancy's eyes. I remembered what she'd said about the orphanage, and I had to admit there was a grain of truth.

I admit it! I liked the *idea* of helping, the idea of doing good. I liked to feel that I was doing my part. If I was—I didn't need to go to the orphanage, I didn't need to visit the soup kitchen. I made my contribution at more of a distance. Is there anything wrong with that?

But as we drove through the countryside, I felt something else floating beneath the surface. A thought that I couldn't quite make out at first, even though I tried to puzzle it through. One night it came to me as a question—a question that surprised me, that I had never considered before.

A question that was most unwelcome.

Was I in love with Nancy? Or was I in love with the *idea* of Nancy?

I spent a lot of time away from her. In the dusty ballparks, the empty fields, the lonely roads of the Midwest. And I realized—in all those weeks and months, it was the *idea* of Nancy that kept me going.

Why not? The idea was all I had!

I could picture Nancy in my mind as I sat on the bus. I could see her standing at the railing in the park, looking out over the Susquehanna River. Walking up the street to her house. Climbing the steps to her porch. Nancy would look down at me from the top step, and I would smile.

I would talk to Nancy in my mind, bantering back and forth, going over the events of the day. What I would say, what Nancy would say to me. I would imagine how it felt when Nancy looked into my eyes, sat next to me on the couch. When she ran her fingers through my hair.

You can't hold on to an idea. You can't draw it close, feel its breath on your cheek. You can't hold its warmth in your arms. But it's something!

If you want to know the truth—as much as I wanted to see Nancy, there was something I liked about that time on the bus, when I was alone with my thoughts. When I could lean back in my bench, look out the window, and let my mind drift. I could think about Nancy, the way I wanted to think about her.

There's something comfortable about an idea. You can see the whole thing inside your head, you can look at it from any angle you'd like, without the diversions, the disturbances of everyday life. All the details that get in the way, that pull your eye in the wrong direction. That distract you from the essence of things, the way they *should* be. Isn't that the most important thing to see?

If you're looking at a painting, you don't want to see the brush-strokes. It's the picture that counts, not all the little parts. Don't the details distract you from the main point? They can confuse you, if you're not careful.

Sometimes I think about that winter I spent with Nancy. The off-season when I lived in Binghamton, when we spent day after day together. Days that were full of little things—you have to do the laundry, you have to figure out what's for dinner. You talk more than you ever expected about hanging curtains in the living room. You organize the bedroom closet, you help sort through sweaters, you argue over where to put the shoes. All these things happen! But they are details, they are not what is important, unless I'm missing something.

When you're alone with your thoughts, you see things more clearly, in a way. You distill them to their essence. You see them in the best possible light! I'm not saying you *change* them—but maybe you make a few adjustments here and there. Edges smoothed, blemishes polished.

I could see Nancy the way I wanted to see her.

What's wrong with that? Do you think the Mona Lisa really looked that way when she sat down for her portrait? I guarantee you there was some imagination involved, that the painter had an idea in his mind when he picked up his brush. And that's what he painted—the *idea* of the Mona Lisa.

I thought about that as we drove through the darkened fields of Iowa, starting our long trip back from the Midwest.

It used to be the best feeling in the world when the bus turned east and headed back to Binghamton. Because I knew what was coming. We'd pull into the parking lot of the Chemung Cafe, wheels crunching on gravel. We'd drive slowly past the plate-glass window, and at first I wouldn't see Nancy—but then somewhere in the back, or off to the side, I'd catch a bit of movement. A flip of Nancy's curls, her shoulders turning as she set a plate of meatloaf on a table. I'd know that in a moment, Nancy would hear the growl of the engine and look around and realize we were there.

Her eyebrows would go up. Nancy's mouth would start to open. My favorite moment—the instant *before* she smiled.

As we drove back from Springfield and Muncie and Akron, I pictured that moment. The moment when we hadn't yet driven across the parking lot, hadn't yet rolled to a stop. When I hadn't raced down the steps of the bus to sweep Nancy into my arms, to hold her as close as I possibly could. My face in her hair, her warm breath in my ear.

When all of that was *about* to happen.

We drove all night but I couldn't sleep. I leaned against that cracked red leather as we bumped along the empty roads of

Pennsylvania. My favorite part of the drive, those last few hours on the deserted highway, headlights gleaming on the road ahead. The bus went around a curve, and I gripped the arm of the bench. The cold iron startled me—as I had been startled, that first time, by the cool touch of Nancy's lips. It hit me like an electric shock.

I knew, all of a sudden, that the idea wasn't enough for me anymore.

I had told Nancy I loved her—many times, as a matter of fact. Sometimes she looked tired of hearing it, if you want to know the truth.

But this was different. I knew it as I gripped that cold cast iron, as my fingers curled around the rail of the bench. As we rode that darkened highway on our Crown Coach Company bus.

I loved Nancy's flat little nose.

I loved her off-center smile.

Her voice, soft and warm and just a little bit throaty, a cat's purr melting in butter. I could sit there all day and listen. It didn't matter what Nancy was going to say—I just wanted to hear her talk.

I loved *her*!

I didn't care about the idea anymore. I didn't want to be alone with my thoughts, picturing Nancy's smile. Her warmth against my side, as we sat on her couch. I didn't want to smooth out the rough edges, to think about Nancy as she *should* be.

What good is an idea, when you come right down to it?

I knew as I sat on that Crown Coach Company bus that I didn't want to distill the essence. I didn't care anymore about fundamental causes—they are buried too deep. The important thing is what you can see, and feel, and touch.

I loved Nancy!

* * *

We pulled in at six in the morning.

I had never been happier to see the Chemung Cafe—the glow of the plate-glass window, a few cars in the parking lot, a couple of seats at the counter already taken. I was glad it wasn't crowded, because Nancy and I would have time to talk. Time for me to take it all back, everything I said while Nancy had stood at the sink. I loved her, for real. I knew it now, and there was nothing more important in the world.

But she wasn't there.

"Where is she?" I asked Virgil.

Virgil scowled at his spatula, to make it clear that he was not happy with me. A single egg sizzled on the griddle.

"I love her," I said.

Virgil frowned again at his spatula, then shook his head. "Off today," he said.

I started walking.

The sun was behind a hill, so the light was filtered and soft. Is there anything better than that early morning light? Nothing showy about it, nothing flashy. Everything fresh and clean, so you see things the way they really are—the world in its underwear.

I walked in the gravel shoulder at the side of the road. A slope dropped away to the left, and a hundred feet below I could see the Susquehanna River, black water lapping at the stones on its banks. The water moving at the same speed I was.

There were trees on the far bank. Thick branches, bark gleaming silver in the clean light. And leaves! I don't think I'd ever seen so many leaves. I had never paid attention before—leaves, water, bark. But now I noticed, as if I had woken from a dream.

I walked by a stand of bushes, bright-red berries, lime-colored needles. I'm not sure what kind of bushes they were, but they caught my eye, the branches angling in interesting ways. I could have stopped for a while if I hadn't had somewhere to go.

Things to look at everywhere—the slick black tar of the road, some kind of bird floating down to the roof ridge of an old garage, its wings spread, lavender feathers underneath.

The sky. Clear and deep with color, the shade brightening by degrees as it stretched from west to east, as you looked from one horizon to the other. Not just one blue—so many blues!

Why would I need a plan? I would tell Nancy how I felt, and that would be it. That was all that mattered! As far as the practicalities, we'd figure something out. Of course we would—I loved her.

What about the team? I didn't know how to answer that question. I didn't want to think about it, I didn't want to debate it with myself. It was the hardest question in the world! But I loved Nancy, and I would do what had to be done.

I turned away from the river. I started to climb Nancy's street as a shaft of sunlight slanted over the top of the hill. The sunlight traveled with me as I walked, sweeping the pavement in front of me. The first light of the day! So pure, before anyone else has seen it. Light as clear as a mountain stream.

Spencer was wrong. Of course he was! Fate decides nothing. The road stretched in front of me. A road that I could follow or not follow, whatever I chose. I set my own path! All that's important is to know what you want.

I knew.

I walked past rows of low front porches, sagging in spots. Flagstone walkways, weeds poking up between the stones. Here and there a flower bed.

A side street wound downhill, where a brick building squatted by the river. Maybe a power plant. Tall smokestacks, breathing puffs of steam into the chilly air.

My breath steamed in sympathy.

One by one, those clouds of steam drifted over the river. They caught the breeze and floated downstream, like stately boats, taking on the light of the morning—dark blue in the center, pearl blue where the clouds grew thinner. As they drifted downstream, they caught the beam of sunlight streaming over the hill—and the rims of the clouds caught fire, they glowed a brilliant pink.

Nancy lived six blocks in from the river. The neighborhood was familiar now, a street Nancy and I had walked a hundred times. Square, conservative houses, with solid timbers and deep foundations, resting on their fat haunches while the morning bloomed around them. The houses looked at me as I neared Nancy's front door, their windows reflecting the rose and bronze of the sunrise.

Look what you've been missing, the houses seemed to say.

Tell me something I don't know, I replied.

I walked past a flower garden—roses and lilies and tulips. The low angle of the light made the flowers look huge and fleshy, like ripe fruit. Sunbeams tangled in the branches of the rosebushes, thorns gleaming like daggers.

The sun grew stronger as it climbed above the hill. Lily stalks were almost transparent, light racing up their stems. Blades of grass were spikes of green flame. Lawns throbbed with a riot of chlorophyll. The street was a river of light! Windows blazing, rooftops on fire. Telephone wires dripping gold.

I stopped in front of Nancy's house, and I had that old familiar feeling. As if a month had not passed. As if we'd never had that terrible conversation at the sink.

We would pick up right where we left off. Why couldn't it work that way? I would tell Nancy how sorry I was, I would take her in my arms, and we would go inside. I was sorry, and I loved her—I'd tell her as many times as she needed to hear. And Nancy would understand. Anyone can make a mistake, she'd say, just don't make a habit of it. Then she'd tell me something funny about the diner, and I'd tell her a story from the road. We'd laugh, and be right back on our path.

I climbed the steps to Nancy's porch.

For some reason, I thought about the stuffed elk in the lobby of the Rockefeller. That look in his eyes, the way he glared across the room, at that painting of a Wisconsin lake. All he wanted was to get back there.

* * *

You already know what happened.

I knocked on Nancy's door.

I knew she would be awake—she got up with the sun, even on her day off. So I knocked again.

And I saw, the instant Nancy came to the door. She didn't even have to open the screen. I saw before she said a word.

I stood there on the porch, and Nancy gave me a good, hard look. Not angry—worse than that. Not a look that said I had mistakes to answer for. Not a look that said there was work ahead, apologies to make to set things right.

A look that lasted for a million years, and told me everything I needed to know.

It was broken.

It could not be fixed.

I had to try, anyway. I started to explain. "Nancy, I have to—"

She closed the door. She didn't slam it—Nancy never slammed doors. But she didn't hesitate either. She closed the door with perfect firmness.

I knocked again and called Nancy's name. I heard footsteps, deep in the room. Then nothing.

"Nancy!" I said.

A window opened in a house across the street. An elderly woman looked out at me and frowned.

"Nancy!" I said again.

The elderly neighbor watched me. Not overly concerned, just taking it all in. I waved and did my best, with hand motions, to tell her that everything was OK.

A mistake had been made, that's all. A little misunderstanding. You can fix a mistake, can't you? Can't you correct a misunderstanding?

I walked around to the side of the house.

The living room curtains were drawn, and the kitchen was guarded by a high bush. I worked my way behind the bush and pressed my face to the glass, cupping my hands around my eyes so I could look into the kitchen. Nancy kept a collection of glass animals on the windowsill, nine or ten figurines that would catch the sun when it came in at the right angle. Other than that, there wasn't much to see. A couple of jars on the counter, the steel faucet curving over the sink. It was strange, seeing the sink from the other side.

"Nancy!" I said again. I tapped on the glass. I waited.

I walked to the back of the house.

I don't know what I thought I would find there. There were no windows in the back, just a blank white wall. I stood in Nancy's yard, a weathered fence on three sides, low shrubs here and there. The bench where Nancy and I used to sit, where sunlight filtered through the neighbor's tree, a tree with thin, silver leaves—I'm not sure what it was called.

I stood in the dewy grass. There were patches of clover, little clusters of dandelion heads, fat and ready to flower. I looked at the back of Nancy's house.

All I wanted was to tell her I was sorry. To hold her, and sit on the couch, feel her weight against mine. But there was a blank wall between us.

A rabbit sprinted across the yard and escaped through the gap under the fence.

I felt far away from my teammates all of a sudden. They would be sitting in the Chemung Cafe now, sipping coffee with Virgil, eating their scrambled eggs. Gossiping about one thing or another. It would be noisy in the cafe, people coming in and out, conversations rising and falling. The clatter of dishes, all kinds of commotion.

I stood alone in Nancy's yard.

I thought about the way Nancy looked at me when she opened the front door. What else could I think about?

Her face had told me everything I needed to know. Even as the words raced through my mind—how much I loved her, how wrong I had been, that I'd do whatever it took to keep us together. There was no hope once I saw that look.

I knew from Nancy's eyes. I might love her—but it didn't matter! That's what her look said. I could love her from here to the moon, but it didn't make the slightest bit of difference. I had made my choice that day in her kitchen. I had decided what was important, what I cared about the most.

I felt weak, all of a sudden, standing there in Nancy's backyard. A bit light-headed. I had to sit down, to catch my breath. But it didn't feel right, to sit on Nancy's bench—the bench we used to share—surrounded by Nancy's soft grass, her clover, her dandelions. The yard that belonged to her.

I bent over and put my hands on my knees. I was breathing hard. Everything was going too fast. I could feel the pounding of my heart, blood racing through my veins.

I would knock again on Nancy's door—and sooner or later, she'd have to answer.

Or I would walk down to the end of the street and wait there. I'd catch up with Nancy when she went to the store, meet her as she walked to work.

I could write it all down, everything I had to say. Some things are better on paper anyway. You can lay it all out, make sure you have the words right. That it means what you want it to mean.

I could find a job in Binghamton! Who said I had to leave with the team? I could rent an apartment, buy a couch, settle in. I'd stand outside the Chemung Cafe every day until Nancy was ready to talk to me.

I shivered. It was cold back there, in Nancy's yard. I remembered the warmth of the Crown Coach Company bus, the throb of the engine, the bubble of light inside as we drove down those country roads, Effie in the driver's seat, my teammates all around.

I could wait for Nancy, and tell her that the rest of life didn't matter. That she would always come first. We *had* to be together, and I would do whatever it took—isn't that what she deserved?

I couldn't look at that blank wall anymore, the back of Nancy's house. I turned my head to the ground and closed my eyes.

I could tell Nancy she was the only thing in my heart. She had a right to hear that, didn't she? She knew how I felt about the team, and I'd be honest—I believed in the cause, I wanted to be part of it. But *she* was more important. I could tell Nancy that none of the rest mattered if it got in our way. That I loved her, and we would make it work. None of the rest mattered!

I could tell Nancy that I didn't have a single doubt.

But I wasn't sure it was true.

*   *   *

What can you do then, except walk back to the bus?

You pitch a game in Syracuse, and you don't even notice whether you win or lose.

You pitch another game, and another. You drive from city to city, all those lonely hours on the bus. You think about writing a letter, once or twice, but what good would that do? What would you really have to say?

She wouldn't write back.

There are diners and rooming houses, coffee shops and cheap hotels. One rusting ballpark after another. Then one day the induction notice comes, and you go off to war. By the time you get back, your arm is old, your legs are tired. The Robins are struggling, the mood in the country has changed. You don't want to quit, because the job is not done—children still go to bed hungry. But at a certain point, history moves on without you.

We hadn't changed the world, in case you are wondering.

What then? You end up teaching school. Not history, because no one wants to tell children the truth. Not civics, because the system is suspicious of your opinions. It doesn't matter that you fought in the war—they don't trust you with young minds.

But no one cares about a gym teacher's opinions.

So you run those kids around the track, you make them do push-ups, you send them up and down ropes. And every spring you take them out to the baseball field, and you climb up on the mound. You show them the ball in your hand. That's why you took the job.

One year, an English teacher catches your eye. She has a sweet smile, soft eyes. She sits next to you at a staff meeting, and you feel something—forty-six is not old, you realize, there's plenty of time ahead. You start to think about her now and then. Her cream-colored sweater, her notebook full of poetry.

The miracle is, she likes you, too. But when you take her out to dinner, it turns out that she isn't Nancy.

One day your hair is gray. They cut down a tree outside the school—a tree that was a sapling when you arrived. You hear the roar of the chain saw, its vibrations rattle your bones, and you realize how much time has passed. So you pack up the things in your little office. You leave a note for the English teacher, because you want to leave one for *someone*. You set the key to your office on top of the desk.

The rest is memory and imagination.

CHAPTER TWENTY-ONE

What about Mike?

They pampered him, they coddled him—of course they did! Irene at his side every minute.

They fed him steaks. They dressed him in a suit. They put his picture on a billboard, his name spelled out in capital letters.

I wasn't there, the day he took the field in Yankee Stadium, the day he walked to the plate for the first time. Pinstripes on pressed white linen, his uniform gleaming in the sun.

The team was in Dubuque that weekend. *Our* team. Not Mike's anymore.

Mike climbed out of the dugout, stepped onto that legendary field. People got up on their feet—a sellout crowd, and why shouldn't they be excited? Flashbulbs popping, a clamor like Mike had never heard in Akron or Reading or Buffalo.

They stamped their feet, they whistled. They shouted at the top of their lungs. A sound that built on itself, a roar that rolled down from the bleachers, cascaded in waves from the stands. People cheered for the Robins, too—but it's one thing when a thousand people cheer, or two thousand. Imagine sixty thousand people! A whole city's worth, and every single one of them is shouting your name. You can't even hear your teammates in the dugout. They are cheering for you, too, but the crowd drowns them out.

Mike probably couldn't even feel his feet as he walked across the grass—the cheers washing around him, lifting him up. I can understand why Mike would want that feeling. Tell me you haven't thought about it yourself, once or twice.

But I wasn't the least bit jealous.

I could have had the same thing, if I'd wanted. Didn't the big leagues need pitchers, too? I might have stood there on the mound, the crowd roaring *my* name instead of Mike's.

I can picture it exactly—let's say a tight spot in the late innings, a tie score with runners on base. A tough hitter at the plate. The batter digs in, he looks out toward the mound with that gleam in his eye. He waves that menacing bat.

But I *know* I have him.

He's fouled off two fastballs, high and away, and I know exactly what he's looking for. He wants the pitch he saw his last time up, the big sweeping curve I struck him out with two innings ago. He knows it's coming, I can see it in his eyes.

I'm going to freeze him instead, with an inside fastball. Tight, but on the edge of the strike zone.

"You're out!" All he'll be able to do is watch it go by, as the umpire rings him up.

I can already see the expression on his face. I can already hear the crowd—they cheer and shout and roar, all of that noise for me.

I can only imagine what that feels like. It must really be something, to stand on the field and hear that sound. The kind of sound that could make you forget things, if you weren't careful.

As Mike walked out to the plate, there were some things I'm guessing he'd forgotten.

Those hours after school in the vacant lot. Our imaginary base runners, our outfield of weeds. No crowds, no fancy equipment, but we had all we needed. A bat, a glove, a battered trash-can lid for home plate. The arc of the ball against the clear blue sky.

Mike might have forgotten, for a moment, about our Crown Coach Company bus. The engine throbbing as we sprawled on our benches, tired out after a game. Unwrapping our sandwiches and spreading the wax paper on our laps. Watching the scenery go by, and talking about the places we were going, the things we meant to do.

Deep down, Mike knew what he believed—I was sure of it. But sometimes, the roar of the crowd can make you forget.

Mike walked to the plate in that dazzling sunlight. Everyone in the park on their feet now.

What did it mean when Mike stepped into the batter's box with that uniform on his back? A team of owners and bosses, a team of luxury and profits.

What did it mean when Mike waved to the roaring crowd? A different crowd than we were used to, bankers in their box seats, executives in neat gray suits. It's true that if you looked hard, you might find carpenters and ironworkers in the bleachers. But no one was there for the cause. No one cared about the fundamental problems with the system, the things that had to be changed. They were *applauding* the system.

What did it mean that Mike had left our side and gone over to theirs?

Mike scuffed the dirt. He planted his feet and waited for the pitch.

He must have been nervous, in front of all those people. But when he saw that fastball, he turned right on it. The swing we knew so well. The infielders froze as the ball shot past them, as it bounced down the left-field line.

A triple in his first at bat! Earning more with that swing than a month on the road with us.

What is it like to hit a triple in front of sixty thousand people? To stand on third base, brushing dirt off your shoes, sunlight gleaming on your uniform. The crowd cheering and clapping and stamping its feet.

What is it like?

He came up again in the third inning. Another fastball, and this time the pitcher reached back for everything he had. Which was plenty—you don't pitch in the major leagues unless you can put heat on the ball. And this one had steam!

He was a big man, the pitcher, muscles carved from granite. Sharp eyes, and that determined set to his shoulders. Not a shred of doubt as he reached back to throw. The pitcher didn't look at Mike—he didn't even look! Just reached back, kicked his leg, and fired that ball right in.

There was no malice. Why would there be? As far as the pitcher was concerned, Mike might as well have been a block of wood. There was no reason to bear a grudge—it was just a question of a message that had to be sent. Nothing personal about it.

Just business.

Ninety-five miles an hour, and you could no more get away from that pitch than you could outrun a bullet. No time to duck, to jump aside. Mike was lucky to be alive, as a matter of fact—lucky he had a hard skull. His head swelled up like a melon, but it could have been worse.

*   *   *

To be honest, it was bad enough.

There were hospitals and doctors, X-rays and all kinds of fuss. How many fingers? Do you know how you got here? Can you see this? Can you hear me? Do you know what year it is?

There were ice packs and bandages, medicines and ointments and dressings.

Where were they then? Where were Spencer and Irene when Mike couldn't get out of bed? When there were headaches, and double vision. When everything in the world was blurred.

Where were Spencer and Irene when Mike couldn't button his own shirt? When he needed help to put on his shoes. When he couldn't walk down a flight of stairs, much less hit a fastball.

Where were they then?

Mike's contract had loopholes, it turned out. The team had options, certain choices it could make. Mike was going to get better, at least he probably would—the doctors said there was reason to hope. But it would be a lot of work, and there were no guarantees. What kind of investment is that?

Ninety-five miles an hour means something against your bare skull. They could have given Mike a helmet—other teams had them, but the Yankees had dragged their feet. You can bet they had guards around Yankee Stadium, insurance on their limousines. They protected their property, but not the man at the plate.

It could have made all the difference. The helmet might have cracked. Mike would have gone down with a bruise. He might have had a headache, but he'd have been back on the field the next day, and they would have cheered him even more.

Would Spencer have been right, then? Mike would have strolled Fifth Avenue with Irene at his side, his name on the front page, women throwing flowers at his feet. Rich as Midas, and he would have spent his money well. The orphanage wouldn't just get a new stove—it'd get a new wing. The soup kitchens could serve roast beef. The poor could live in the Waldorf Astoria.

Would Spencer have been right? Can you do more from the inside? Do you have to work *within* the system to change it? If that ball had gone an inch to the right or the left, Mike would have had a chance to prove it. But he didn't.

Weeks turned into months. Where were they then? The cheering fans, the roaring crowds. Where were the headlines, the popping flashbulbs? Where were the boys lining up for autographs when Mike struggled down Fifth Avenue with a cane? Where were the women throwing flowers?

Where were Spencer and Irene?

They were just where you'd expect them to be.

They were somewhere else.

CHAPTER TWENTY-TWO

I went back to see Nancy. Many years later, when I happened to be in Binghamton for one reason or another. An errand of some kind that I don't remember exactly—there are plenty of reasons to go to Binghamton, aren't there? So I looked her up.

Maybe I went just to see her.

Nancy had moved to the outskirts of the city, to a little neighborhood set off from the main road. A freshly paved street, the asphalt smooth, a little wider than necessary, I thought. Who needs that much pavement? A road has a purpose to serve, like anything else. There's no need to build an airport runway.

The houses were pleasant enough, but the lawns were too neat, the bushes overly trimmed. Although the landscaping wasn't extravagant, compared to what you might see in some other neighborhoods. There were no bushes carved into giraffes, no wrought-iron gates. No benches overlooking formal gardens—or, God help us, an ornamental fountain, a tarnished brass fish looking embarrassed as a stream of water spouted from his mouth.

But the grass was too neatly mowed, if you ask me. Not a weed in sight! The hedges too carefully tended, every branch clipped to exactly the same length. One more thing I'll never understand. Who spends their time clipping hedges? When there are so many problems in the world, so many things to be fixed. Why would you give a hedge even a moment's thought?

Nancy's house looked like all the others.

It took all the courage I had to ring the doorbell.

* * *

Nancy was nice to me—I'm not sure why. She smiled when she opened the door, as if she were happy to see me. She invited me into the house, hung my coat in the closet, asked me to stay for dinner.

She introduced me to Bruce.

Bruce.

Why wouldn't Nancy be married? You'd be crazy not to marry her if you had the chance. Bruce was tall and solid—head a little on the square side, if you ask my opinion. But he looked right at you, a direct look, nothing to hide. The look of a man you could trust.

I liked him, if you want to know the truth.

Bruce built houses for a living—nothing fancy, he said. No marble counters, no imported tile. Three beds and a bath, for people just starting out. But the houses were sturdy, Bruce said. He believed in a good foundation.

I knew, without asking, that Bruce had built that very house. The house that he and Nancy shared.

"How are you?" Nancy said.

I told her about the school. I told her about the blue-eyed English teacher, and I made it sound like more than it was. What was I supposed to do? Nancy was sitting there with Bruce, her husband, a builder of houses. She leaned against him every once in a while. They smiled at each other, and their fingers touched.

I couldn't tell her I was alone.

I had seen Sweetie Malone a few years before. I'd never thought Sweetie would settle down, but there he was in Sioux Falls with a house and a yard and three tall daughters, all with dimples in their chins. A little shop where he ran his carpentry business. His wife, Gladys, was bossy and round, but she had bright eyes, and smiled like she meant it, and Sweetie followed her around like a puppy.

"I fell like a ton of bricks," Sweetie said. "I saw her smile, and I was gone."

Gladys taught piano, and canned jellies, and made the best beef strudel in Iowa. An apple pie you'd lose a finger for. Why shouldn't she be round, if she could cook like that? Sweetie was chubby himself, by then, not the same man who dove into the stands for a sinking foul.

They showed me around the house, and then Sweetie and Gladys sat on their porch swing, fat and happy, while I drank lemonade and reminisced about the dusty ballparks, the open road. I could still hear the rumble of the engine, I said. I could feel that old cracked leather.

"I don't miss it," Sweetie said. "All that time, looking for something you could never find."

I was happy for Sweetie, that he'd ended up where he wanted. Why wouldn't I be happy for him? What's wrong with drinking lemonade on your porch? Is there anything the matter with canned jellies, with beef strudel?

And why shouldn't Nancy sit next to her husband at the dining room table, lean against his shoulder, touch his hand with her fingers?

Nancy didn't look young, anymore, she didn't look girlish. Her face was more filled in, and a lot of things were softer. She was thicker in places—*solid*, if you know what I mean. I was surprised how well it suited her.

There were creases around Nancy's mouth, little wrinkles at the corners of her eyes. Not quite a double chin but a hint that one might be coming. I realized, all of a sudden, how many years had gone by.

Where had I been?

I looked at the lines etched in Nancy's forehead. Where had I been when those wrinkles started to grow? When the hair at Nancy's temples began to gray?

The Chemung Cafe had closed, Nancy said. Business had gone off when traffic moved to the highway, so Virgil and his wife, Claire, had opened a restaurant of their own. His lasagna was famous in three counties. People stood in line on the weekends, they drove in from Horseheads and Whitney Point. Virgil wouldn't tell you his secret. He'd just nod in Claire's direction and say, "You have to put in the love."

Nancy had helped out when Virgil opened, managing the dining room, but she gave it up when she married Bruce. Now Virgil had four teenage boys to wait on tables while Claire balanced the books.

I asked Nancy about her cinnamon rolls, and she laughed. That was a long time ago, she said. She hadn't made them for years. She wasn't sure she still knew how.

"Tell him about the bakeries," Bruce said. Nancy shrugged, as if it weren't a big deal. She had knocked on the door of every bakery in town, and some of the restaurants. And now at the end of every day, she drove her station wagon around, or her volunteers did, and picked up leftovers to serve in church basements. Or at the Salvation Army. "Two hundred people a night," Bruce said. "They'd go to bed hungry if it wasn't for her."

I excused myself to go to the bathroom. I turned on the sink, splashed water on my face. There was a basket of soaps next to the sink—fancy little soaps wrapped in cellophane. They must have been handmade. They were all different colors, and they looked almost like candy. What are you supposed to do with soaps like that? You don't want to unwrap them, they're too fancy to use. Who wants to wash their hands with colored soap anyway? One more useless luxury, one more thing people don't need. There's something *wrong* with fancy soap—a good, practical thing turned into an extravagance.

Give me a plain white bar.

I knew that Bruce didn't buy those soaps. Nancy must have walked into a store one day, and there they were—a collection of colors and shapes, probably set near a window so the sun would fall on them, would shine through the wax and light them up from the inside. So you'd look at those soaps and think they had an inner glow.

Why wouldn't Nancy be drawn to that translucent light? The glitter of the cellophane wrappers. I thought of the windowsill behind the sink in Nancy's old apartment. The row of glass animals she used to keep there, their crystal bodies sparkling when the sun came through the window. I used to look at those animals when I rinsed dishes, the way they caught the light and splashed fragments of rainbow onto the wall. I thought they were silly—who needs glass animals in their kitchen? But Nancy lined them up behind her sink, and as I looked at that basket of colored soaps, I realized something.

This was the kind of life Nancy wanted. The kind of life where you could have glass animals, where you could have a basket of soaps.

I had to stop myself from crying.

We ate dinner, something with spinach and rice and cheese. I'm not sure what it was, but it was nice and warm—it was very good as a matter of fact. Nancy told me what it was called, but I can't remember.

I looked around the dining room. I thought about Nancy and her husband sitting there, eating dinner every night. After dinner they would clear the table. They would go into the kitchen, put water on for tea, do the dishes. A little music on the radio, Nancy washing while Bruce rinsed and dried.

Nancy would talk about her day, and she would tell Bruce everything. Every little detail. And Bruce would listen, he'd be interested, he would ask her questions. They would take their tea to the living room and talk some more.

They would go through the mail. Letters that were addressed to the two of them together.

They would look at the newspaper, maybe a magazine. Make a fresh pot of tea while they listened to the record player. Bruce close enough on the couch to feel Nancy's soft hair, her warm breath. The heat of the steam of the tea.

It would get late. Nancy and Bruce would walk to the staircase with its polished oak banister. The stairs carpeted, so you couldn't hear their footsteps as they climbed to the second floor, to their bedroom, to their bed.

* * *

We sat around that dining room table, the three of us. We had tea, with some kind of cake for dessert, not frosted but dusted with powdered sugar, sweet with raisins and apples. The kind of cake you didn't want to stop eating. Bruce helped himself to a second piece.

He talked about some land he was buying, where he was going to build houses. A beautiful spot, he said—a stream ran behind the lots, a great place for children. Nancy asked questions, and as we talked, I watched Bruce chew his cake. He looked like anyone you'd see in the street. Not the most interesting man in the world, by any means. Nothing special about him. Bruce might not understand the way things worked, at a deeper level, the root causes. He didn't see the flaws in the system itself—that it would take more than a few houses to fix what is wrong.

But he built houses. And Nancy fed two hundred people every day. What had I done?

At some point, Nancy went to get an album of pictures. She set the book on the table and unsnapped a little case and took out a pair of silver glasses. I had never seen her wear glasses.

I watched Nancy as Bruce walked up behind her, as he put his hands on her shoulders. Shoulders that were softer, more rounded than I remembered. I knew the angle of those shoulders, I understood what it meant, the way Nancy held them. The way she looked when she was comfortable.

I watched Nancy as she sat in front of that picture album. She had the same flat nose, the same off-center dimple in her cheek. Her blue eyes were still flecked with gold. There might be wrinkles around Nancy's eyes, a touch of gray at her temples, but even so— she looked exactly the same.

The world had followed a path to get here. To the point where Nancy sat at her dining room table wearing silver-framed glasses, Bruce's hands on her shoulders.

Who chose this path?

I had a part in it. Of course I did! There were things I said, things I did—I thought, at the time, that they were the right things. You know how that goes.

Maybe, looking back, I wish it could have been different.

But how much is really up to you? You set a goal, but at every turn, there are mistakes just waiting for you. All kinds of distractions and miscalculations, little bits of wrong thinking. The choices aren't clear—you're not smart enough to figure out all of the angles.

All you can do is weigh the options, puzzle it through. Balance the pros and cons until your head spins.

Did I choose this path?

Nancy opened the album, to show me a photograph of her son. He was away at camp for the summer, fifteen years old, an assistant counselor. A big shot! Nancy smiled when she showed me the picture.

He had Bruce's eyes.

Nancy's son had Bruce's eyes.

The two of them sat there, touching elbows. They finished each other's sentences, they patted each other on the knee. At one point Bruce put his arm around Nancy's shoulder, and looked at her in a certain way. At that moment, I knew: Bruce loved her 100 percent.

We drank our tea.

Nancy told me about her new job. It had something to do with publicity, with public relations, maybe—I'm not sure of the specifics. But Nancy liked it. Her eyes sparkled as she talked. She was proud of what she was doing, she was good at it.

They walked me to the door.

Bruce shook my hand. "Come back anytime," he said.

Nancy gave me a little hug.

I walked down their driveway and got in my car. I closed the door. I turned the key in the ignition.

I drove this way and that, through the neighborhoods of Binghamton. Houses just like Nancy's, cars parked in the driveways, lights in living room windows.

I thought about Nancy as I drove down streets where the stores were closed. Barbershops and shoe stores, groceries with cans piled in the windows. Bakeries and hardware stores, shops where you could have your toaster repaired. Signs in second-floor windows for lawyers, dentists, plumbers. A fortune-teller's shop with a red neon palm: YOUR FUTURE, ONE DOLLAR.

I passed churches and banks, gas stations and schools—maybe one of them was the school that Nancy's son had gone to. I drove through the empty streets, waiting at traffic lights when no one was there.

I thought about Nancy as I drove past a bowling alley and a firehouse. My headlights lit up warehouses and lumberyards, a used-car lot, prices drawn in grease on the windshields. A train yard, locomotives hulking on their sidings.

All those years, since the last time I had seen her. Years when I had imagined how she was doing, pictured the way she was living.

All those years I had missed her.

I used to feel responsible, in one way or another, for the way things turned out. Let's be honest—I felt guilty. Guilty for the things I said that day, as Nancy stood at her kitchen sink. For the things I *didn't* say.

Guilty for all of it. For not seeing what was right in front of me. Not understanding what Nancy meant. Not realizing, in time, exactly what I had.

How many people do?

As I drove through the streets of Binghamton, I pictured Nancy sitting at the table with her photo album. Bruce behind her, his hands on her shoulders. And I began to understand—I didn't need to feel guilty. I didn't need to feel bad for Nancy, I didn't need to feel responsible. Not at all. Because Nancy was fine!

She was fine, in a way that I was not.

She had lived her life.

CHAPTER TWENTY-THREE

It calms me down when my nurse walks into the room.

I can feel it happen. I'll be sitting on my bed, beginning to get upset. A dispute with a man on my hall, some minor unfairness in the cafeteria. The latest outrage from management—the doctors got a raise, but not the orderlies. The janitors have to work on Saturday, without overtime.

Injustice everywhere—and that's just in this building! Heaven help me when I open the newspaper.

It's not good for me to get so worked up. But what am I supposed to do? There are plenty of things to be upset about, if you look past the surface, if you see what's really going on.

I feel better when my nurse comes in the room. Not because she reminds me of Nancy—that's not it at all. It's her manner, the way she has about her. She walks over, puts her hand on my arm, looks at me with those soft brown eyes. A nice steady look.

I melt a little.

We walk together down the hall. Everyone is jealous when they see me with my nurse. That blonde hair—who wouldn't want to run their fingers through it, to feel that silk against their palm?

People stare as we head for the front door, and I stare back.

I feel a bit off-center sometimes. Let's be honest—I can get grumpy, and it takes me a little while to shake it. But my nurse is patient. She will talk me through it.

If it's a nice day, people will be on the lawn with their canes and crutches, their aluminum walkers. Here and there a wheelchair. Men and women who have seen better days. Less a social gathering than a collection of artifacts, a museum of the distant past.

At least they're still moving.

My nurse has something to say about everyone. Something interesting, maybe even amusing. People who are just annoyances to me, who get in my way, who are on my nerves—it's surprising how many there are! But they don't annoy my nurse. To her, they are one more thing to talk about.

She leans in close. She whispers some tidbit, a funny story. I feel her breath in my ear, her cheek against mine, and it makes sparks run down my spine.

I begin to enjoy the sunshine. The warmth feels good as we walk across the lawn. A squirrel scampers up a tree, a bird pecks at a gum wrapper. I nod at a woman with a red ribbon in her hair. It's not bad out here—I'm starting to see things from my nurse's point of view.

She makes one of her little comments, and I laugh.

When the time is right, we stop at a wooden bench. Not because I'm tired. Because *she* wants to sit for a while.

My nurse sits close to me on the bench, I feel her breathe in and out. Her side is pressed against my side. I swear I can feel our hips touch.

If I were forty years younger!

We sit on the bench and look out over a pond. More of a marsh, really—cattails along the edge, weeds rising out of the water, patches of purple flowers.

A couple of birds circle. The sun beats down. The water is still.

I listen to my nurse breathing.

Sometimes, the future seems so close—all those open doors, the thrill of the road ahead. The adventures that are *about* to happen. The victory that is sure to come.

Sometimes, you'd rather look back. Your mind is drawn to things that were important once—things you let go, but wish you hadn't. You didn't *know* they were important at the time.

Maybe you weren't paying attention.

You think about the things you missed, that slipped away. Who wouldn't want to go back, to try it all again? Make it come alive. And why can't you? Whose idea was it to build a wall around the past, to fence it off like a foreign country? It doesn't make any sense. Isn't the past your own backyard? Why can't you walk out there and visit, as easily as you walk from your kitchen to your living room?

People tell you to live for the present. That's a big mistake, in my opinion. The present is here only for a moment—by the time you notice, it's already gone. What's so great about a single moment? There's a lot more going on in the past, if you ask me.

Whose plan was it to divide things up this way—past, present, and future? It doesn't make any sense. It's all the same thing, if you really pay attention. You're just looking from different angles. The lines blur, if you let them. Things spill across the border. So why do we push them apart? Why invent that kind of separation? It's a trick of words, when you come right down to it.

People say the present is what's real. But I'll tell you what's real to me. The throb of the engine on the bus. The weight of the ball in my hand. Nancy's soft curls against my cheek.

The Chemung Cafe is the place that's real, as sharp and clear as yesterday afternoon. And that Crown Coach Company bus, with my teammates on those cast-iron benches. The smell of grass-stained uniforms, of old leather, the cornfields of the Midwest gliding by. Who dares to tell me that's not real? I see it as plainly as I see you.

Maybe it's just my imagination. I'm tired, and I won't argue if you tell me the past is only an idea. So what? Maybe an idea is enough! What else do you really have in the end?

I sit on the bench with my nurse, looking out over the pond. We can sit there forever, as far as I'm concerned. The shadows will lengthen, and we'll keep each other company. The sun will go down, the air will cool, the sky will darken. We'll sit by the pond together, and I'll listen to my nurse breathe. Our fingers *almost* touching.

We'll sit there all night long, and then the sun will come up, morning light on the water. Birds circling overhead. We'll taste that fresh, sweet air, warming as the sun rises, cooling again with the passing of the afternoon. Once more the shadows will lengthen.

The days will come and go. The seasons will change, the world will go by. My nurse and I will take it as it comes, the hardship and the sorrow, the disasters and the disappointments. We will face it all!

As long as we are together.

* * *

There's someone new in the hall next to mine. A woman with sharp eyes, steel-gray hair. Posture straighter than you have a right to expect, at our age.

I saw her in the lounge last week, sitting at a little table, the newspaper spread in front of her. Shaking her head as she turned the pages. A lot of people don't read the paper, here—it makes no difference, they tell themselves. Why bother with the outside world at this point in our lives? What are you going to do about it?

But I saw her reading the newspaper, scowling at one thing or another, turning the page and clucking her tongue. She caught me watching and she looked up, for a moment. She didn't smile, but she didn't frown. I thought I saw something in the tilt of her head.

I thought I saw a spark.

"Her name is Helen," my nurse said. "She worked for the garment union, a long time ago. I think she set up picket lines."

My nurse can't possibly understand what that means to me.

I might see Helen, later in the lounge. You never know! I might sit down at the next table, open up my own newspaper and read it, making clucking sounds with my tongue. I might look over at the right moment and catch Helen's eye.

The sun is climbing over the pond.

As we sit on the bench, my nurse shows me a picture of her son. He's some kind of organizer, he works all the way downtown. He's setting up a food co-op, he's cleaning up vacant lots. He's leading a rent strike. In this day and age! God bless him.

I can picture him speaking at a meeting. He's in a church basement, talking to a group of tenants, standing on a little stage. The same place the choir stands when they practice their hymns.

My nurse's son looks out at the group of tenants, and they look back at him. They drink coffee from paper cups while he talks to them about fairness, about justice. He talks about the power they will have if only they stand together.

He has a good, honest look, my nurse's son. He believes what he tells them, every word of it. By the time he's done, they believe it, too.

I look closely at the picture. He's twenty-six, my nurse says— but he looks like a boy to me. He is wearing a blue work shirt, some kind of vest. His hair is as dark as my nurse's is blonde. His eyes are sharp, his smile mischievous.

I stare at my nurse's son, and I see the look in his eye. A look I haven't seen for a while, but I remember it. A look that says: there is hope.

* * *

Mike got well. Of course he did! He had that kind of determination. But by the time he was strong enough to walk to the plate and take his swing, the war got in his way, just as it got in mine. He fought in the hills of Italy, and what can I tell you? Things went the way they go in that kind of thing.

When Mike came back, he bounced around the minor leagues—but his eye was off, his bat was a bit slower. You can hardly blame him, after what he'd been through. He kept running his drills, though. He kept taking batting practice. What else was he supposed to do?

I drove down to Florida one year to see Mike at spring training. School let out for a week, and I packed some clothes and headed into that unnatural warmth. There's something just wrong about Florida—the way the heat softens you, puts you off your guard. You have to watch yourself, or you'll slip into a lazy dream, where all you'll do is relax and eat fruit, rest your toes in the warm sand, listen to the sound of the waves.

There are hotels where you sprawl by the side of a swimming pool even though the beach is five steps away. The ocean is not good enough—they have to put in a pool! You stretch out in a lounge chair, and waiters come by and bring you lemonade. At least, I've heard there are places like that.

It isn't natural. I don't know why anyone lives in Florida—maybe the heat confuses you, the heavy air. You lose your sharpness after a while. You start to forget the point of things.

Mike was in camp near Jacksonville. I drove past acres of weeds, clusters of tar-paper shacks. Coconut palms with their white trunks, their wide floppy fronds. What's the point of a tree like that?

I drove past a swamp, half-drained, a stack of lumber piled on a sandy rise. The wood must have been there for quite a while—there were weeds growing up around the bottom of the pile, and patches of black mold, where the water puddled after a rain.

I bumped along an asphalt road, a narrow path winding between orange groves. I drove past streams and ponds and canals. A long way from the fields of the Midwest.

It wasn't much of a training camp—a couple of long cabins where the players slept. A shed for the equipment. Only one real building, a low square box with a sheet-metal roof, yellow paint peeling from the stucco. They probably cooked their meals there, had meetings where they sat on folding chairs, sweating in that thick Florida heat.

I parked on a patch of dirt. I walked out to the field.

Players were scattered around, playing long toss, shagging fly balls. Dressed in powder-blue uniforms. The cotton was faded, and the lettering was hard to read. You wouldn't have heard of the team anyway—a team of hired hands, a team that didn't stand for anything when they ran onto the field.

The ballpark itself wasn't much to look at. The grass was badly mowed, there were patches of weeds everywhere, and left field faded into a swamp. There was a sagging fence with some of the boards missing—they hadn't even tried to paint it. Base paths were made of sand, not dirt. What do you expect, in the minors? A rusted backstop, rotting dugouts. A few bleachers nailed together from worn-out pine. The wood had long ago turned pale in the Florida sun.

The manager stood between third base and home. You could recognize him by his shabby sport coat, his potbelly. His scowl as he glared at the batter's box. Why does the manager always look like that? Is there some kind of special training where they pass out secondhand sport coats? Where they show you how to grow a potbelly, groom eyebrows like underbrush, spill mustard on your shirt? How does it work to look like you always need a shave? They must teach you how.

They show you how to skimp on expenses, how to throw a tantrum. How to grow one of those pencil-thin mustaches. One of the worst mistakes a person can make, growing one of those pencil-thin mustaches.

When you graduate, they hand you a box of cheap cigars and send you out to rule the world.

The manager glared at the batter's box. At Mike.

I stood there at the side of the bleachers, and watched.

Mike had the same blue eyes, the same dark curly hair, but he looked different. Some of the air had gone out of him. The bat looked heavy when he held it over his shoulder. You know what I mean.

Mike did the only thing he could do. The only thing he knew *how* to do. He planted his feet in the batter's box and dug in a little, to get a grip in the sand. Wiggled the tip of his bat, as if it still had the same magic, the power he still remembered.

Mike stood there in the batter's box, looking out at the mound. He watched the pitcher go into his windup.

The pitch sailed in. Mike let it go by.

I watched him stand there as the catcher threw the ball back. I watched Mike plant his feet, grip the wood of the bat. Another windup, another pitch—and Mike let it go by.

Then another.

Mike didn't swing until the fourth pitch. Even then, he bare-ly connected—just a little tapper, the ball dribbling toward the mound.

For a moment, Mike looked surprised. Then he dropped his bat and trundled off toward first.

The manager stamped his feet in disgust. He scowled. He kicked up a cloud of dirt.

"Run, you big dummy!" he shouted. "What do you think we're paying you for? Run!"

ACKNOWLEDGMENTS

Thank you to Karyn Ginsburg, Howard Moraff, Jay Weber, Tamar Haspel, Jeff Purcell, Steven Schlang, Rishi Reddi, and my amazing children, Carol, Daniel, and Laura, for reading drafts and providing helpful comments and encouragement; to my editors, Terry Goodman, Kate Chynoweth, and Elizabeth Johnson, whose insights brought out the best in this book; to my parents, Linda and Howard; and to Karyn, the love of my life.

ABOUT THE AUTHOR

Ken Moraff grew up in Ithaca, New York, and now lives near Boston, where he has been an environmental lawyer and a Red Sox fan for more than twenty years. He and his wife, Karyn, have three children. This is his first novel.